T0284300

About the Author

Paul Cosway has had a long career in education as a teacher,
school adviser, inspector and International Education Consultant.
He now devotes his time to writing for adults and children.

Dedication

To Maureen, whose support and encouragement helped
to make this book possible.

Paul Cosway

OSIRIS

AUSTIN MACAULEY
PUBLISHERS LTD.

Copyright © Paul Cosway (2015)

The right of Paul Cosway to be identified as author of this work has been asserted by him in accordance with section 77 and 78 of the Copyright, Designs and Patents Act 1988.

All rights reserved. No part of this publication may be reproduced, stored in a retrieval system, or transmitted in any form or by any means, electronic, mechanical, photocopying, recording, or otherwise, without the prior permission of the publishers.

Any person who commits any unauthorized act in relation to this publication may be liable to criminal prosecution and civil claims for damages.

A CIP catalogue record for this title is available from the British Library.

ISBN 978 1 78455 186 5

www.austinmacauley.com

First Published (2015)
Austin Macauley Publishers Ltd.
25 Canada Square
Canary Wharf
London
E14 5LB

This book is a work of fiction. Names, characters, places and incidents are imagined or used fictitiously. Any resemblance to actual people, living or dead, events or locations is entirely coincidental.

Printed and bound in Great Britain

Acknowledgments

I wish to acknowledge the help and support of the publishers, Austin Macauley, whose faith in this project has brought this work to publication.

OSIRIS

A terrible tragedy is about to strike one of the world's greatest cities. Only four children can save the world from the terror. But these are not normal children...

1. AN END AND A BEGINNING...

Imam Khomeini International Airport, Tehran.

The security officer picked the plastic bag containing toiletries out of the tray and stared suspiciously at the three large tubes of toothpaste contained within it. He looked up at the passenger waiting to go through check in. 'These are yours?'

'Yes sir! They are within accepted limits, yes?' The passenger smiled pleasantly at the security man, showing a mouth full of teeth, each one a different shade of yellow. The officer shrugged and waved him on. He smiled to himself, thinking that if anyone needed three large tubes of toothpaste, it was this man. He did not notice the spring in the man's step as he went through the metal detector and on towards the departure gate.

The man with yellow teeth was elated. The staining had worked well and could soon be removed. These three small containers, disguised as innocent tubes of toothpaste, held the final batch of liquid explosive on its way to London. Nothing could stop them now from wreaking a terrible revenge on the West for the wrongs that had been committed in their country. Actually, he was wrong. One person could – but he was just a boy, in a deep coma in an English hospital.

Poole General Hospital, Dorset, England.

He didn't remember anything about the accident. They hadn't expected him to survive. Even if he lived, they told his mother, the family must prepare themselves for irreparable brain damage. A vegetable, they said. But as the weeks passed, he emerged, slowly, from the darkness. He saw flickers of light. He saw shapes that could have been people, but there was a glow around them, like multi-coloured halos. Only much later would he begin to learn their meaning.

Then the voices. Not speaking to him. Echoing and distant, going about their business.

Talk of monitors and medication.

References to gossip and to television programmes that he had not seen. The ephemera of their lives. Disconnected phrases.

Although he was aware of what was happening around him, he couldn't move. They didn't suspect he was conscious. They drifted round him, sometimes attending to his needs. He wanted to move his arm. To touch them. To speak. To tell them: *'I am here. Notice me. Speak to me!'* But his body lay like lead. The signals he sent his muscles were ignored, like messages tapped into a phone that has lost its charge. The frustration of that time he remembers all too well – and the fear. The terror of hearing distant voices weighing up his chances; the horror of realising that they were considering turning off the machines that kept his unresponsive body alive; the impossibility of screaming *'NO!!!'* and being heard.

At last, after many weeks imprisoned in his unresponsive body, he could fully open his eyes and blink. Everything changed. Suddenly the voices became business-like. They taught him to respond, to blink in answer to their questions. He became a human being again, with needs beyond liquid feeds and injections of antibiotics. Best of all, his mother held his hand.

And wept for joy.

The process of healing was slow, agonisingly slow. But he could hear and understand. They told him, bit by bit, how it had happened. The trip to the coast with his family – to his favourite beach, where he could build castles in the sand and watch the trains roar by on the track that ran parallel with the seafront. He'd been overjoyed, because he had been allowed to sit in the front of their new car, alongside his father. He'd felt grown-up and excited – he would see the road as if he were the driver, just as his father did.

We can never tell what fate has in store for us. It sometimes seems that it's when we are at our happiest that it plays its cruellest tricks. They never reached their destination, because boys in a fast car were joyriding on that same road. Fearless and exhilarated by their daring, they overtook a slow moving lorry just as his father, in their family car, reached it. The collision was head-on. His father swerved left so that he would take the greatest force of the impact. He was crushed and died instantly. His mother, in the back, suffered only minor injuries – whiplash, cuts and lacerations from broken glass. But his seat belt was too loose to hold him securely. He shot forward and a piece of debris from the car in front pierced his skull in the middle of his forehead. The boys in the car that hit them, driving too fast and on the wrong side of the road, were not using their seat belts. Seat belts are for wimps. All four of them were killed.

The physio was kind and had infinite patience. Some of his face muscles began to respond to endless manipulation. Then two of the fingers on his right hand. He began to regain the power of speech, though his words were slurred and he felt as if he were speaking through sludge. Sometimes no-one understood. But his mother, most often by his side, was best at interpreting his needs. He saw a haze around her, golden but flickering with anxiety. He learned that the gold represented kindness. His physiotherapist also glowed, but with a touch of pale green that he began to associate with gentleness. But not everyone had a kind nature. He had once assumed that all adults in healing professions, especially those who dealt with children, loved their work and their charges. He was gradually discovering that life was more complicated than he had ever imagined, especially as far as grown-ups were concerned.

One of the nurses, often on night duty, had a different aura. It was hard edged and dark with bitterness. He sensed much about her. He did not know how he had come to understand such a lot about her past, but somehow he did. She was angry with the way the world had treated her. She had been a regular churchgoer, giving to deserving causes. But one day her husband left her.

A younger woman had tempted him away. Her once devoted husband had found more pleasures in that woman's sin than in his wife's many virtues. Now she worked nights to avoid the lonely and empty evenings ... the childless times. For that was the unkindest cut of all. They had had no child together, but with his new woman, out of sin, he had a baby boy. And she burned with resentment.

He sensed that danger lurked in her, but she was a nurse, an authority figure, committed to caring for the sick. He could not mention his feelings about her to anyone, even his mother. But he watched. And some nights the anger burned in her like a living flame, consumed her, filled her mind with dark thoughts. On nights like these he was afraid to sleep.

His physiotherapist – he called her Mary now, although he knew they were not really friends – would praise him every day. She told him he was her best patient, that he was making excellent progress. She had thought it would be many more months before he would gain so much movement of his hands. He knew this was true. She exuded kindness and honesty. But there was a tidy, professional aspect to her aura. He knew that when she said *'We'll have you out of here in no time!'* it was not totally true. It was the doctor in her, wanting to cheer him along. He was just another patient to her, when it came down to it. But he liked being with her. And when he could lean his head against her, feel her softness and her warmth after a long session of muscle manipulation, he felt a pleasure he had not sensed before. It would make him smile.

Could he confide his fears to her?

'Mary, can I tell you something? It's about the nurse who does nights...'

'Which one? Nurse Blackmore?'

'Yes. I'm afraid of her. I think she'll do ... something bad.'

'Like what? Put such silly thoughts out of your head! She had a difficult time ... in her personal life. But she won't harm you! You couldn't be in a safer place! Everyone here wants to help you. To make you better!'

Grown-ups do not believe children who criticise those around them. It is fantasy, they think. He realised that it would be unwise to take it further. He rested his head against her arm. But he knew it was not him in danger. He had one last try.

'She won't harm me. It's Jonathan...'

'You're tired. Settle down now and get some rest. And stop thinking these nasty thoughts.' She made a mental note to mention this to one of the counsellors. It was not surprising. After all that he had gone through, it must have affected his mind. He needed some psychiatric involvement. She would see if Dr Pryce was in her office when she went for lunch.

He settled on the pillows and turned the pages of his book. It was from the library trolley that trundled around every other day. He had begun it and enjoyed it – a story of youngsters in sailing boats, playing at catching pirates. But he couldn't concentrate on it now. His gaze wandered across to Jonathan's bed. He was the golden child of the ward. Everyone liked him. Parents visiting other children would look enviously across at his bed.

'How is he today?' they would call to his parents. 'You're so lucky! Such a lovely boy!'

His parents would smile their thanks in return. 'Yes ... and he's borne all this so patiently. We hope he'll be out next week.' And Jonathan would smile his sweet smile, beneath his blonde curls. In truth he was a nice enough child, but he was mean to Sarah in the bed next to him. She would lend him her crayons – anything he wanted – but he gave nothing in return.

Selfishness, he came to learn, most often came with the prettiest children.

But Nurse Blackmore did not spoil and coo over Jonathan. The more she saw him, the more she resented him. *'Why should others have such beautiful children and I none at all?'* He could sense her anger. And when it happened, it happened quickly.

As she worked her way from bed to bed, he knew that this was an especially bad night for her. Something had gone very wrong. Her aura was dark and menacing. As she reached Jonathan, asleep in bed, he gasped. He felt the full force of her hatred of him and it took his breath away. These were emotions beyond his comprehension. He almost cried out in fear. She walked, quick and determined, to the nurses' station and opened the drug cabinet. She filled a syringe. Looking round furtively, she paced to the bed and took his limp arm. In went the needle with deadly precision.

His heart beating so loudly that he thought the whole hospital could hear it, he pressed his emergency button. She rushed across. 'What's wrong?'

'Don't...'

'What's the matter with you, child?'

He couldn't tell her. He needed someone else to come. 'A pain...'

'Where? How bad? On a scale of one to ten ... where ten is the worst that...'

'Ten! Ten!'

'All right. Wait a minute!'

She went to the phone and mumbled some urgent words. He looked across at Jonathan. He was slipping away ... he could sense his life aura fading. Desperate, he waited. After an age a junior doctor came running, his stethoscope tangled in his white coat.

'Where does it hurt?'

'It's not me – it's Jonathan – quick – he's dying!!'

The doctor did not know Jonathan, but glanced a professional eye in the direction he was pointing. 'Nurse! The boy in bed three. Is he OK?'

'Perfectly fine. I checked him not five minutes ago.' She tried to sound dismissive and confident, but she was surprised at the question and suddenly apprehensive.

The doctor turned back to him. 'There. Nothing to worry about! Just a bad dream. We'll give you something to calm you down and then you'll sleep.' The doctor remembered overhearing a conversation between a physio and one of the psychiatric staff. It was something about a boy who had been in a terrible accident and was having belated problems, imagining things.

'You'll be fine in the morning.' The doctor was trying to calm him down.

'Please ... please believe me ... he's going ... I can tell!!!'

'Now how can you do that? You've become the doctor now have you?'

Between his bed and Jonathan the nurse fluttered like a black crow. He could sense her anxiety, turning to panic, then relief as the doctor ignored his pleas. He could not help himself. He began to cry. 'It's true ... you must listen ... there's no time...'

The doctor felt sorry for him. He shrugged. 'I'll tell you what – just to make you feel better, I'll check him over.'

The nurse screamed at him. 'NO!!!'

'What?'

'He's fine, I told you! You're needed back in casualty! Now!'

'There's been no call...'

'I've checked him! You'll be wasting your time!'

The doctor was astonished at the intensity of her reaction. He realised that something was wrong. He walked to the bed as she flapped around him in extreme agitation. The doctor leaned over the unconscious child and lifted his eyelids. He was immediately professional, concerned, barking out instructions. 'Notify A and E that we have an emergency on the ward. Locate a bed in intensive care...' He was feeling for a pulse. The nurse flew away, automatically following his orders. An oxygen mask was clamped over Jonathan's mouth as the doctor spoke into a cell phone. More staff came rushing in – an injection – a porter – the bed wheeled away. The doctor paused before he left. 'Well, you may have saved him. How did you know to call me?'

'Will he be all right?'

'I don't know. We have to find out what's caused this. His whole body is shutting down.'

'The nurse ... she gave him an injection...'

The doctor stared at him and then picked up the notes that had fallen off the end of Jonathan's bed as it was rushed away. They had spread across the floor. He glanced through them. 'Are you sure? He wasn't due anything...' And then he saw the empty syringe in the waste basket that the nurse hadn't had time to empty. He picked it up, turned it over in his hand, confused and concerned.

'I'll have to get this to the lab. Hopefully there'll be someone working this late. Now don't worry. I am sure we can sort this out. You try to get some rest. You've been very helpful.' And he was gone.

In a very real way, this marked the end of his childhood. He was growing into teenage years anyway, but this was the end of his carefree days – of his innocence. What had happened marked him out as an object of intense curiosity and everyone, it seemed, wanted to see him.

To examine him.

To probe him.

To try to understand how he was functioning, without accepting the evidence that was so clearly before them. But this is jumping ahead. Jonathan? There was enough in the syringe to identify the drug – just a heavy overdose, but enough to kill. They saved his life, but only just in time and it affected his heart. The muscles were weakened. The golden child would live a reasonable span but would never enjoy the athletic, carefree life that had been his destiny.

And Nurse Blackmore? He was kept ignorant of her fate, but she never appeared again round the hospital wards. There was a court case, he knew that, and he had to give a written statement. The lawyer helped him to word it carefully. Some details, he was told, were better missed out because it would affect his credibility. He was excused a court appearance of course, on account of his youth and his state of health. There were newspaper stories – laughably sensational. 'Boy saves friend from certain death!' – that sort of thing. His mother was so proud of him. *'You might get a medal!'* she breathed, with stars in her eyes. But he did not want a medal. He did not want all this fuss. Already he realised that he had drawn too much attention to himself and this could change his life, not necessarily for the better.

The Docklands, East End of London, England.

The estate agent drove up to the huge building and tried to be as positive as he could. It towered over them, gaunt and derelict. Most of the windows had long ago been smashed by well-aimed bricks or inclement weather. Starlings flew in and out of holes in the masonry, attending to their young, who screamed impatiently for more food. The wind howled eerily through the long abandoned corridors. The estate agent was new to the agency, and getting a rental agreement here would be a feather in his cap. He pulled up by an opening that gaped like a dark, open wound and had once been the main door. He turned to his companion and whispered, apologetically, 'It doesn't look much, I'm afraid.'

'There is no door?'

The agent gazed at him. The stranger was inscrutable. He wore a shabby business suit with a pair of trainers that were new and clean, but cheap. He would smile humourlessly, showing two rows of uneven, yellow teeth. Was he a time waster, or an eccentric millionaire businessman from overseas? It was impossible to know what he was thinking, but he did not seem to be totally phased by what he was seeing.

The agent crossed his fingers behind his back and tried to sound positive as he answered the question. 'There's a secure door to the part of the property that's for letting. Come on in!'

They walked into the cold, derelict building. Behind a staircase was a strong metal door. The agent produced a key and it opened with a reluctant groan. Inside was totally dark. The agent groped for the light switch and a flight of stairs was revealed, leading to an enormous basement area. Only the first few of the fluorescent tubes had flickered into life and so it was not possible to see the far end of the space. Rows of iron columns supported the ceiling and piles of junk lay everywhere. The agent tried to hide his sense of despair.

'This building – it is for demolition, yes?'

'No. It has a preservation order on it, believe it or not. But it's proved ... difficult ... to let any of the floors. This is the only part now that's fit for use. It's very secure. And there would be no-one else here but you. It's got good parking and two entrances. One is by the dockside, so you can access it from the river or the road...'

'It may be what I am looking for...'

The agent swallowed hard. He couldn't believe what he was hearing.

'What is it for? Storage? It's ideal for that.'

'Maybe. We are importing things. We need quiet and security.'

'It's got that all right! And we can give you an incentive package to start. The council will waive council charges for the first six months to help business start-up, and the owners will give you the first month rent free to help to cover your set-up costs.'

The stranger grinned. 'This will suit us fine. We'll take it!'
It would cost him nothing. He would be gone by the end of the
first month – and so would part of London...

Poole General Hospital, Dorset, England.

His legs still would not respond. He had to be pushed in a
wheelchair, because his arms were not strong enough or co-
ordinated enough to work the chair himself. But all the time
there were slow, but sure, signs of recovery.

The doctors talked of him going home and even of
schooling. Of course he must continue with his education,
although he could read and write well enough, and was
competent with numbers. He struggled to think what they
could teach him now. He felt strangely wise, much older than
his years. But you could not know what you did not know until
you learned it. There could be much that would be useful to
him. They may teach why women try to kill small children.
Why grown men ignore the words of young boys. This would
be worth knowing, worthy of an education.

But first, he must attend sessions with the psychiatrists.
Not one consultant, as had been mentioned, but three and then
four. They questioned him gently, probing his mind. He was
cautious with his answers, remembering the lawyer's advice.

'How did you know that Jonathan was in trouble? Why did
you suspect the nurse of doing wrong? What gave you such
feelings of acute anxiety?'

'I don't know. I just felt it.'

Three shook their heads and shrugged. But the fourth,
called in late, was different. He sensed that this lady had a
mind that could accept the impossible. She had long nails,
painted vivid red. Her wrists were festooned with gold bangles.
Her hair was drawn sharply from her face, making her pointed
nose prominent and emphasising her eyes, which were piercing
and heavily made-up, even though she was old. '*Mutton
dressed as lamb,*' his mother breathed, glancing disparagingly

at her short skirt that exposed two bony knees. But he knew that this was not entirely true. This woman was not deluded, believing that she could pass for twenty when she was clearly in her sixties. Far from it. She was dressing as she did to make a statement. He could sense an aura around her of sheer, bloody-minded rebellion. She was what she was and she was proud to be herself. She didn't care what anyone else thought. This was what Hilary Fleischman (for that was her name) was: someone who liked heavy gold jewellery, long, ridiculous earrings and loads of make-up. And she was old enough and important enough to be whatever she wanted.

Hilary could see more in him than the others did. She guessed how much he was concealing. She waited till they were on their own, even his mother gone.

'Can we play a game?' she asked, pleasantly.

This seemed a welcome relief. He was drawn to her, to her extrovert but comforting presence. He sensed good in her.

'You see these cards? They have pictures on them. Simple pictures. Look – I'll turn one over. It is a swan, do you see? Now, can you tell me what any other pictures there are? You will get a chocolate for every one you get right!'

He stared at her, perplexed. The cards were face down on the table that was drawn across his bed.

'But they're upside down,' he complained.

'Of course. It would be too easy if the picture side was facing up wouldn't it? Concentrate on them. Try hard.'

'Ahh...' (He wanted to please her) 'I see, they've got some clue on the back, some pattern that I need to spot?'

'No.' She looked at him steadily. He sensed that she was not angry or disappointed with him. She was analysing, thinking things through. 'Let's try another way. I'll pick up a card and look at it. You see if you can tell me what I am looking at.' She picked up the card nearest to her and held it away from her so that she could see it, but he could not. 'Now, I am picturing what is on the card. Can you tell me what it may be? Guess if you like.'

But he did not have to. Her aura was shifting. He could see patterns, colours.

'It's a train.'

She stared at him, and, for a brief second, there was a look of astonishment in her eyes. She gathered herself. 'Can you tell me what kind of a train?'

'A steam train.'

'What colour is it? Can you tell that?'

'I think that it's red.'

Two more cards followed: a cat (black) and a boat (with green and white sails). Hilary looked at him strangely, as if she had seen a ghost. She passed him three chocolates, one for each correct answer.

'You are a clever boy! That's enough for now. But I would like to come and play with you again soon. Would you like that?' He nodded, his mouth too full of coffee cream chocolates to make any sort of intelligible noise. She did not scold him for stuffing his face, as his mother would. She walked away, as if in a daze. Believing herself out of earshot, she talked into her phone.

'Extraordinary. We have never had results like this. I'll write it up tonight, you'll have a full report by morning...' And with a tinkle of gold bangles she was gone.

And his life was about to take another, most unexpected, turn.

2. OUT OF HOSPITAL, INTO...

His mother was distressed. He wasn't sure why. He couldn't hear what was being said. She was behind glass with a doctor and a man in dark suit – strong and athletic with curly black hair. He could tell the man was efficient and matter-of-fact. There was no gentleness or compassion, but no evil either. He was doing a job – whatever that was. Eventually they shook hands and his mother emerged from the room and walked over to his bed. She stroked his forehead. He wished he could move his arm more freely. He wanted to take her hand.

'How is my treasure this morning?'

Love and concern flooded her eyes. Love surged in his heart in return.

'I'm fine, mum.'

'You're so brave. I'm so proud of you. What did you have for breakfast?'

When there were so many other things to be worried about, her concern for his eating always astonished him. But he played his part.

'Eggs ... and toast ... and juice!' he added, to make sure she realised he had had one of his five a day. 'How are things at home?'

She knew that he was asking about the changes they were making. The insurance was paying. Doorways were being widened; a bathroom downstairs would be specially equipped for him to use. The work had been going on for weeks. When it was finished, he would be able to go home. For short breaks at first, whilst he still needed very regular treatment, but eventually for good. He wanted to be home, to have familiar things around him.

He could tell immediately that something was wrong. The light – the aura – around his mother begin to flicker alarmingly. She was distressed, but fighting to conceal it from him.

'They should be finished soon. The plumbers are in today ... but there might be...'

'What? What's happened mum?'

'Nothing. It's all right. But there could be a bit of delay. They want to move you somewhere for a while ... I'll be coming too...'

'Where? Why?'

'Some more tests that's all ... I don't really know what it's about. But it will just be for a while. And I'll be with you, they've promised me that...'

He could tell that she did not know much more and that his questions were causing her distress. He stopped the interrogation and let her chatter on about his cousin's new puppy and a hundred other family things without really listening. What was this about? Why wasn't he going home? He waited until Hilary came for her regular 2pm visit. She was even more tanned than usual and her gold chains struggled to compete with the bronze of her skin.

He got straight to the point. Somehow he knew that she was part of this. 'Where are they taking me? Why can't I go home?'

'Oh – you've found out! She smiled. We'll have to remember: there's no keeping anything from you!'

'What's going on?'

'You are being moved. For a while. Somewhere you'll be safe and we can do more tests.'

'Safe?'

'You're attracting a lot of interest, even though you don't realise it. You seem to have developed some remarkable abilities. We just want to see how we can help you.'

'But why?'

'And there may be people who, if they found out, might want to ... exploit you. You'll have to trust me on this. Do you trust me?'

He looked into her eyes. He could tell that she was sincere, but she wasn't telling everything. She only wanted what was best for him, but there was more to this than she was saying. He nodded.

'Good.' She smiled again, and there was nothing but relief and friendship in it. 'You will like it. There are other children there – teenagers...' she added, realising that 'children' did not necessarily mean the same thing to him as to her, 'around your age. And it is a lovely house in the countryside. It's where I work. You'll have your own room, next to your mum when she visits' (when she visits – he thought she'd be staying there too, all the time) 'and we organise trips – to the coast, to theme parks...'

'The man in the black suit?'

'He's from the government. They fund the work I do. That's all.'

For some reason, the mention of 'government' worried him more than anything else she had said. She sensed his sudden withdrawal. 'Don't worry. We'll have a great time. And it won't be forever.' She leapt to her feet with a dazzling sparkle of jewellery. She was departing quickly before he quizzed her further. He sensed no ill will towards him, but somehow felt trapped without knowing why. And then she was gone.

The Docklands, East End of London, England.

The small boat chugged gently towards the landing stage. There were three people in it – two middle aged men and a younger woman. She was tall and slim, with a mouth that was set and stern. Her head was covered modestly with a white scarf. They tied up and climbed out, each carrying heavy packages. One of these was being handled with extreme care.

The man who had made the deal with the estate agent produced a large key from his pocket and opened a heavy door. The woman looked round. 'This is good. We cannot be observed.'

'Is right ... we can slip in and out of here undetected.'

'It is ideal...'

They entered the cavernous basement and switched on the lights. This time more of the tubes flickered into life. They looked round at the dust, dirt and rubbish all around them. The place was dank and filthy. Somewhere in the gloom a rat scurried for cover. A strong smell of rodents filled the damp air. They walked up to a group of empty packing cases and used them to make an improvised work bench. Carefully they began to unpack the packages they had brought. The one that contained the explosive gel was left until last. Only the size of two or three shoeboxes, it contained enough highly refined nitro-glycerine to blast the whole building off the face of the Earth.

Poole General Hospital, Dorset, England.

When it was time for him to leave, it all happened very quickly. There is something both very personal and totally impersonal about hospitals. When they admit you and are caring for you, doctors, nurses and orderlies are all over you like a rash. But when it comes to discharge, you are just another number, not of any concern. He realised that the nurses who had cared for him like guardian angels could not be lifelong friends. They had to switch on and off. They were programmed to forget you. If they became emotionally involved with every patient who passed through their hands, life would become intolerable. They would break down under the strain of it all. They said they would miss him as they put him into a wheelchair. And then they put him out of their minds.

'You'll be glad to be going home at last!' the orderly said, as he pushed a door open with his foot and then pulled him through towards the big, grey metal lift that smelled of disinfectant. He saw no point in trying to explain that he was not going home. The man would ask why, and he did not really know.

'How long have you been here?'

'Three months, I think...'

'Blimey! You'll qualify for a pension!'

He laughed politely. He knew the man was trying to be kind.

The entrance hall was full of people. Posters on the walls offered a bewildering range of advice, from blood in your urine to sexually transmitted diseases. Rows of brightly coloured chairs looked comfortable and inviting until you looked more closely and saw the stains. Then he spotted his mother near the door. She had a large suitcase for herself and a smaller one that he knew would be for him. She waved to him and smiled. He raised his hand as much as he could in acknowledgement. Then she was hugging and kissing him. He would have squirmed in embarrassment if he could.

'There's a car outside for us!' She was impressed. She had always avoided taxis as much as she could, afraid that they would not come on time – or at all – or overcharge. He looked outside. A large black BMW was parked directly by the exit doors, obscuring the NO PARKING sign painted on the tarmac. Two men in dark suits were seated inside, smiling out at them. One got out to open the car doors. The other stepped out to take the cases. Then he was lifted into the front passenger seat and the wheelchair, folded, was swallowed up into the trunk.

'Are you sitting comfortably, young man? We thought you'd like a front seat! Howd'you do, by the way? My name's Tom!' Tom was the same man he had glimpsed in the hospital. He had blue eyes, black curly hair and trendy dark stubble that made him look like a film star. In the rear view mirror he could see his mother, a contented smile on her face as she sank into the soft leather seat.

'Where are we going?'

The driver touched the side of his nose and winked. 'Can't say, son. Sworn to secrecy. If you ever found out, I'd have to shoot you on the spot!' He winked again, to reassure him that he was joking.

'Have you got a gun?' The man pulled his jacket aside and showed the glimpse of a holster.

'Don't worry. It's not for you. Standard issue. We're armed protection officers. We escort important people like you. You and your mum – you're VIPs!'

Before he could ask him why, the officer squeezed an unseen switch on the steering wheel and spoke to the dashboard. *'OSIRIS to convoy. We're ready to roll!'*

The dashboard answered him with a crackle. *'Roger, OSIRIS!'*

And then, astonishingly, two motorcycle outriders appeared from nowhere and swung in front of them and a black Range Rover pulled up behind them. *'Move out!'* barked their driver, in a tone very different from the friendly one he had used up to then. Several voices were heard to respond almost simultaneously. Blue lights began to flash, first on the motorbikes and then on the 4X4 behind them. A siren wailed and the convoy moved swiftly and smoothly into the road. Alarmed he looked back at his mother. She was excited and beaming with pleasure as they accelerated away, well above the legal speed limit, cars moving aside to let them pass. They say that everyone has five minutes of fame and this was hers. He realised that she was imagining herself a film star and enjoying every second of this. But it made no sense to him. Where were they taking him and why all this fuss? Whenever they approached a set of traffic lights, the bikes shot ahead and then slowed to a halt, stopping all traffic so that the two cars could sweep through without slowing. Then the bike riders screamed away to pull back in front. But what was so important? And who was in the second car? Was it Hilary? He wanted to ask, but the noise of the sirens made conversation impossible. He had never realised how deafening they were, or how they made adrenalin race.

Within minutes they were on the motorway and the office blocks and rows of houses gave way to green fields and trees. A herd of black and white cows was lying on the grass to get cool in the heat of the day. His mother leaned forward. 'Look! A tractor! A red one!' He fought back a sob. Seven months ago he was still a child and would have been thrilled to see it. His mum still saw him as that child. But so much had changed since then. He managed a nod to please her. But he was beginning to see into the darkness of men's souls and he wondered whether such childish, innocent things would ever thrill him again.

3. FOXES HOLLOW

The convoy swung off the motorway and slowed slightly as it made its way along minor roads. They passed occasional quaint country pubs with names like 'The Dog and Anchor' and 'World's End'. Brightly coloured cars were parked outside them and people sat at picnic tables laughing and drinking. This cheerfulness seemed to contrast oddly with his own feelings. He wished he had paid more attention when his father had taken them out for car rides. He had no sense, he realised, of geography. He had no clue where they were. They went through a small town of grey stone buildings. The shops on the high street thronging with people. A small child was screaming – hot and bored. The pedestrians stared at them as they raced by, but the darkened glass gave them total anonymity. Some large houses set back behind trees, a railway crossing, a petrol forecourt and then they were back driving past fields and high hedges. After what seemed an age, they turned off the road into a narrow unmarked lane. It twisted between enormous shady trees and they pulled up by large iron gates. Two men came over to the car, peering in, calmly but seriously. The driver showed his pass. Not a word was spoken. The gates opened electronically and the two cars drove through, leaving the escort bikes behind.

The drive wove between tall trees and then emerged into a vast grassy space that led up to the house. He learned later that the clear open space was for security: any interloper would be spotted long before he reached the shelter of the building. The house itself was large, a mansion in the Gothic style moulded out of cream stone. The windows were mullioned and multi-paned, reflecting the sun like clusters of diamonds. In Jacobean times, the house had been lightly fortified. A wall about a

31

metre and a half high of matching stone ran across the front of the large gardens. The wall was crenellated by tall regular stones stood on end every metre to conceal a defender. Two small towers with arrow slits guarded the heavy wooden entrance gates. The path from here ran in a straight line up to the grand entrance doors of the house itself, at the top of sweeping stairs. To the left were large buildings in a plainer Gothic style that had once been stables, carriage sheds and barns, but now were store rooms and garages. The house was U-shaped in plan, with two matching wings coming forward from the central block. The gardens were mainly laid to lawn, but there were island rose beds and beautiful herbaceous flower beds, filled with lupins, delphiniums, geraniums and aquilegias in the English country garden style. His mother's eyes shone. It was the loveliest house he had ever seen. It had three turrets, one taller than the other two, and a coat of arms carved in stone over the heavy wooden front door. It swung open with a creak and to his delight Hilary emerged, followed by Mary, his physiotherapist. It was such a relief to see a friendly face!

The man in the back got out of the car and opened the other passenger door for his mother, before retrieving the wheel chair. Then he was lifted out and lowered gently into the chair. Hilary reached down and hugged him, her heavy perfume falling over him like a cloud of incense.

'It's wonderful to see you! How was the journey? Welcome to Foxes Hollow! Aren't you glad to be out of that hospital? We're going to have such fun here!'

No response was needed to these questions, even if there had been time to squeeze one in! Hilary and Mary pushed him round to the side of the house where there was a door at ground level, more manageable for a person in a wheelchair. The dark suited man who had travelled in the back helped his mum with the cases. The driver remained seated, watchful, looking round carefully. The 4x4, with darkened windows, remained behind the first car and no-one got out.

They entered the house. The contrast between the light outside and the dim light within made it difficult for him to see at first. He was in a dark, wood-panelled hallway. Hilary pulled open the doors of an old, metal lattice lift and the four of them squeezed in, just.

'We're so lucky to have this. It was put in a couple of years before the war, when this was a family home, to help the servants move heavy trunks upstairs to the luggage store. It creaks a bit I'm afraid!' Mary was right – it did creak. And squeak. And jolt rather alarmingly. But it got them to the second floor.

'We'll take you to your room first, so you can settle in, and then you can meet the others!'

The door to his new room opened automatically and a faint smell of new wood and fresh paint greeted him. Work had been completed very recently to adapt it to his needs. The bed was at the perfect height for him to swing onto from his wheelchair. The doorway was widened to give him easy access to the adjacent bathroom. But it was not these physical changes that impressed him.

'My pictures!'

The precious things that had been in his own bedroom at home had been collected and installed here: his toy cars – most especially his favourite model of a James Bond sports car, with silver paintwork and working cannon; his transformer toy that changed from a big truck into a fearsome robot; and the pictures – of David Beckham, Wayne Rooney and Stuart Broad. Tears welled up in his eyes – partly because he was happy to be with familiar things again: partly because he realised, with a sickening thud to his stomach, that his daydreams of one day becoming a sporting hero were over forever. Hilary crouched down beside him. She saw the tears that he was fighting to hold back.

'Do you like it? We have tried to make it nice for you!'

He swallowed hard. 'Thanks – it's great...'

'There's a guest room down the corridor where your mum can stay when she's here.' (Every time they mentioned her, it became clearer that his mum was going to be far from a permanent fixture at Foxes Hollow.) 'And you have your own television. And an Xbox. But you'll spend a lot of time with the others. Shall we go down and meet them?'

He couldn't speak, but he smiled a yes. She swung him around and the door sighed as it swung itself open. 'You can leave your things here,' Mary told his mother. 'We'll show you your room later!' They all trooped back to the lift and down to the first floor. The corridor was carpeted and there were mullioned windows giving disjointed glimpses of a sunlit lawn through small diamond panes. The corridor smelt faintly of dust and lavender polish. A large wood-panelled door opened itself as they neared it. Beyond was a large room with three comfortable-looking sofas; a cupboard, half-open, with neatly stacked, brightly coloured board games; and shelves of books and DVDs next to a flat screen television. A cartoon was showing, but the sound was down. On one of the sofas three young people were sitting, on their best behaviour.

The most striking of the three was a girl. She had dark hair in a ponytail and large, brown eyes that seemed to smile kindly at him. He guessed that she was a few months older than he and she looked somehow more sophisticated. It made him feel shy and awkward, but he sensed that she was open and ready to like him. The other two were boys. One was short and freckled, with blonde, unruly hair. He had a mischievous glint in his eyes that made one warm to him instantly – though not perhaps if one was an adult! The third was the eldest, at least a year older than the girl. He was tall and rather lanky, with the gawky awkwardness of a teenager who was not yet developed into a young man. Hilary moved across and stood behind them to make the introductions. 'Ladies first! This gorgeous young lady is Beth!'

'Hi!' said Beth, with a welcoming smile. She was obviously used to Hilary's gushing descriptions and so was not phased by them. He smiled back.

'And this cheeky monkey is Archie!'

Archie smirked. 'You OK?'

'And this is the dashing Lothario of our company: this is the handsome George!'

'Good to see ya, ' said George, and again he sensed nothing but friendliness in him. But Hilary came across and crouched beside him. She knew that he was too quiet, that something was bothering him.

'Don't worry – they're really nice. You'll be great friends.'

But it wasn't that. He had expected them to be like him. If this was a special place where he would be cared for and helped to recover – why were the other children not like him? He struggled to understand. These were perfectly healthy young people. They had no physical disabilities at all. This didn't make sense.

Hilary stood up behind him to complete the introductions.

'And this is the new member of our little gang – the one you have been dying to meet for weeks, ever since I told you about him! This ... is Zahir!'

Two years earlier, Southampton University.

Doctor Hilary Fleischman was hot and annoyed. Her academic gown, with its richly decorated hood, was pulling at her shoulders and making her back ache. She refused the glass of sherry she was offered and asked for a cold spritzer. She hated these events, when the faculty was put on show at a boring reception. She understood the reasons. University departments needed all the additional funding they could find. It was vital to finance their research. Student fees paid the basic tuition costs and salaries, but left little spare cash for anything else in the way of academic work or expensive new equipment.

Invitations had been sent to anyone in business who might possibly support them. Hilary hated the false politeness. She dreaded the endless small talk and the forced smile that seemed to freeze on her face. It left her jaw aching by the end of the evening. And anyway, it had always seemed pointless. Psychology was not the sort of department that attracted the support of big business. It was the science and technology faculties that drew the money. Business leaders were eager to invest in research that might give them an advantage over their rivals. The funding always went to those departments, ones doing research into electronics, medicine or particle physics. So she had to spend an evening chatting to boring men who had come for the free drinks, leered at her legs and forked out not a single penny at the end.

She walked out through the French doors onto the lawn to get the most out of the evening sun. Then she heard her name being called. She spun round and saw the Vice Chancellor waving at her. Reluctantly, she turned back to join him. His eyes glistened with excitement.

'A gentleman here desperate to meet you, Hilary!' he beamed. 'He's been asking me about your work on the paranormal! But this won't be news to you, will it Hilary? You'll have seen it in the stars!'

He tittered at his own witticism. Hilary glared at him, barely disguising her disgust, and then turned to look at the visitor. He was wearing a smart black suit and a tie held in place with a tie clip. His hair was dark and neat, his eyes a bright blue. She held out her hand and introduced herself. 'Doctor Fleischman...'

'Yes. I'd been hoping to meet you.' He did not offer his name in return. She wondered who he was and what interest he could have in her work.

'Take him to your office, if you want, to have a quiet chat,' suggested the Vice Chancellor.

'Shall we?' the nameless visitor asked.

As she passed him, the Vice Chancellor hissed in her ear: 'Find out if he's got money. See what you can get out of him!'

She ignored him and led the way down a long echoing corridor to a plain green door with her name on it.

'Come in.' She manoeuvred herself round to the far side of the desk. Books were crammed everywhere in the tiny room and space was at a premium.

'Thank you.' He squeezed in next to her.

'How can I help you?'

The man looked round the small office as if to check no-one was hiding under the desk. Then he looked her straight in the eyes and smiled.

'I'm sorry to seem so secretive. I assume it is safe to talk here?'

'Of course.'

'My name's Tom, by the way. Tom Asquith. I want to be completely open with you. I have an offer to make. You may not accept it. Whether you do or not, I need your absolute assurance that what I say will never be repeated to anyone.'

His smile had disarmed her slightly. For the first time, she noticed that he was quite handsome. He had the look of an athlete, despite his smart suit, and she liked the way the light reflected in his curly black hair.

'I can assure you that I am not a gossip.'

'I guessed as much. I can't be too specific about my role, but let's just say that I'm part of the team that this country has mobilised to track down terrorists.'

'I'm sure you are. But what has this to do with my research?'

'You will know that we use electronic surveillance to try to keep one step ahead of our enemies. It may not always be enough. We aren't looking for mystics or ball gazers, but we have heard interesting things about your work. It is possible that – if you are willing – we may be able to add – how shall I put it? – psychic surveillance to our repertoire.'

Hilary stared at him coldly. 'You want me to use my research for military purposes?'

'For defence only.'

'I'd be putting my patients at risk.'

'I hope not. You and they would be offered the highest level of security.'

'I'm not sure...'

'I know that you and your faculty are short of funds. We can offer considerable financial help, along with a secure site. And your patients – I understand that they are mainly children?'

'Yes. The research I am doing is into the psychic skills that some young people possess, but lose as they get older.'

'The children can stay together. We'll supply the domestic staff and education facilities. You'll be able to progress your work much more quickly with the support we can offer you.'

Hilary was thoughtful. She doubted that George, Beth or Archie would be much help to him. But this offer sounded too good to refuse.

4. IT BEGINS...

FOXES HOLLOW, THE PRESENT DAY.

It was over an hour before Zahir met the others again. He and his mother were taken upstairs to unpack and then Beth, now dressed in frayed blue jeans and a sparkly top, popped her head round his door.

'We're having tea in my room. Want to come?'

Before he could answer, she had taken hold of the handles of his chair and wheeled him out and into the corridor. Skilfully she steered him round a right angle bend and past the main staircase before entering another corridor in another wing of the house. '*The girls' side*,' she whispered.

'Are there more girls?'

'No. Just me, but Hilary sleeps next door and Mary too, now that you've come. And your mum will be here when she visits you. Most of the staff live out and security are in the stables.'

'Security?'

'At least two on guard, day and night. You've no need to feel nervous.'

'Why? Should I be?'

'Not sure. This is mine!'

She kicked open a door covered with brightly coloured notes ('Keep Out! This means you! Girlzonlyzone!') and pushed him in. The walls were bright pink. Almost everything was pink, even the television. She had large posters on the walls, some of boy bands and some of fluffy kittens. Every spare space was covered with a very odd collection of objects, even including large pebbles and pieces of broken pot. Several items of cutlery were arranged in a row. A large bar of soap had pride of place, along with two old watches. In fact, there was a huge assembly of what to Zahir looked like useless small items of junk. Beth didn't explain her collection; she pushed aside a pile of books and magazines and flopped on the bed.

'Are the others coming?' He had never been alone with a girl in her bedroom before. It was disconcerting. He sort of felt as if it was slightly immoral, without knowing why.

'Soon. They're raiding the kitchen. Want a drink?'

He panicked, afraid that she was offering him alcohol, but he had nothing to fear. She stretched gracefully over the bed, reached under it and produced two bottles of cola. He couldn't see any tumblers. She took a swig out of the bottle and flipped the bottle top expertly into a waste paper bin six feet away. He had never drunk straight from a bottle before. He tried it. It felt surprisingly good. It gave him a feeling of freedom that he was beginning to enjoy – although it scared him – of being able to do things he had not been allowed to do at home. His father was very conservative and would have chastised him severely for doing what he was doing now – even just being in a girl's room. At the thought of his father, he felt suddenly heartbroken. Beth seemed to know what he was feeling. 'I'm sorry about your dad. I haven't got one – never knew him... I miss him sometimes.'

'Can I ask you something? What is this place? What are we doing here?'

'Hmm. I should probably leave it to the grown-ups to explain. Mind you, we're a bit of a mystery to them, I think! It's a sort of school...'

'A school?'

'Yes. They have to teach us, because we're of school-age – compulsory education and all that. We have English, maths, science just like other kids. Only we are all in the same class because there are only three of us – four now. And we only have one teacher for everything. He's crazy. You'll like him. Then in the afternoons we work with Hilary and the others.'

'Others?'

'They vary. Usually one other, sometimes more. They come and go.'

'But why? Is it to make us better?' He glanced down at his crippled body.

'Better, yes – but not the way you mean!'

'Then better at what?'

'Better at what we can do. We've heard such a lot about you – Hilary is over the moon about you. But we're all here because we are a bit ... different...'

'You mean like I can see things...'

'Yes. Things that other people can't see. I am a toucher. Give me something of yours. Anything. Your watch. It will tell me about you. You'll see!'

He stretched out his arm, with difficulty. She undid his watch and held it cupped in her hands. Then she closed her eyes and touched the watch to her cheek. Suddenly tears welled up and she wept quietly.

'Beth ... are you OK?'

'I'm sorry. I'm so sorry,' she sobbed. 'I didn't know. Your helplessness ... you were trapped inside your head all those months and ... your dad...'

Just then the atmosphere was shattered by a commotion outside the door and George and Archie burst in. Beth turned away and wiped her eyes so that they would not see that she had been crying. There was so much more that Zahir wanted to know, but it would have to wait.

'We got cake,' chortled Archie, 'and sausage rolls!'

'Do you eat meat?' asked George, realising that they may have been very inconsiderate.

'I don't mind. I shouldn't really, but I don't mind.'

'We could go and get something else...'

'No, it's OK, really.'

Beth fussed, putting towels on the bed so they wouldn't cover it with crumbs. For a few minutes everyone was quiet as they munched happily. Zahir decided that sausage rolls were over-rated, but enjoyed the cake. It's carrot cake! Archie confided. Zahir laughed politely, assuming that this was one of Archie's jokes. It was nothing like a carrot.

'Beth said we all have special skills,' he said hesitantly. He wasn't sure whether or not they would want to talk about them, but he need not have worried.

'George is amazing,' whispered Beth. 'He's an OBT!'

'A what?'

'An OBT. Out-of-body traveller.' Zahir was no wiser. George made a gesture to show he was too modest to talk about it. 'He goes into a kind of trance and his mind can leave his body and travel to other places.'

'Not too far yet,' interrupted George.

'No, but he's getting stronger all the time. They test him by placing an object in a closed room and he sends his mind into the room and then tells them what it is...'

'I can tell what people are saying in other rooms without being able to hear them,' offered Zahir.

George was not to be outdone. He ran a hand through his thick, wavy brown hair. 'Yes, I can hear things too. But I see them.'

'And Archie, well he's Archie...' said Beth, with a giggle.

'I read screens,' spluttered Archie, spitting crumbs in his eagerness not to be missed out.

'Read screens?'

'This is too weird!' exclaimed Beth. 'We half think he's making it up!'

'Am not!' cried Archie, annoyed by her teasing.

'He stares at blank screens,' explained Beth, 'and sees things in them.'

'In the attics,' added Archie, helpfully.

'The static!' corrected Beth.

'Like television screens?'

'Any sort,' said Archie, proudly. 'Computer screens, phone screens ... if I stare into them for a long time, I start to see pictures.'

'Of what?'

'Things that haven't happened yet...'

George was not going to be outdone. 'I can make my mind leave my body and look down at it as if I was on the ceiling. And then I go through walls into other rooms...'

'How far?'

George looked slightly crestfallen. 'Only around the house yet. But I'm getting stronger all the time!'

At this point, Hilary burst in and put an end to any further questions. 'Here you all are! Right you three – you've had an easy day so far, because Zahi was coming. But Fenton is waiting in the schoolroom. An hour's lesson before supper.' There were moans from the trio, but Zahir sensed that they didn't really mind. They obviously liked their teacher. Hilary turned to him. 'Lessons start for you tomorrow, my dear. But Mary is waiting in your room to give you some physiotherapy. We need to get you as mobile as we can!'

The West End of London, England.

She stepped back into the doorway, so that no-one would see her. She was excellent at not being noticed, but she did not have to try hard here. No-one was interested in the slim, dark woman waiting quietly at the roadside. She gazed across at the tall, classical building facing her. She shrugged herself tighter into a corner of the deserted doorway to avoid the bright electric lights that covered the facade. The street was busy at this time of the evening and, if this was to be their first target, this would be the time of day that they would need to enter and deliver the package. It looked easy. A single person would be difficult to spot amid the crowds - some still shopping, some going home from work after stopping for an evening drink at the bars.

She could see three entrances. Any one of them would do. She felt confident – elated. When the time came, this would cause a sensation all across the world. What a victory it would be for their cause! And what a wonderful revenge for her and her family! She needed to get inside, to plot where and how the bomb would be planted. She slipped across the busy street. Gaining entrance would be easy for her. She was confident of her special skills, believing herself to be unique. She knew nothing of the four remarkable children, over a hundred miles away, about to settle down for a very eventful evening meal...

5. A SUPPER TO REMEMBER
FOXES HOLLOW

He was aching after the physiotherapy session with Mary. She was pleased – it meant that he was beginning to get feeling in more parts of his body. She pushed him to the lift and they went together to the dining room. He felt comfortable with Mary. She was strong and clean, devoted to mending broken bodies, and he knew that she would do all she could for him.

'Do you think I'll ever walk?' he asked, tentatively, not sure whether or not he wanted to know the answer.

'We're really pleased with how it's going. You've already made more progress than we dared hope. We can't tell how far you're capable of going.'

He'd have to be satisfied with that. She was telling the truth, he could tell.

The door to the dining room opened. Large French windows opened onto the garden. Small vases of flowers graced the tables, of which there were two, one for the children and one for the grown-ups. Zahir had never seen tables set so nicely. This was much better than the hospital. The cutlery gleamed and the plates were made of bone china – not plastic. Instead of paper cups, lovely glasses sparkled in the rays of the evening sun that lit the room. Mary pushed his chair into place and then his mother came in with Hilary.

'Isn't this beautiful, darling?' she said, beaming and pecking him on the cheek. He blushed. Her aura was dancing. She would have so much to tell his uncles and cousins when she got back home. Or so she thought. The others came in with Hilary and a man Zahir realised was Fenton. He resembled a bat, with a hunched back and a long black coat. He had piercing eyes that twinkled at Zahir, and he liked him immediately.

'So you're the famous Zahi?' he joked. 'Well, tomorrow you'll begin lessons again. You've months to catch up, I understand. We'll soon get you racing through the National Curriculum, won't we guys?'

The others laughed. 'Don't worry!' they reassured him. 'Fenton doesn't set much store by National Curriculums!'

'Shush! Do you want the Secretary of State to hear that I'm leading you all astray? He'll take my job and then you'll find out what a crazy old bore HE is!'

A rosy glow around Fenton promised kindness and joviality, but Zahir saw also a depth of colour in the man's aura that implied he cared deeply for his charges as well as for all types of learning. Zahir wondered if Fenton was his given name or his family name, and resolved to call him 'sir' as he had done his previous teachers, until he was sure. '*Fenton*' seemed rather familiar, if not impertinent.

He looked properly at the table for the first time. He had never seen a setting like it. Neat place mats, dark in colour, contrasted beautifully with the white linen cloth. The napkins were not paper, such as he had seen at parties, but of stiff cotton, bound up inside silver napkin rings. Each place had not a single knife and fork as he expected, but a line of cutlery, beginning with a large round spoon. He wondered what it was all for. Then bowls arrived and were placed around the table by a lady dressed in black. The plates steamed with a spicy fish smell that made him realise with a start that he was aching with hunger. Fresh bread was passed round and he noticed that the others placed it on a small plate at the side of the forks. He saw his mother watching all this round-eyed. Quickly she copied what the others had done and then, like them, picked up her large round spoon and began to taste the soup. At first she scooped the soup towards her and then noticed that Hilary was moving the spoon away from her body, towards the back of the bowl, before lifting it to eat and so she did the same.

He could tell that his mother now adored Hilary and mused on this. It was strange, because they were so different. His mother was so diffident and unassuming. She kept a scarf over her head whenever she was out in public and never wore make-up or jewellery that would draw attention to her. She would regard it as immodest to be flaunting herself in any way, especially in front of men. Hilary was entirely the opposite. She was a jewellery shop on legs, Zahir joked to himself. She wore far more make up than a woman of her advanced years should and so his mother should be shocked by her. Yet he could tell that she secretly admired her for her self-confidence as well as her intelligence. She understood that Hilary did not present herself as she did because she was trying to attract male eyes, but simply to express her identity and her right to be whatever she wanted to be. And of course his mother loved Hilary for what she was doing to help her son win back his independence and his control over his body. She was a simple and trusting woman and Zahir loved her for it. She had no idea that there were any hidden motives behind the attention that was being shown to her beloved son.

Luckily Zahir had no reason for him to worry about picking his way through the minefields of cutlery and etiquette that constituted this formal supper gathering. Mary was at his side, guiding his still unsteady hand to the correct item of cutlery and then helping him to spoon the hot soup out of the bowl and bring it to his lips. She pressed against him as she did it, and he enjoyed the warm touch of her against his side and the smell of her hair. The soup was good and a feeling of content began to creep over him. This, he decided was much better than the hospital ward. This was a new beginning. He had even begun to solve the conundrum of the row of cutlery each side of his plate. He realised that there was an order and that the ones to use first were on the outside. As these were finished with they would be taken away and the next ones would take their place. He resolved to explain this to his mother when they were alone to banish her confusion. But not tonight. For suddenly a darkness was taking over his mind. A feeling of imminent danger began to turn his stomach and tie it in knots. Unable to control his neck muscles, his head swung wildly from side to side, knocking the soup out of the spoon and over Mary's hand. A moan rose from deep in his chest and grew in intensity as he became more and more distressed. Hilary shot to her feet, her chair falling backwards behind her. She rushed to his side and knelt by his chair, on the opposite side to Mary.

'Zahi!! Speak to me! What's wrong?'

'I...I don't know...'

'Are you ill? Is it pain? Sickness?'

Zahir shook his head. It was hard to speak. His mouth felt as if it were full of sticky treacle.

'Something's scaring you?'

He nodded dumbly. Hilary moved like lightning. She grabbed a phone out of her bag, but if it was a phone she did not need to dial. She pressed on it and called: 'Security team. Condition red. This is not a drill. Repeat – this is not a drill!'

A scratchy voice answered her. 'Roger. Condition red.' As he spoke, sounds like bolts moving came from every window in the room and metal shutters dropped, plunging the room into darkness. 'Access safe room.'

'Accessing now,' replied Hilary calmly, and led them all back into the hallway. Mary swung Zahir's chair around and pushed him first through the wide door. Hilary glanced up and down the hall to check that it was clear and then slid aside a wall panel. Behind it was a concealed metal door. She pressed her finger tips against a small panel at the side and a tiny light glowed from red to green. The door slid silently open and she led the way through, closely followed by Zahir, Mary, the children, Fenton and Zahir's bewildered mother. As the door closed automatically behind them, lights came on illuminating a small chamber with chairs, television screens, a drinks machine and, to Zahir's shock, a rack of automatic weapons. There was one occupant, one of the men who had driven with them from the hospital.

'Hi! OK, you're safe now,' he smiled. 'Safe room accessed,' he told a screen.

'Ground search underway,' the screen replied, and Zahir saw a picture of men with dogs walking warily around the outside of the building. 'Nothing in the immediate area,' the voice said, 'widening the search. How sure <u>are</u> we that this is a code red?'

Hilary looked at Zahir, who was shaking. Sweat was pouring from his brow and Mary was taking his pulse and shaking her head at Hilary. 'As sure as we can be. Something's seriously wrong!' She came up close and put her arm around him. 'Zahir ... it's all right ... you're safe here. Is the danger still there? Can you feel it? Can you tell me what you feel?'

Zahir tried, but his head was rolling and the words stuck in his throat. The security patrol had found nothing. 'Come back to the main house,' suggested Hilary. 'Let the dogs go...'

On the screen they saw the dogs being released. They barked and began to run in different directions, but did not seem to be finding anything that alarmed them. Hilary turned to George.

'Can you help, George? Lie back. Scan the grounds.'

6. BEYOND BELIEF

Hilary knelt down beside George, but it was Fenton who spoke to him next. He gently massaged his shoulders and then took his hand. 'Relax, Georgie ... don't worry about anything ... just let it come...'

George's eyes closed and he began to moan quietly in a long monotone. Fenton glanced at Hilary and nodded – an unspoken reassurance passed between them. The others seemed to hold their breaths for a long, long time. Beth clutched Archie's hand – they both looked full of concern for their friend. 'His spirit is floating free,' she whispered to Zahir. 'He's outside ... searching.' Then George's eyes popped open. He looked startled. The moaning stopped.

'There's a man ... by a small window ... he's hiding behind a bit of wall that sticks out ... above the ground...'

Hilary was on the intercom immediately. 'Security! We've found the intruder ... look by the yew tree ... he's not at ground level ... that's why he's hard to spot... He's hiding in the corner of a buttress.'

'Roger. We have him. We'll bring him in.'

Zahir's mother looked both bewildered and shocked. Hilary noticed her dismay and signalled to Mary, who began to lead her towards the steel door. 'Don't worry!' she reassured her. 'This is just an exciting game we play with the children to stop them being bored. Come on – we'll go and have a cup of tea...'

'You're lucky!' laughed Hilary, playing along. 'I wish I could join you! But we have the game to finish, don't we children?' They nodded and Mary left with her very confused charge. Hilary addressed the intercom again. 'It's clear in here. Code blue. Bring him here for questioning.'

'Roger. On our way.'

'Sit here, Beth. We won't need you, George and Archie, but listen carefully and if there's anything you notice pass me a note.' They nodded dumbly, just as the beep alarm sounded and the door slid open again. Two uniformed men entered, pulling between them a dishevelled-looking stranger. He was dark skinned, with a short but untidy beard. His eyes darted around the room, whilst he pretended to be amazed at his treatment. He seemed relieved to find the room contained only four harmless looking children and an elderly – if eccentric-looking – maiden aunt. His looks changed from amusement to dismay as he was placed roughly in a chair by the security guard who had escorted him there and his hands were handcuffed behind his back.

'Look here – there's been something of a mistake.'

'I'm sure, replied Hilary, icily. 'And the mistake was yours I'm afraid.'

'I can explain.' His voice, which had been a good imitation of received pronunciation, began to shift towards an Eastern European accent as sweat broke on his brow. 'My car broke down, just outside your garden wall ... I didn't want to come straight to your door in case you were ... I wanted to check someone was at home ... I was looking for a phone ... didn't want to disturb you unless it was absolutely...'

Zahir was recovering his composure. The danger he had felt was gone. He saw the man's aura darken and called across to Hilary. 'He's lying. He's very clever. He came looking for information. He's scared.'

'The boy says you are a liar.' Hilary stared coldly into the man's eyes as Tom entered the room.

'The boy! You know what boys are like! It's a little fantasy to him! He's just a boy!'

'You think so? Well let's see what a girl can do.' Hilary held out her hand to the security men and they passed her a wallet, a mobile phone and a key. 'Is this all he was carrying?' Tom nodded. 'It will be enough,' Hilary said and she turned to Beth.

'What can you tell? Try the phone first.' Beth cradled the phone in her hands and then closed her eyes. Fenton stood behind her and rested his hands on her shoulders, protectively. The stranger looked at Fenton in surprise. He had not noticed him before. He took in his beak like nose and receding chin, his dark, wispy hair. He was trying to place him. His amused nonchalance was gradually changing to perturbation and even fear.

'Just ask me questions! I can tell you anything you want to know! There's no need to bother the children...'

Hilary dismissed his offer with a sardonic smile. 'It's no bother. They're going to enjoy this! What can you see, Beth?'

Beth spoke slowly and quietly, so that they all strained to hear. 'There are so many things. Airports. Meetings. A woman. It's hard to focus...'

The man smirked. 'She's good isn't she? It's just a phone...'

Beth closed her eyes and concentrated hard on the messages coming to her from the inert mobile phone. 'Boris. He meets with Boris. He goes to his flat. It's number 12.'

The stranger lunged forward. The chair began to topple before the security men restrained him.

'My God! Give it back!' He struggled desperately now.

'The woman lives there ... called Elspeth... She works in a very important place. It's a huge building. Round ... with computers everywhere...'

The man's face was ashen. Unable to move his body, he began to grimace wildly with his mouth. Tom looked alarmed. 'Hold his mouth open! Don't let him break a tooth!'

One of the security men forced his jaw open. Tom rolled a wad of paper and jammed it between his teeth. The terrified stranger shook his head and tried to spit but he could neither dislodge it nor cry out. Tom barked at the intercom: '*Security! We need a safe prison with a dental unit! And an armed escort vehicle!*' He turned to the prisoner.

'Well ... a false tooth with a suicide pill! And you say that your car broke down? Unusual accessory for a man with a broken car!' The prisoner glared at him with hatred in his eyes. 'And a friend who works at GHQ. Called Elspeth. Not difficult to trace.'

Hilary smiled. She was glad that her little team had been so effective. 'Only a girl, eh?' She taunted the stranger. 'Well, the girl did well, didn't she?' The man swung his head wildly back and forth in impotent rage.

Tom took over. 'Get him to the car. Take him as soon as the escort arrives.'

As he was dragged from the room, Hilary turned to Beth, her expression now calm and kind. 'Does anyone know he is here?'

'I don't think so. I don't think he meant to come. I think he was passing and was curious about the security gates.'

'We'll have to disguise them so they won't attract attention. But he wasn't sent by anyone?' Beth shook her head. 'Zahi?'

'No ... he seemed to be frightened because he was helpless. No-one knew where he was...'

Tom breathed a sigh of relief. 'That's reassuring. If this had been planned it would mean that someone had traced us and our cover was blown. MI5 will handle it now. A fake accident will explain his disappearance.'

Hilary touched Zahir's arm gently. 'Zahi – do you think you can go with Mary and talk to your mum? Tell her the game is over and it was fun?'

'Yes. She trusts you.'

'That's good to know.' She smiled wryly. 'I'm not sure I do myself sometimes! Now, let's finish our supper!'

7. AND SO TO BED

Zahir snuggled down into his soft nest of a bed. His mother was slumbering at his side, curled in a large chair. She was staying with him tonight, in case he needed help with the bathroom in the night. She was leaving in the morning, so she was glad for this extra time with him. He could tell that she was no longer concerned about last evening's excitement. She believed their cover story and was glad that he was having fun with the others. He was surprised at how easy it had been to feel at home here. He liked his new name – *Zahi*. Even though it was only one letter shorter than his full name, it sounded pleasantly friendly and familiar. He had never had a nickname before. He felt he belonged. And most important of all, he was with others who, like him, were very different from ordinary children. He was no longer alone. No longer a freak. He could begin to open up, knowing that his strange new abilities would be valued here, rather than ridiculed. These kind people would help him to become stronger, not only physically but mentally too. He glanced round at all the pictures and toys that he had treasured before the terrible accident. But deep down he knew that these were becoming childish things. He was growing into a new person.

He lay awake, taking in the faint smell of his mother's perfume. It was so much better than the disinfectant smell of the hospital ward. Trees were swaying gently outside and the moonlight made ever-changing patterns as it was filtered through the dancing leaves. He began to think through all that Hilary had told him as the others went to watch television before bedtime.

He had asked her what would happen to the man they had found, trying to break in to their home. She assured him that he would not be harmed. She doubted that he was terrorist. More likely he was paid to collect information and when he realised that the game was up, would work just as readily for our own government as he did for his current employers – whoever they were. And Elspeth? She had already been identified, he was told. Listening devices would be placed in the flat she shared with Boris. Everything they said and did would be secretly monitored. Their contacts would be traced. Every so often, Elspeth would be given access to information that would seem useful and credible to a foreign power, but would in fact be totally incorrect. Without realising it, she and Boris would become a way of spreading confusion and misinformation instead of being useful spies for their countries. Eventually, they may be 'discovered' and revealed to the world as espionage agents. This would only happen when and if it became important to embarrass, for any reason, their governments in front of the rest of the world. The ways of international espionage and diplomacy were complex and strange. But they would not be killed or tortured. It was no longer the way.

Then Hilary had gone quiet. She looked at him seriously and gravely. 'Let me tell you how I came to be here and something of what we are about.'

Zahir faced her, equally serious. 'We're special, aren't we?'

'Yes and I was a little like you when I was young. I was special too, but no-one knew. And I didn't realise. '

'What was it? What was it you could do?'

'I seemed to hear people's thoughts. As if they were speaking aloud to me. I'll tell you how it happened, but keep it to yourself...'

'Sure I will.'

'It started when I was seven – or eight. I was playing in our back garden with my brother and sister. We were playing rounders with our friends. I don't think boys play it – it's a game like baseball. My sister – she's younger than me – swung the bat at the ball. Instead of going forwards, it bounced off the top of the bat and went backwards, in a high arc, out of the garden into the backyard of the woman who lived behind us.'

Zahir leaned forward, curious. Hilary was deep in thought, recalling a distant memory from her childhood. Her eyes were half closed. She seemed a long way away. 'We were scared of her. We thought she was a witch. She wasn't of course, but we were only little. Once I lost a ball in her back garden and I knocked on her door to ask for it back. I asked very politely and thought she would be kind, but she wasn't. She shouted and swore at me. Told me to get lost. Said we were a rowdy, bleeding nuisance. No-one had ever talked to me like that before. I suppose she was annoyed with the noise we made, but we thought she was evil.'

Hilary paused, remembering her feelings as a child. 'We should have left the ball or one of the older ones should have gone for it. But we were selfish. We made my little sister go for the ball. She was terrified. She was crying. I should have gone instead, but I was scared too. She didn't go to the door. She crept in through the back gate. We ran into our house and hid. Everyone held their breath ... and then I heard her say, 'Got it!' I looked round at the others and said, 'That's great!' And then slowly realised that they didn't know what I was talking about! And worse, from where I was hidden, I couldn't possibly have heard her. When she ran into our garden I hugged her and told her that I was afraid she'd been caught. She said she'd been really, really scared. I asked her what she had thought when she found the ball. 'I just thought, Got it!' she said.'

Zahir nodded. 'So you were hearing what people thought?'

'Not all the time ... not at all. The next time it happened was when my little sister got lost in the town centre. We were Christmas shopping with my mum. The shops were packed. It began to rain and we were getting soaked and so mum dragged us into a dress shop. I was staring at the beautiful evening gowns. I'd never seen such clothes. They had hundreds of sequins sewn on them in wonderful patterns so that they sparkled in the Christmas lights. I was captivated. I asked my mother if she was going to buy one, but she told me, sadly, that these were much too expensive for her and she never went anywhere where she could wear one. I felt indescribably embarrassed and sad for her. One day, I vowed, I would always wear glamorous clothes, like the stars I saw at the cinema.'

'And did you?'

Hilary laughed ruefully. 'Most people think I do too much – like mutton dressed as lamb!'

'I like the way you look.'

'Well thank'ee kindly, young sir!' She acknowledged his compliment with a mock curtsey and laughed. 'But just as I was losing myself in daydreams, my head was filled with a most terrible wailing. It was my little sister. I looked round, but she was nowhere to be seen! I screwed up my eyes and soon worked out why she was so distressed. I cried out: 'She's lost!''

'Who?' asked my mother and then she looked round and realised. 'Leah!' she cried and we ran out of the shop into the rain.

'Where are you?' I shouted, but of course Leah couldn't hear me. So I concentrated as hard as I could and thought the question, hoping she would pick it up. At first there was nothing but whimpering, but then I heard her voice again inside my head.

'I'm lost, Hil!'

'Where are you, Leah?'

She was panicking and too young to read street names. 'Don't know!'

It was so strange, because I could hear her as if she was standing next to me! 'What can you see?'

'Lots of people ... and a boy with a dog ... and a telephone box.'

I ran to where my mother was weeping, staring desperately up and down the busy road. 'I'll find her!' I cried, and raced down the street before she could stop me. The nearest 'phone box was outside the newsagent's. But when I got to the shop, there was no sign of Leah. I pushed my way through the shoppers. They must have thought I was demented. A portly, middle-aged lady tut-tutted as I brushed past her. 'Young people today! No manners at all!'

I muttered under my breath, 'Fat old cow!' But then I sighed with relief as I saw Leah talking to a store assistant who was trying to help her. 'Oh Leah!' I cried out, so happy that I had found her.

'Are you her sister?'

'Yes...'

'Where are your mum and dad?'

'My mum's just down the road.'

'Take her back to her mum then. You nearly lost her.'

'Yes, sir. Thank you!'

Holding her hand tightly, we half walked, half ran back to where my mother was. By now she was extremely distressed and a policeman was taking notes as he gleaned information from her between sobs. She was overjoyed to see us and threw her arms around us. The policemen closed his book and smiled at me. 'Well done, young lady! You saved the day and no mistake! Where d' you find her?'

I told him. He looked surprised and stared down the road. 'That's a long way back. How did you know where to look?' I didn't want to tell him. You understand why, don't you?'

Zahir nodded and smiled.

'There are some things we instinctively know that adults will not believe.'

'Can you read my thoughts?' Zahir wondered.

'It hasn't happened for a long time. I realised that I only picked up these thought messages when people were extremely agitated or afraid. And then even that stopped. But it made such an impact on me that when I grew up and went to university I specialised in ESP – much to the horror of my professors!'

'ESP?'

'Extra-sensory perception. It means being able to hear or see things that are out of the range of the normal human senses.'

'So that's why you're so interested in Beth and the others?'

'And you. Partly, but getting the funding I needed for all this (she waved her arm around the room) I had to promise the government agencies more than just pure research...' She grimaced.

'But back to my story. The more I studied it, the more I realised that many children are born with special gifts that defy accepted science as it is taught in our schools. And indeed everywhere else! Let me give you another example. This is from a case we studied as part of my university research. We found out from a local news reporter in Dorchester that something strange was happening in an old Victorian vicarage nearby. What we found was so mind boggling that we have never been allowed to publish it.

The house had been sold after the previous occupant, a vicar who lived alone, had died. The church was ill attended so the vicarage was surplus to requirements. A young family had moved in and began to redecorate. It meant disturbing the fabric of the house.

It was the daughter who was causing concern.

The reporter had heard about the problems and thought it would make a haunted house story for his paper. But his editor dumped it. So he passed it on to us.'

'The little girl!' guessed Zahir. 'Did she see dead people?'

'Yes. And how! Lindsay she was called. Cute little thing, just three years old. And it was her age that was so curious.'

'Why?'

'Because there was so much that she could not know, except by seeing ghosts. Her mum and dad became worried when Lindsay began to talk about the people who came to visit her in the night. At first, of course, they thought she was dreaming or inventing it. Children often have imaginary friends – especially little girls who don't have anyone to play with. She was an only child and they'd only just moved to Dorset. But there was something strange about these 'friends'. They wore odd clothes, like the little girl would never have seen before. The lady who walked through her room at night had a bunch of keys hanging from her belt. This was a fashion in the late eighteenth and early nineteenth centuries, two hundred years before Lindsay was born. These keys would have opened the silver cupboard, the tea caddy and the drinks tantalus. The lady of the house would keep these locked to prevent any of the servants or trades people stealing from them. Even sugar and spices were very expensive then and had to be locked away.

And then there was the little boy she saw, who she called Dickie. Oddly, he always wore a dress. Her parents tried to persuade her that this was a girl, but she insisted that he was a boy.'

'So why was he in a dress?'

'It turned out that until late Victorian times – and sometimes later – it was quite normal to dress boys, while they were toddlers, in frocks. It was more comfortable for them and made them easier to clean if there were 'accidents'. But how would little Lindsay know that?'

'Maybe she'd seen pictures of people from long ago...,'Zahir guessed.

'We needed to check that out. We went through every book in the house and then every film and television series that Lindsay might have seen to discover if any had featured scenes of Victorian life.'

'Were there?'

'We couldn't find any. And remember, she was only three years old, so would she have remembered anything if she had seen it? But that was just the beginning – things got even weirder.'

Zahir trembled. 'I've got shivers going up and down my back! Lindsay must have been well scared!'

'Oddly enough, no. In fact her parents heard her laugh at night. She said that these people were funny, because they didn't come in through the door like everyone else. They walked in through a solid wall...'

'Cool!'

Hilary laughed. 'It probably was! Most ghostly visits are accompanied by a marked drop in temperature! It's thought that to appear they must draw energy from the air. But we were university researchers, remember, so we had to carry out a full investigation. Some of us volunteered to spend the night in Lindsay's room.'

'Did you see the ghosts?'

'No. Her mum had done it before us and she hadn't seen anything either. The ghosts, it seemed, only made an appearance when she was alone. That made us a bit suspicious, so we went to the local records office to find out who had lived in the house in the past. And that is when things began to turn very nasty.'

'How?'

'The church records showed that in 1909 a new vicar moved into the parish with his young wife. Six months later they had their first child. A little boy. And they called him Richard.'

'Just like Lindsay had said!'

'That's right. 'Dickie' she'd called him, which could have been his mother's pet name for him. It was a common abbreviation. Just a coincidence? Possibly. But something very sinister had happened at that old vicarage.'

8. A MACABRE DISCOVERY

Hilary paused in her story to pour herself another cup of coffee. Zahir watched her, fascinated. Supper was over and they had remained in the dining room after the others had left. She was not drinking instant coffee from mugs, as he was used to. Instead, on the brilliant white table cloth, she poured the dark brown liquid from a silver coffee pot. She added a small amount of sparkling brown sugar from a silver spoon and then drank it, to his surprise, without adding any milk. The smell of coffee was strong and invigorating, but she passed Zahir a bottle of coke and a straw. He was grateful. It was still an effort for him to raise his hand to his mouth, and the straw made it easier for him to drink.

'You said something sinister?'

'Oh yes. But let me tell you first why the newspaper had lost interest in the story. There was an odd aspect to it. You see the little girl said that these strange visitors were floating.'

'What?'

'I know. But she was absolutely positive about this. They didn't walk on the floor of her room. They walked in the air, floating about 30 centimetres above her bedroom carpet.'

'So they thought she was making it up?'

'They didn't believe her anyway, but this was the final straw – too much for their readers, they thought.'

'How did she know it was 30 centimetres?'

'She didn't, of course. She told us they were just above her knee. But I haven't told you all that we found out from our research into the archives. You see the national press became involved when this little boy disappeared. It was in 1913, as he approached his fourth birthday. One day his mother went to the nursery to wake him from his afternoon nap and he was gone. The nursery door was closed, the window was locked, but there was no sign of the child. The Daily Chronicle picked up the story and made a national sensation out of it. A reward was offered of one hundred pounds for his safe return – a fortune in those days.

Search parties were organised by the parishioners and as time went on men and women from far and wide got involved. There was genuine concern for the family as well as the promise of riches if the boy was found. The country side was searched for miles around, not as methodically as would be done today but thoroughly nevertheless. There were reported sightings of a small boy matching his description in Ramsgate, in Putney, in Croydon. But all came to nothing. After a couple of weeks, as with all these things, it was no longer news any more. The great British public gradually forgot all about it.'

Zahir was totally absorbed in the story. 'But how awful for his family. They must have been gutted.'

'Gutted? Hmm. Well, it was heartbreaking for his mother. But coming back to the present and the case we were investigating, something worrying had happened to Lindsay. We had a text message from her mother to say that one of the visitors had made her cry. When we got to the vicarage, Lindsay was still sobbing and refusing to go back into the room. She said that the man – we assume that this was the Reverend Johnson, the boy's father - had come into her bedroom in a violent rage. He was shaking a belt and – although she could only rarely hear the words that these visitors said - was obviously very, very angry with the child. The mother was trying to defend him and the little boy seemed to be screaming.'

Zahir was perplexed. 'I wonder why?'

'We'll never know. But Lindsay moved out of the room and for a while slept with her parents.'

'Is Lindsay going to join us?'

'No. She lost it.'

'Lost it?'

'This is what happens. That's why you and the others are here. Once she moved out of her own room she stopped seeing the spectral visitors and never saw them again. You see, Zahi, as adults we use only a small part of our total brain. Some sections just seem to lie dormant. It appears that some young children are capable of firing these parts of our brain into use and they become aware of things that the rest of us cannot detect. Like me, they can hear thoughts. Like Lindsay, they can see people long dead. But as they grow older it goes.'

'Why?'

'We're not sure. It could be that like anything that isn't used enough it fades away. Or it could be that children are taught that what they think they can see or sense is impossible, so their brain eventually rejects the 'spiritual' side and accepts only the rational and scientific. What we decided to do was to find children like you who have these special gifts and instead of ridiculing you, encourage you – even help you to develop your skills further.'

'So we're like ... guinea pigs!'

'I'd prefer to call you subjects in a university research project!' she laughed.

'But why are we being guarded? Why the police escorts?'

'Ah, you're too sharp, Zahi!' Her face became suddenly serious. 'We could not have done this without government funding. And the interest is at a very senior level. Think about it ... with a hundred Zahirs, one in every rail station, at every airport, no-one with evil intent would escape detection. If we can work out how you do it and share your gift, this country will be a much safer place.'

'That'd be good...' said Zahir, thoughtfully.

'Yes, but unfortunately every terrorist organisation would see you as a major target if word got out. That's why we were so worried when that agent almost got through our security. We were very relieved when it turned out he was acting on a hunch and our cover hasn't actually been broken.'

'I see...'

'Don't worry. We're going to look after you and the others very, very well. But I can't pretend to you that this is not without risk. It's a lot to take in, Zahi. You'll have to reflect on all this and we'll talk again.'

'I feel as if I sort of belong here...'

'That's good. That's what I want. But let me tell you the rest of the Lindsay story. It has a rather gruesome end. Once Lindsay had moved out of her room, we asked for permission to investigate it in depth. We were very interested in the wall which her visitors walked through when they entered the room. If these were spirits of some kind, why would they enter the room through a solid wall?'

'It's what ghosts do!'

'Only in stories and films! So we stripped the old wallpaper off the wall. But there was nothing there – just old plaster. But when we searched out some of the original plans of the house, they showed that there was originally a link door in this wall connecting the nursery with the master bedroom. So, after promising to make good the damage, we brought in a builder to remove the plaster where the doorway was supposed to be.'

'And you found it?'

'Much more. There had been many alterations to that part of the house. The first things to come to light were holes that had once held floor joists. It turned out that the floor in that room had been lowered at some time. It had originally been about thirty centimetres higher.'

'So the ghosts were walking on the original floor? That's well scary!'

'It was exactly as Lindsay had described it. And if she hadn't actually seen the ghosts, how could she possibly have known where that door had been and that the floor had been changed? And yes, we did find the door, plastered over, just where she said the people walked through that wall. And then the most macabre discovery of all.' She reached for his hand

and held it tightly. 'When we pulled away the remains of the old door, rotting away behind all that plaster, we found the mummified body of a small boy. We found the lost boy, Zahi.'

As Zahir lay in bed he went through all of this again in his head. He was very glad that his mother was with him, dozing in the armchair beside the bed. He was conscious that this house too was very old. Were there ghosts here also? He wondered what would happen if he opened his mind to them, invited them to show themselves to him. A cold shiver ran up his spine. Maybe he could do it, but this was not the time. It was hard enough to cope with the strange skills he had already found in himself. He felt suddenly very serious. And he made a quiet promise to help Hilary all he could. If he could make the world a safer place for everyone, then that is what he would do. And then he fell into a deep sleep, as all around him the unquiet spirits that still dwelt around that old house murmured and stirred in their graves.

9. A MORNING SCARE

Zahir woke on his first morning at Foxes Hollow to sun streaming in through the many tiny panes of his window. Motes of dust drifted slowly across the beams of sunlight. He tried to stretch, but his legs did not respond and he remembered his damaged body with a sickening thud.

But then he remembered his new friends and his new surroundings – so much more pleasant than the hospital ward. He breathed in. No smell of antiseptic and stale air – instead a warm and gentle breeze stole in through a slightly open window and from somewhere the faint smell of fresh toast. He looked over to where his mother had been dozing. The chair was empty. He called for her, just the slightest edge of panic in his voice, as he recalled the danger they had faced the evening before. But all was well. Her smiling face appeared at his bedroom door.

'Ah! You're awake my little sleepy head!'

He grimaced slightly at the baby talk. 'Yes. I wondered where you were.'

'Packing now. I have a home to look after! But I'll be back to see you at the weekend! Are you ready to get up?'

'Uhmm.'

She turned and looked down the corridor. 'Mary! Can you help me, dear?'

Soon the two of them had lifted him out of bed and into his wheelchair. He was proud that now he could manage some tasks for himself in the bathroom, though he would need help with dressing. Mary smiled. 'There! You're getting quite independent now! After breakfast we'll do some work on your arm muscles to try and strengthen them!'

And then a loud scream rang down the corridor. Mary left him and ran to the door. She yelled, '*SECURITY!*'

But before half the word had left her lips, Zahir heard the bolts flying that sealed the house from the outside. Hilary was running down the corridor towards Beth's room. 'Are you all right, Beth? What's happened?'

'That was way out of order!' Zahir could not see Beth but he could tell from her tone that she was extremely angry. 'Don't you dare try that again! Ever!'

He steered his chair to the doorway, wheeled it down towards the girls' corridor, and gazed in alarm at Beth. She was standing outside her door wrapped in a large bath towel, red in the face and talking, apparently, to thin air.

'Once more and you're dead!'

Hilary was the only one who understood what was happening. She spoke first to the tiny intercom on her lapel. 'Security, this is Hilary. Stand down. Repeat, stand down.'

'Roger. Return to code green.'

And then she knocked on George's door. 'George! Out here, please. Now.'

A pause, and then his door opened an inch or two. 'What's up?' asked a voice, dripping innocence.

'Out here! Now!'

George, looking very sheepish, slid through the half opened door in his dressing gown. 'What d'you want?'

Beth flew at him, with fire in her eyes. Only the fact that she had to hold tight to her towel to prevent it from falling saved him from serious harm! Hilary restrained her. 'What's happened, Beth?

'I was just getting ready – for my bath – and I sensed him,' she gabbled, barely coherent she was so angry.

'What? I've been in here all the time ... I never...'

Hilary turned and looked at Zahir. He could see the guilt written all over George's face. His aura was filled with disturbances. Both Hilary and Zahir knew that George did not need to physically leave his room to spy on Beth. Hilary saved him the embarrassment of 'snitching' on his new friend. She turned back to George and made it clear that his behaviour was not going to be tolerated.

'The gifts we've got are not there to be abused, George. I'm disappointed in you. If we're all going to live together we have to able to <u>trust</u> each other.'

'I didn't do nothing...'

'Don't give me that. We all have a right to privacy. Do anything like this again and I'll have some hard decisions to make about you staying here.'

'It w'only a joke anyway!' George was red-faced now and very discomforted by being told off in front of his friends. 'I wouldn't have stayed while she...'

Hilary contradicted him very firmly. 'It's a joke to you, George, but not to anyone else. None of us will trust you if you ever, <u>ever</u> do anything like this again.'

George could take no more. Muttering something under his breath that, luckily, nobody could properly hear, he slammed his door as he retreated back into his room. Hilary turned.

'Let's put this behind us now. Breakfast everyone! Beth – get dressed and come down to join us. I'll sort out George. When he comes down, Beth, just be normal with him. We don't want this to spoil things between us.'

Beth, still seething, spun on her heels and stomped into her room. Hilary sighed and knocked on George's door. Not waiting for a response that probably wouldn't come, she turned the handle and walked in. None of us would have wanted to be George at that moment. Zahir was surprised by Hilary. She had always been gentle and concerned in all their dealings. But now he saw a different side to her. Her aura shone like polished steel. He knew that she was determined to sort this out and she reminded him for a moment of the headteacher of his school – a long time ago it seemed now – on the warpath when some miscreant had been identified and was being brought to justice. Determined and stern, she was a force to be reckoned with. For Hilary, this was indeed a crisis that had to be resolved and quickly. The unusual skill that George had, and which was developing well under the guidance that he was getting at Foxes Hollow, was in fact essential to the operation. To lose him would be a disaster. Her face set, she began to explain again that personal privacy is an inalienable right and had to be guaranteed in any 'family'. What he thought was funny was far from amusing to everyone else.

There were things in George's background that, she knew, went some way to explain his actions. It had been a risk taking him on, but she believed in him and in her ability to make something of him. This incident, however, came as a timely warning. It was difficult to over emphasise the unpleasant experiences that he had suffered as a young child. He had been badly neglected by his parents, who had never wanted him. They were addicted to alcohol and, she suspected, drugs as well. His presence in their home was just a nuisance to them and most of the time they were incapable of caring for him. At night, they would go out drinking. The young George was left in the house in the care of his uncle, a youth of 18. The uncle was quite happy to be left alone with George. Gradually it became clear why.

At first George would scream and cry when his parents left, but they took no notice and so he eventually became resigned to his fate. Once they were alone, his uncle abused him, night after night, in ways that were gross and disgusting.

It's impossible to imagine the effect that this pervert's actions had on the mind of the young boy. Ask George about it now and he retreats into a shell. The nightmares that he suffered have been repressed. And that, it seems, is how he dealt with the terrible assaults on his body. He left it. Somehow, he became able to detach himself from all that was happening and drift away. It was as if his body no longer belonged to him and he was able to float away into different rooms to escape from his attacker. He couldn't feel what was happening to his physical body – he was on another plane of reality. And he liked it there. And so it might have continued for years longer, but the uncle, having succeeded so easily to get his way with George, became overconfident. He began to molest one of George's school friends. This boy had parents who listened to him and cared about him. When he told his dad what the man had tried to do to him, his father went straight to the police.

George was saved – his uncle was behind bars. But he could not remain with his parents. They were judged to be unfit to care for children and he was taken into local authority care. He was given counselling to help him to overcome the trauma he had been through. That was when his extraordinary ability to detach himself from his body came to light. While a psychiatrist was talking to him, asking him to go over with her the abuse he had suffered, George's eyes glazed over. He was unwilling to live through the experiences he had just been rescued from and said that he wanted to play with the computer next door. The psychiatrist was taken aback. This was George's first visit to her office, so how did he know what was in her private office behind the closed door?

As she probed further, barely believing what she heard, she quickly realised that this was something out of her area of expertise. A little research later, she found references to a university project that was investigating psychic abilities in young children and the next day Hilary arrived to take George into her care. He was the first recruit to OSIRIS. He was the first young resident at Foxes Hollow.

George had grown into a tall youngster with grey blue eyes and a head of light brown hair that he combed back, but that often fell over his forehead in a nonchalant and rather appealing way. He had more confidence now and she hoped that the scars of his young days were largely healed. She was almost convinced that this incident of voyeurism was going to be a one-off. She was determined that he would not be allowed out of his room until he fully understood that girls were not objects, but people with a right to privacy and deserved to be respected. She sighed. She also knew that this would be a very difficult interview and would test her skills to their limits. And she knew that abused children often grow to be abusers themselves when they became adults.

10. ARCHIE PERPLEXED

Breakfast passed very quietly. When George came down with Hilary he looked very sheepish and whispered an apology to Beth.

'OK. Forget it,' replied Beth, clearly unconvinced.

Zahir wanted to do something to bring them all back together, but he was the newcomer here and didn't want to say anything that would make the situation worse. Archie had missed everything and munched happily on his breakfast cereal, unaware of the strained atmosphere. Mary and Hilary began a conversation about the weather to fill the silence. Zahir's mother was packing in her room. It was Fenton who relieved the tension.

Fenton did not live in and he arrived as the meal was ending. He breezed in full of good humour. The sun was shining and he was sure they could spend some time out of doors. He wasn't the sort of teacher who liked being shut up in a classroom. He believed that there was so much that we could learn out in the environment and today he planned a hunt for minibeasts. This sounded fun and lifted everyone's spirits. They'd work in pairs, and luckily he had not paired Beth with George. Fenton would work with Beth, Mary with George and Zahir would pair up with Archie. He wondered if he was working with the youngest boy because he was thought to be a little behind in his schooling. Did they think that his command of English might be poor because he was not white? He looked carefully at Fenton, but could not detect any hint that he had doubts about Zahir's educational competence. He was being oversensitive, perhaps. But it made him determined to work as well as the others, even those older than he.

Breakfast cleared away, George, Beth and Archie went with Fenton to gather the equipment they would need, while Zahir hugged his mother goodbye. He was glad that he could do this away from the others, so that they would not see the tears that both of them shed. His mother was all he had now, except for this new family that had adopted him. But, as they both assured each other, they'd be apart for just a few days and he was better at Foxes Hollow. Here he would get the care he needed. And, as if to prove this, Mary stepped in then to begin half an hour of intensive physio with him whilst his mother drove away in her taxi.

By the time Zahir was ready to join the others, all the troubles of the morning seemed to have been forgotten. The others had been hard at work and had constructed three wooden frames, a metre square. Three plastic containers had been 'borrowed' from the kitchen along with plastic tumblers to help to trap their prey. Archie's eyes shone when he saw Zahir. 'We'll win!' he shouted.

For Archie, the object of the exercise was to collect as many minibeasts as possible – it was a contest. Fenton tried unsuccessfully to correct him, but he was irrepressible. They switched on the tablets and entered their theses. Fenton had asked them what type of ground would contain the highest number of insects – dry meadow, lawn grass or heavy shade. Zahir and Archie opted for dry meadow grass, as did Beth. George thought that damp, shady conditions would give the tiny creatures the most chance of food and drink and so that is where he would find the most.

Each pair had to investigate each of the three soil types, count and collect the insects and other small creatures they found within their metre squares, and then bring them back to the classroom to identify them. They tapped in their introductions and listed the equipment they were going to use, full of enthusiasm. Archie was keenest of all to start fieldwork. Outside the sun was bright and was warming the ground. It was hard to believe at that moment what darkness there was in the world beyond Foxes Hollow, or how this day would end.

As they walked out into the hot sunshine, security staff followed at a discrete distance. It still seemed vaguely disturbing to Zahir, as he eyed the bulges that concealed their guns, but the others took it all for granted by now, after months of close protection. Archie led Zahir, his chair pushed by Tom, to the meadow grass beyond the lawn. Hilary was watching them through a window, whilst sipping tea. She was resting after the difficult conversation she had had with George. Zahir realised with a start that she was really quite old, and needed regular rest. Up to now, she had always seemed to him full of energy and immune from harm. She opened the window and called, 'Archie! Don't go past the haha!'

'I won't!'

'What's a haha?' Zahir asked him, puzzled.

'This ditch,' Archie told him, pointing to a long ditch that ran the full length of the lawn, separating it from the fields beyond. Zahir had not seen it until they were almost in it!

'Why is it called a haha?'

'Dunno. 'Cos it's funny if you fall in it?'

Zahir doubted this. It may be funny to Archie, but it wouldn't be funny to most people, especially as the bottom of the ditch was boggy and smelled bad. Archie flopped down on the ground, as Tom retreated to leave them to it and resumed his surveillance duties. Zahir used the strength in his arms to lift himself from the wheelchair and fall down beside him. He wasn't going to be just an observer and leave the collecting to Archie. He was determined to prove that he could be as useful as anyone. They brushed the grasses to one side and immediately found minibeasts aplenty. Archie had struck gold. He had happened by chance on an ant run. A small army of tiny creatures was marching in a thin line from some unseen ant colony to a source of food somewhere down the slope. Archie squealed in pure pleasure. 'Look at them! Thousands! We're sure to win now!'

Zahir smiled. It was clearly going to be a waste of time trying to convince Archie that this wasn't a competition. He helped him to scoop ants into the plastic box they had been given to preserve their specimens. Unfortunately, Fenton had never planned for the sheer quantity of tiny living creatures that Archie had stumbled upon. The ants were refusing to cooperate. As fast as the two boys scooped them into the container, they ran out again. Archie tried to trap them in the box by holding the lid down and then lifting just a corner to slip more in. The ants were too clever for him. They climbed over each other and moved at such speed that there were always more leaving the box than he could stuff in. He screamed in frustration. 'Stay in there! Ge'back!!'

'Use the plastic cups,' suggested Zahir. 'Scoop them up in the cup, keep your hand over it to stop them getting away, and then drop them in!' It sounded easy. It wasn't. The ants seemed able to cling to the sheer sides of the plastic cup and refused to drop out into the box. In the meantime, every ant in the box escaped. Both frustrated now, they tried different approaches. Zahir made a bridge of paper to lead the ant column into the plastic container whilst Archie, resorting to force, began to squash the ants to stun them and then dropped them into the box.

'We just have to collect 'em,' he explained to Zahir, 'and nobody said they had to be alive!'

Zahir nodded his agreement, though he thought this tactic was a bit hard on the ants. Despite all their efforts, progress was still very slow. Archie's attempts to squash the ants into submission were largely unsuccessful. The ants seemed indestructible. Most of the ones he squeezed between his hands came back to life after a couple of seconds and scurried away. The ones that stayed dead seemed to be food for the few ants remaining in the box after Zahir had coaxed them in. One of the two security guards who had brought the intruder into the safe room wandered over to them. Archie was keen to recruit him as an assistant. He pointed at the ants. The man crouched down so that he could see them properly. 'They won't stay dead, Ben!' Archie pouted, clearly feeling that the ants weren't playing fair. Ben sucked in his bottom lip and considered the problem. 'Shoot 'em!' shouted Archie, pointing to the bulge in Ben's jacket.

'Uhmm ... a bit drastic,' said Ben, dubiously. 'You need a way of keeping them in the box. You could put some treacle in...'

Zahir was impressed by this logic, but Archie had a new problem that was fully occupying his mind. The ants had begun to fight back. They were running all over his arms and legs and biting him fiercely. They may be very small, but boy could they nip. Archie began to dance around the field, trying to brush himself clear of minibeasts. Zahir started to laugh at the antics of his friend, but then realised that lying on ground infested with tiny ants was not a great idea. He squealed in dismay as he felt hundreds of ants crawling between his clothes and his skin. Unable to get up, he rolled on the hard ground in a sad attempt to squash the ants to death. Another security guard ran across to help Ben and between them they got the two boys back to the house. Then there was the ignominy of being stripped and bundled into a shower before they were both finally clear of their unwanted guests!

Dried and dressed in ant-free clothing, they joined the others in the classroom. Beth and George had had plenty of time to finish their assignments whilst the two younger boys had their mishap. They were researching minibeasts on Google to identify the many species they had collected. Fenton passed Zahir and Archie their plastic box with a sorry collection of thirty or forty ants in varied stages of distress.

'Don't worry, lads,' he said, kindly. 'You can go out later and find some more. But it's nearly lunchtime. Just record these for the time being!'

Archie ignored the tablets. He had decided that if he had not got the largest collection of minibeasts, at least he would use the biggest computer. He liked the big 20 inch flat screen monitor. Zahir watched the stag beetle that Beth had captured. He was fascinated by its hard shiny back, iridescent black. He turned to Archie to ask him to come and admire the giant insect. But there was something wrong. Archie was staring at an empty screen. And Zahir could see that his aura was very disturbed indeed. Whatever Archie imagined that he could see was leaving him stunned and speechless...

11. A WORLD IN DISARRAY

'What's up?' Zahir felt some responsibility for Archie because he was his partner, and anyway nobody else had noticed his distraction. They were all too busy writing up their results. Archie did not answer – did not appear to have heard the question. Mary turned away from the work she was doing with George and noticed, for the first time, Archie's fixed stare. She moved to Zahir's side.

He turned to Mary for help. 'What's the matter with him, Mary?'

'It's OK. This is how he goes. He can see something on the screen.'

'But there's nothing there!' Zahir protested.

'In a way there never is,' Mary explained. 'Whenever we look at a screen, there isn't really a person or an object. All that's there are lots and lots of tiny coloured dots. Look at any screen with a magnifying glass and you'll see them. But our brain turns all those dots – pixels they're called – into a picture that we can recognise.'

'But there's no picture at all,' Zahir whispered.

'Not that we can see,' Mary whispered back. 'But somehow, in a way we don't understand, Archie's brain sees pictures that we can't. To him they're just as real as the ones we see when we're watching television.'

'But what's the matter with him?' Archie hadn't moved. His stare was fixed on the screen and his face was ashen.

'I don't know. I've never seen him like this. Beth, can you get Hilary?' Mary moved up to Archie and gently took his hand. She began to take his pulse. Hilary was quickly by her side. By now, all the others had turned and were watching the drama unfold.

'Archie listen to me.' Hilary's voice was quiet and steady. 'Talk to me, Archie. What can you see?'

A sound came out of Archie. It was not his normal voice. It came from somewhere no-one would want to go. Hilary was worried. Zahir could see that her aura was dimmed and deep colours reflected how hard she was concentrating on bringing Archie back to them. She tried again.

'Archie. What is it? Come back to us, Archie!' But he continued looking fixedly at the screen, his eyes staring strangely and his skin a ghostly pallor. Hilary changed tactics. She motioned to Fenton, who stood behind the little boy and began to massage his shoulders. He spoke quietly into his ear and something about his deep voice began to stir Archie back to life.

'Come on, laddie. We're all here for you. Talk to us, kid. What's up?'

When the boy spoke, the word came from deep in his throat like a message from a distant planet. It was one word.

'Blood...'

Hilary grabbed his arm. 'Where Archie? Where's the blood?'

The boy's head turned further, Zahir thought, than a head should be able to do. The eyes stared forward, not recognising them. The hairs stood up on the back of Zahir's neck. The aura was almost gone. Where the boy's aura had been, was a black mist. He did not know what it meant, but he knew that things were very, very wrong.

'Where is it, Archie, this blood?' Fenton was keeping his voice calm, but he was signalling secretly to Mary to be ready to alert A & E.

Archie's head turned back to the screen and then spun slowly round in the opposite direction. It was as if it was moving on ball bearings.

'*Everywhere...*'

Mary clutched Hilary's arm. 'I'll call an ambulance!'

'We may have to. But give me a few more minutes ... I have a feeling about this.'

'His pulse is dangerously slow!' Mary warned.

'I know. Just two minutes. Archie. Where are you?'

'*Big ... .big place...*' Again, the voice seemed too deep for Archie's tiny frame. It resonated around the room.

'What's happened, Archie?' As Hilary continued to ask questions, Mary took hold of his limp wrist once more and felt for a pulse.

'*Bang ... big bang,*' responded Archie. His eyes, staring at the screen, glowed eerily in the light reflected from it. All of them now were gazing at the computer monitor, trying to make out anything in it except random dots.

'What can you see?' Hilary persisted, still ignoring Mary's increased agitation at her side.

'*A hand. No arm. Just bits ... bits of people...*'

'Was it a bomb, Archie?'

'*Fire ... big bang ... smoke ... screaming .. .hurt...*'

Hilary looked up at Mary. Mary frowned. 'No more than another minute, Hilary. He's stable, but very weak...'

'Archie! We need to know where you are. What is it like?'

'*Big...*'

'Yes – a big room?'

'*Smoke everywhere ... hard to see...*'

'You're inside?'

'*Lots of chairs ... hard to move...*'

Hilary jumped to her feet. She hit the intercom on her lapel. 'Tom! We're in the schoolroom! Get here quick! Fenton – switch it off. We've got to bring him back!'

Fenton moved with a speed that surprised Zahi for such a big man. He wasted no time. He pulled the plug on the computer and the screen went black. He picked Archie up like a rag doll and took him away with Mary following.

Hilary reassured the others. 'We'll put him to bed with a sedative. Mary will monitor him until he's back to rights. But we've got work to do. All of us. Tom!'

Tom entered with an air of urgency and authority. 'Are you OK?'

'We are, but lots of people won't be unless we act quickly. We've good reason to believe there's about to be a bomb attack. From what we can tell, it will be on a cinema or theatre – a large building with multiple seating.'

Tom latched on to this faster than the rest of them. 'If it's a bomb, it will probably be against a prestige target. A first night or a film premiere.'

'Can you find out if there's one happening tonight?'

Realisation dawned on Tom with a terrified suddenness. 'My God – there is! It's a royal premiere in the West End!'

'Can we stop it?'

'I doubt it. There's extensive television coverage. We'd need considerable evidence...'

'Which we don't have. Well everyone – this is going to be our first big test. And we'd better come through!'

12. LONDON – AND FAST!

The M3 Motorway, Southern England.

The children looked out of the speeding car in stunned silence. The convoy had been put together incredibly quickly. As they drove, Hilary and Tom had been on phones for at least half an hour, making arrangements for their arrival in London. The police outriders in front switched on their klaxons as they approached any junction or traffic light and so they made swift progress through the English countryside. They were approaching the outskirts of London before Hilary had time to turn to them and fill them in.

'OK, guys, listen carefully. We can't be sure about anything. Archie may have imagined the whole thing. If it's true, we may still have misinterpreted what he told us. We've very few clues and we've just had to guess at what it all meant. You saw the state he was in. We couldn't risk asking any more of him. But this is where we are. We think he saw something that is going to happen, but hasn't happened yet. That's the normal pattern with Archie. And because it hasn't happened, maybe it can be avoided. That's what we have to hope. Because if it's true, and we don't stop it, lots of innocent people will die very horribly.'

'And if it's going to happen, we can't be sure where. It could be anywhere, anywhere in the world. But as it happens, there's a prime target in London this evening. A new Lloyd Webber musical is due to have its premiere tonight. That would be enough to make it a high profile occasion. But crucially there's more. The royal family is on the guest list. This could be a world shattering event. And it could be that only the four of us stand between this country and a terrible disaster.'

Beth's face was deadly serious. 'And we can't have the premiere cancelled?'

'No. Our government's policy, ever since the Brighton bombing, has been that terrorism should not be allowed to disturb the normal business of our lives. We'd need very firm evidence indeed of possible danger to the royal family to have an event like this cancelled. And we don't. We can't even be sure that this will happen today or even in this country, No – it's up to us.'

George's earlier totally inappropriate behaviour was now forgotten. 'What have we got to do?' he asked, his voice very serious indeed.

'Find the bomber. It's as simple as that. We'll be able to park our convoy outside the theatre where we can see everyone who goes in and out. Zahir?'

'What if the bomb's in there already?'

'Good point! But that's very unlikely. Because this is a royal event, the preparation has been particularly thorough. The whole theatre has been searched from top to bottom, and then sniffer dogs went through the building. They're trained to detect the faintest trace of any explosive. So we're as confident as we can be that if there is to be a bomb, it will have to be brought in. And that's where we are depending on you, Zahi.'

She was sitting in front alongside the driver. She turned completely round and took Zahir's hands in hers. 'You have a unique ability to read people's intentions, Zahi. We need you to observe everyone going in and out of the theatre and, if you see anything that seems to you disturbing or suspicious, let us know.'

'It all depends on me?'

'You've already shown an astonishing ability to see – I don't know – into the souls of people. Remember the nurse who deliberately gave a drug overdose to the other boy in the ward?'

'Jonathan.'

'Jonathan, yes. Somehow you saw what she intended to do. You knew she was going to harm him, didn't you?'

'A darkness...'

'Yes. You see it. You sense it. And when the man broke through our perimeter and almost got into Foxes Hollow, you were the one who sensed it and alerted us to the danger.'

'I just felt something was really wrong.'

'And you were right. You can do it again, Zahi. If someone out there is going to try to murder hundreds of people, you're the one we can depend on to seek him out.'

So much praise in front of his new friends made Zahir feel very proud – and a little embarrassed. But this was too much – too much responsibility. He had never felt under so much pressure. He remembered taking tests at school and knowing that his mum was expecting him to do well. His dad too. Oh – more and more now his father's death was drifting to the back of his mind. But because this had brought his loss back to the forefront of his thoughts, tears welled up in his eyes and he felt sick in his stomach. Hilary did not know what had affected him so suddenly, but to his surprise she leaned round her seat and put her arms round him. He was pressed against the soft warmth of her breasts and breathed in the perfume of her hair. Emotions that he had suppressed for months washed over him like a tsunami and he felt as if he was drowning in grief. The small tears welled up into uncontrollable sobs. He could barely breathe and was gasping for air. Tom pulled over onto the hard shoulder and the outriders formed a defensive ring around the car.

Beth and George were shocked and watched helplessly. They had no idea what was wrong with Zahi. George sat frozen while Beth reached for Zahir's arm and stroked it, not knowing what else to do. Hilary got out of the car and opened the rear door next to the weeping boy. She squeezed in next to him and cradled him in her arms. Soundlessly, George opened his door and took Hilary's place next to Tom in front. He sort of guessed that the present situation was best dealt with by women. The male's dread of excess shows of emotion had taken over and he needed to distance himself from this outpouring of grief.

Hilary spoke quietly and soothingly to him. She sensed that it may not matter what she said, as long as she the tone was comforting. What was wrong with him? As she went through in her mind all that had happened to him, she became gradually more and more aware of the true horrors of his young life: the loss of his father; the loss of his home; the terrible damage to his body that had left him crippled. How brave he had been up to now to remain as calm and controlled as he was. She was not sure what she whispered to him. It may have been just baby talk, she thought, when she recalled this situation later. What can you say to someone who has been through so much?

Beth was sitting at the other side of Zahir. She hugged him too and tried to tell him how important he was to them. 'We're here for you, Zahi. Don't cry. You're safe with us. Stop, or you'll make me cry too...'

Slowly, Zahir began to pull himself together. His sobs were no longer continuous. He began to breathe better. Hilary stroked his hair. 'We're so sorry. We've never thought of what you've been through. We're asking too much of you. You don't need to do anything. Just stay in the car. We'll have every chance of finding the killer, I'm sure. We shouldn't have asked you...'

'No...' Zahir's words spluttered out between the tears. 'I'll try. It's not that. It's my dad...'

13. BETH'S STORY

'Oh Zahi!' Now it was Beth's turn to cry. Like George, she had neither a mother nor a father. She had grown up in a children's home in the north of Ireland. It had been founded by a group of nuns almost a hundred years ago, to care for the illegitimate children of single mothers. They ran it as if the children had inherited the wicked ways – as the nuns thought – of their parents and so the strictest discipline was needed to teach them the path to goodness and salvation. Although the nuns were long gone, the tone they had set had been continued by their successors.

For Beth, it was not a happy childhood. Life was regimented: out of bed at seven in the morning; the queue for one of the two washrooms; the ridicule and beatings if it was discovered that you had wet your bed; the unfulfilled longing for any sign of affection. One day, when she was eight years old, she had been left in the communal dining room whilst all the others went to watch an hour's television before an early bed. She had not finished her meal. The meat in the greasy stew she had been given to eat had been so gristly that it was impossible to chew. Round and round it went in her mouth, becoming dryer and more like rubber with every minute. The cook told them that they had to finish their main course. They had to be grateful for the good food that the ratepayers supplied for them. It was far better than they deserved. Nobody wanted them. Their own parents had dumped them. They were fit for nothing.

All the others had managed to swallow the disgusting food, or had succeeded in stashing it away to dispose of later. But Beth was both honest and strong willed. She was determined not to swallow the lump of gristle that seemed to be getting larger and larger by the minute. So she sat there alone, the smell of overcooked cabbage still lingering in the cold, draughty hall. Not even the clothes on her back were hers. All clothing belonged to the home. When it went, twice a week, to the laundry room, where the older girls worked, you would not get the same dress or underwear back. Provided the shabby garments were roughly the same size, any would do. She owned nothing, had nothing to call her own. Bored and lonely, she shuffled her feet under the table and to her surprise her toes touched something.

She ducked down and saw a large bar of carbolic soap. It had been left there by one of the girls with the job of scrubbing the dining room floor. She picked it up. She liked the weight of it; liked the feel of it in her hands. At that moment it became hers. She had stolen it, strictly speaking, but it was the first thing she had ever had that was hers and hers alone. It was comforting to stroke it and feel it next to her body – like cuddling a pet or a tiny baby. Her heart was filled with affection for this unlikely object and she vowed to conceal it and keep it.

After an hour, it was time for bed. One of the minders came to shoo her upstairs, but when it was discovered that the lump of gristle was still uneaten she was shouted at and beaten before finally being allowed to spit it out into a foul smelling bin. She slipped the bar of soap into the large pocket at the front of her apron. She managed to keep it hidden by bending forward slightly so that the bulge would not show. The other girls – for this was a home only for girls – looked at her sympathetically as they walked alongside her, but dared not speak. In the dim light of the dormitory she folded her apron and dress neatly, slipped her shoes under the bed and pulled the worn cotton nightdress over her head before removing the rest of her clothing. Then she slipped under the coarse blanket and waited for the other girls to go to sleep. Eventually she felt it was safe to retrieve the bar. She snuggled deep into the bed with it clutched to her chest. Then she fell into a deep sleep, the best night's rest she had ever had.

At the first grey light of dawn, she woke and squeezed the soap between the bed frame and the mattress, where it would be safe. And in the ensuing days, she collected more objects. It became an obsession. She stole a large old spoon from the kitchen. She collected small pebbles from the barren yard in which they were allowed to exercise. She saw a broken hairbrush in a waste bin and added it to her treasure trove. She was happier than she had ever been in her life and the other girls began to notice a change in her. She had never had any friends because she was always miserable, but now she was able to join in their conversations and was accepted more readily into their company. But whenever she could, she would steal away to the dormitory to be with her precious things. She began to cradle them, one at a time, in her hands. She cooed to them like small pet animals. She told them her thoughts and wept with them when days were hard. She held them close and stroked them while she talked to them.

And one day they began to talk back.

It wasn't exactly talking. And it could have been just her imagination. But there seemed to be stories coming from the objects, as if they were replaying their histories to her. It wasn't the story of the object really – the spoon did not tell her of the day it was forged in a white hot furnace. It was the people who had owned the things that she learned of, as if their thoughts and feelings had been recorded in the objects they owned. As she stroked the hairbrush she saw it travelling through the long blonde hair of its first owner. Then she felt the despair when those locks were roughly hewn from her and lay in tangles on the floor. One large pebble told her of its first contact with mankind, when it had been heated in a fire. Then it was dropped into a cooking pot by a woman from the Stone Age centuries ago to bring her water to the boil. To Beth, who had so few friends, these stories were wonderful. The more she stroked and hugged the objects the more they revealed to her of their past. For weeks she was happy and her collection grew.

She wanted to share her pleasure with the other girls. Her generous nature proved to be her undoing. She told the one in the next bed, Jane, of her new friends and how they could talk to her. Handling them as carefully as the most valuable porcelain, she introduced Jane to her large pebble, her spoon, her bar of soap. Unfortunately, none of them spoke to Jane. In fact Jane seemed surprisingly underwhelmed by these new additions to her circle of acquaintances. Worse was to come. She went on to tell the others of Beth's talking pebble. Soon, Beth was an object of derision amongst the girls, who giggled every time they saw her.

'Hi Beth,' they would say, 'how's your pebble? Looked a bit stony faced last time I saw him!' At which they would scream with laughter. 'And your friend the spoon! Been stirring up trouble again!'

Beth withdrew back into her shell. Her true friends, she realised, were not these fair-weather ones, but the precious objects that comforted her at night. Her retreat, however, proved to be her undoing. One of the girls, who tried to be popular with the minders by snitching on the others, told them of Beth's secret hoard. The dormitory was raided and her precious things were confiscated. When Beth went berserk, she had to be restrained and tied to her bed. As more of the story emerged, the adults became convinced that Beth was showing lunatic tendencies. The local authority called in a psychiatrist and it was through him that Hilary found about this strange girl who believed that she could have conversations with inanimate objects. Hilary realised immediately the terrible privations that Beth was suffering in the institution and within days she was moved into Foxes Hollow.

And so, when Beth heard Zahir say that he was missing his father, she understood the pain of having no-one to love and care for you. She leaned over and kissed him on the cheek. Zahir was so surprised that he stopped crying. He looked in amazement at Beth and then turned to Hilary.

'I'm sorry. I'm all right now. I want to do it – to try to help...' he said, bravely.

'Are you sure? If it's too much for you...'

'You need me, don't you?'

'Yes we do. And if you can help, it will be a great relief to all of us.'

Zahir straightened and sat up on the back seat of the car. He looked round and saw that they were parked on the hard shoulder of the motorway. 'There's no time to waste. Shouldn't we be going?'

Beth laughed delightedly and gave him a big squeeze. 'Oh, Zahi! I'm so proud of you!'

He rubbed his red eyes with the back of his sleeve and said nothing, but inside he was suddenly aglow with pride. Hilary squeezed his hand. 'You were destined for this, Zahi!' she told him. 'Do you know what your name means?'

'What it means?'

'Yes. In Islam, Zahir means the exterior, the surface meaning of things. Isn't that strange? Because that's what you can do for us to save all these people today. You can watch them and see something on their surface that other people can't. Something that tells you whether they're innocent bystanders or a mortal danger to everyone around them.' She turned to Tom. 'OK, let's get on our way.'

14. A RIDE INTO DANGER

The sirens wailed. The convoy left the side of the road and began to race, much faster than before, towards London theatre land. George, Beth and Zahir were excited by the speed and the noise. Adrenalin pulsed through their bodies and they stared at the rapidly changing landscape as the motorway rose above the streets around them and became an elevated artery rushing them to the heart of the city. They saw cars and lorries move aside to let them pass, suburban housing give way to office blocks, restaurants and, finally, smart, brightly lit shops. They didn't slow down until the gaudy lights of huge theatre frontages swung into view: 'The Prince of Wales', 'Drury Lane', 'The London Palladium'.

'Right,' said Hilary, 'here's the plan. There are two armed snatch squads, one at each end of the block. Zahi, you're going to walk with Tom along the lines of people queuing to enter the theatre. The doors have been kept closed until we got here. It's now (she looked at her watch) forty-five minutes to curtain up, so once they start to move, they'll move quickly. If you spot someone you suspect, Zahi, don't say anything. We don't want to put you at risk. No-one must realise that you've identified the person we are after. Just indicate to Tom in some way and we'll take it from there... Tom, how could we do this?'

'How about this?' Tom responded. 'If you see someone, Zahi, get close to them and then turn the wheelchair as if you've forgotten something and we'll move slowly back towards the car. I'll lean over you and you can describe the person to me. Then we take them out.'

'Is that OK, Zahi?'

'I think so...'

'Talk to Tom while you're going along and tell him what you're seeing. Move along as if you're friends. And we have to bear in mind that there could be more than one of them. It could be a group of two or three...'

'That's all right. They'll be easier to spot.'

'Good boy. Once you've spotted them, come straight back to the car and we leave. If things get nasty, I want you all to be safe.'

The Theatre District, West End, London.

The outriders had melted away and it was a perfectly anonymous car that slid to a halt opposite the theatre. The children could see dark blue minibuses with darkened windows at each end of the street. These contained the two groups of armed police, ready to respond whenever Zahir identified the suspect. He gulped. For the first time he realised fully the enormity of what he was being asked to do. Their car was partly concealed by a large outside broadcast van. Tom opened the driver's door of the car and stepped onto the road. He spoke briefly into his phone to tell the backup squads that they were ready to begin. He opened the trunk of the car and lifted out the collapsed wheelchair. He was strong and agile. A couple of swift movements opened the frame and locked it into shape. He helped the boy into it.

'Just over forty minutes now,' he said to Zahir. 'They have to start letting people in or we'll be holding things up. And the royal family don't like to be kept waiting!'

Concentrating hard, Zahir began rolling down the street with Tom pushing him. It was dark and just beginning to rain. The crowds were jostling forward. Most were queuing up to the entrance doors, which were just opening. A large crowd was milling around by the main entrance waiting for a glimpse of the VIP guests. Zahir tried hard to identify all the individual auras that swirled around him. Never before, since his accident awoke his new-found skill, had he tried to use it in such a busy environment. It was totally confusing. These men and women were so close together that their auras were merging and the colours were so confused that he could make no sense of them. A group of excited teenagers had flickering lights around them that were like dancing rainbows. Their auras were so bright that they drowned out the detail of the older people around them.

A man and woman were nearby and their auras were dark and sombre – but not because they were a threat, Zahir realised, but because they were unhappy. One of their parents had just been diagnosed with cancer and they felt guilty being here, enjoying themselves. A lady was showing signs of desperation – but this was because she had been standing a long time and she didn't dare leave the queue to find the ladies'! Zahir groaned. This was impossible. He gently tugged Tom's sleeve. Tom swung around immediately. 'Which one?'

'No ... none of them. There are too many Tom. They're all merging together. They're too close...'

15. IT'S ALL GOING WRONG

'I don't see how we can thin them out,' whispered Tom, seriously worried. 'Let's walk more slowly. Is that better?'

'A bit...' Zahir wanted so much to get it right. He tried harder as they wandered more slowly past the throngs of people. The danger now was that their cover might be blown. One or two in the crowd were looking with undisguised curiosity at this tall, athletic white man and the brown boy in a wheelchair, moving very slowly past them. They pushed past a policeman with a sniffer dog on a lead. The dog was edging up to each person as he or she walked past, pushing his nose towards any bag or package. To Zahir's surprise, the policeman seemed to recognise Tom. He stood to attention and said, 'Nothing yet, sir!'

'Keep up the good work! Geoffrey, isn't it?'

'Yessir!' The policeman seemed very pleased that Tom had known his name.

'We can't take any chances. If you have time, go over as much of the crowd as you can a second time.'

'Will do, sir!'

Zahir was surprised that Tom, a security guard he thought, was on first name terms with the police and seemed to command their respect. But there wasn't time to dwell on this. Things were not going well. It was easier now to pick out individual auras, but they were so varied that there simply was not time to read them all. Then Zahir spotted a figure crouching in a darkened doorway.

He grasped the wheels of his chair to stop it and tried to get a better view of the man who was half concealed between the people moving in a stream towards the theatre entrance.

There was a sour, disturbed light around him – he had a deep and bitter grudge against the world. Zahir was stunned by the man's dour, unforgiving hatred – for that's what it was. He despised all the people walking past, heading for the warmth and comfort of the theatre, looking forward to seeing royalty. It angered him that they would be boasting tomorrow they were there, at this special occasion – the first to see this new and exciting musical. He hated them because they were, in his terms, rich and successful. They did not deserve their success any more than he deserved failure, poverty and distress. Hunger gnawed at his stomach. His thinking was muddled by the alcohol he drank to make the misery more bearable. This man sat in the foul stench of his own vomit. Tom was reaching for his phone and turning Zahir quickly away to safety. But Zahir detected no threat in this sad human being. He had so much bitterness in him, but no real evil. He was pathetic in many ways, but incapable of hatching a plot to destroy all the people whose success he so resented. In some ways he had opted out of society and he knew it. He had accepted this lifestyle and there was little harm in him. He motioned to Tom to put away the phone. He glanced back at the sad figure wrapped in ragged clothes that could barely be keeping him warm. The beggar gave him a toothless grin that was really more of a sneer. He stretched out a bony arm. 'Go'any change, laddy?'

Zahir shook his head nervously. He was beginning to despair. Tom spoke to Hilary by phone. 'OSIRIS – we've been all the way down the queues and drawn a blank. The people are too crowded. Zahir says they're merging together, he can't make much out.'

Hilary was very worried – for the audience in the theatre and for the safety of her young charges. 'Bring him back, Tom. You're becoming too obtrusive.'

'There's always a chance that Archie was wrong.'

'Hmm.' Hilary sounded unsure. 'But if he's right... It's a big call.'

'How about one last throw of the dice? We may stand a better chance in the theatre itself. Most people are in their seats by now. While they're sitting in neat rows, it'll be easier for Zahi to scan them. I'll take him in.' Tom swung the wheelchair towards the theatre entrance and – apparently from nowhere – an armed police officer moved alongside them. Zahir began to understand that Tom was no ordinary security officer, but someone of considerable importance.

'Don't take him in, Tom! If there's a danger of an explosion I can't risk him or you in there!'

Tom never flinched. 'I don't think there's any danger yet. The royal party is still behind the scenes meeting the cast. If a bomb is planted, it'll be set to go off after they've entered the auditorium. These people will want the maximum impact.'

'It's a big risk, Tom. I don't like it at all...'

'We'll not stay long. Let's just see what Zahi can make out when he goes in. If it's a no go, I'll bring him straight out!'

In the protection of the car, Hilary turned to George. Both he and Beth were white-faced, sick with worry. They had had so much confidence in Zahi and in the abilities of the four of them. But could they be fallible? Was Archie wrong about the whole thing? Was Zahi less skilled than they had thought? Suddenly the situation was out of control and things could go terribly wrong. It had all seemed so exciting and secure – the police convoy had been so impressive that they felt invincible. Hilary and the other adults had seemed so competent and reassuring that they trusted them and felt perfectly safe, even in the face of a bomb threat. Now it all seemed much less certain. This might have been a wild goose chase after all and they may all look like fools in the morning. Worse still, if their premonitions proved correct, Tom and Zahi could be in mortal danger. Without realising it, they were subconsciously straining their ears for the sound of an explosion tearing and ripping through the building in front of them.

'George...' Hilary's voice sounded more tremulous than they had ever heard it. She looked straight at George, holding both his arms with her hands and staring into his eyes. 'Can you go in there and help Zahi? You'll be safe, because your body will be back here with us. Can you go in and see if you can see anything that will help Zahi?'

'I think I can ... I'll try...'

Beth gasped and put a hand on George's shoulder. Fenton wasn't with them. Normally he helped George to relax and slip out of his physical body. She felt she must grow into his role. She would try to do what Fenton did. As George slumped back, she gently massaged his shoulders. *'George ... it's going to be all right ... just relax, George ... drift away...'*

The low moan began. George was above them now, looking down on the car. As he drifted towards the theatre, he could see Hilary and Beth crouched over his empty body, still speaking soothing words to him. He could no longer hear them. The bright lights were drawing him in, past the posters advertising the royal premiere, into the lushly carpeted foyer. His physical senses were deserting him. He could not hear the music playing over the hidden speakers in the walls. He could not smell the wood polish that had been lavished on the wood panelling on the walls, or the perfume of the carpet cleaner that had left the red carpet glowing brightly. He was floating along in a mystical silence into a danger he dared not think on.

In the meantime, Zahir was struggling to cope with the pressure he was under. Tom had shown his pass to the ushers at the door and they had been allowed to enter the auditorium without question. They paused at the top of the stalls. Zahir gasped. He had never imagined that the theatre would be so large inside. It was cavernous. There were thousands of people in front of them, seated in long rows of red plush chairs. The lines of rows swept down to a highly ornate proscenium arch, with its enormous rich red curtains. Hundreds of tiny candle bulbs filled the space with sparkling lights and from all around him came a subdued buzz of conversation. The audience was expectant, quietly excited, totally unaware of the horror that might well explode in their midst.

Zahir began by scanning the people seated on the back row. Now that they were still and in orderly rows, his task was easier. He could make out their individual auras. But he was emotionally overwhelmed by the sheer numbers involved. It would take many minutes to scan each row thoroughly. Every second brought a possible disaster nearer. It was difficult not to give way to the panic that was stealing over him and threatening to make it impossible for him to do his job. Tom sensed his anxiety and leaned over to whisper in his ear. 'Just do what you can, Zahi. When you feel you can't take any more, just tell me. I'll get you out of here.'

'There are so many, Tom.'

'I know. Take a row at a time.'

It wasn't just the size of the task that was scaring Zahir. It was the complexity of what he was seeing. Up to now, since the tragic accident had so altered him both physically and mentally, he had not been in any room with more than five or six adults at a time. Furthermore, apart from the nurse who had been so evil to Jonathan and the intruder at Foxes Hollow, all of the people he had spent time with had been caring and compassionate. Hilary and Mary, Fenton and their security guards, the children who were his new friends and almost all the hospital workers: all had been concerned for others; not solely interested in their own welfare. How different it was now!

As he scanned the lines of audience, he saw some who were gentle and looking forward to a cultural and intellectually stimulating evening. But many were very different. It was hard for Zahir to separate selfishness from evil as he glossed over their auras. He was filled with dismay as he tried to understand the complexities of some of these people. Their feelings and motives were so far from his young experience that he was totally confused. These were some privileged citizens and yet their wealth and status did not, in every case, make them into contented people. Next to him a man in a smart suit with an old school tie had an aura that flared purple. He was obsessed with a divorce settlement and was mentally calculating how many of his considerable assets he could squirrel away to keep them from his wife.

A few seats further on, a power dressed woman with immaculately coiffured hair was seething with inward anger at the actions of her boss, who she believed was undermining her position in the firm. She was going over in her mind a plot to accuse him of making inappropriate advances towards her in the hope of discrediting him. All around him was a sea of egocentricity and greed. A beautiful young woman who would grace a perfume advertisement was sitting with a handsome young man. She was wearing a designer dress that must have cost him a fortune, but she was facing slightly away from him, thinking how boring he had become, and assessing the men sitting in the VIP boxes and hoping to catch someone's eye. Zahir was stunned by the darkness in men's hearts – and women's. He was growing up faster than any boy should and this was hardly the time to have to come to terms with so many unpleasant truths.

Meanwhile George was desperately trying to enter the theatre auditorium. He had never travelled so far before. After reaching the foyer he was pulling on the umbilical cord that connected his spiritual self to his body as he strained to move further, through the darkened doorways into the huge hall. Hilary and Beth clung onto his empty body as he moaned and groaned in the car in desperation. They could do nothing to help, except to hold him and to whisper reassurances. He could see through the entrance ways; he could see Zahir and Tom as they moved painfully slowly to only the third row of seats from the back – still so many to go! He could sense their anxiety at the seemingly impossible task they faced. But with a sickening certainty he realised that he could go no further. He was at the end of his strength.

Then he began to drift upward. Slowly he rose through the ceiling of the foyer and into the dress circle that had been built above it. To his relief he realised that he did not need to stretch further from his body to see into the theatre – from this heightened position he could look down on almost all of the auditorium. He began to look for any clue that might help Zahir to track down the killer.

Below him, Zahir and Tom heard the beginning of the announcement they dreaded: '*Lords, ladies and gentlemen, welcome to the Princess of Wales Theatre for this very special occasion: the premiere, in the gracious presence of members of the royal family, of a new production of...*' The house lights began to dim. Within minutes the royal guests would be ushered into the royal box and, if Archie was correct, the tragedy would begin. Tom realised that their time was up. They had done their best. He could not take a risk any longer with Zahir; they had to move out of the theatre and find safety. He was desperately unhappy not to have succeeded and dreaded to think what was going to happen after they had withdrawn, but it had turned out to be a brave but futile attempt. OSIRIS had done all it could.

The best he could hope for now was that he could perhaps persuade the royal protection squad to prevent their charges from staying for the entire performance so that they, at least, would be safe. With a very heavy heart he laid his hand on the wheelchair to turn it back towards the exit. Zahir, tears in his eyes, was trying to scan blocks of seats ahead but it was too difficult and there was still more than half of the front stalls to go. Unaware of George, looking down from high above, they began to move towards the nearest exit.

It was the tiniest movement that caught George's eye. From anywhere else, he would not have seen it, but in this elevated position, high above the rows of tiny seats and ant-sized people below, his attention was drawn to an odd flicker of an arm. He would not be able to say, afterwards, what about this had made him aware that something was wrong – it just did not look right somehow. It was as if a wire was being pulled out of clothing and a push switch being readied. It could mean anything, but worryingly this was happening in a seat just below the royal box. Furthermore, the person (he could not see a face because he was looking directly down onto the top of the head) seemed to be trying to disguise the movements being made. He had to get back, to tell them what he'd seen so that Tom and Zahir could be told where to direct their search. In a split second, like a long length of elastic that had been stretched to its utmost, he flew back into his body. He opened his eyes, and found Hilary inches away, full of concern. 'George ... speak to me. Are you OK?'

'Zahi?'

'He's still in there! We're pulling him out. Don't worry, he'll be all right.'

'No! Tell him I saw something ... he's gotta go further in.'

'Oh George!' Beth's threats to him earlier were now forgotten. 'You found him! That's so cool!'

'Can you describe him, George?' Hilary was ready with her phone. 'Tom! Stay a minute! George has a lead!'

'OK, Hilary, we'll wait, but be quick. I'm getting very nervous.'

The announcer was preparing the audience for the imminent entry of the special guests: 'Lords, ladies and gentlemen, please be upstanding...'

George was pulling his thoughts together. 'I dunno what he looks like, but I saw him, with some wires ... he was sitting just under the royal box...'

Hilary gently shushed him and became ultra efficient. 'Tom, the suspect is seated below the royal box. Wheel Zahir down there straight away. Tell him to concentrate only on those seats. If he hasn't seen anything within two minutes get him out as fast as you can...'

'We're moving down now.' He leaned down to whisper to Zahir, letting him know why they were moving back into danger. Zahir nodded and looked towards the ends of the three or four rows nearest to the box. The royal box was spotlit, ready for a grand entrance. Everyone would want to see these important guests, would want to applaud their arrival. It was called a box, but it was not box-like. Like others it was set into the side wall of the auditorium, above the seating rows, and was shaped like a large pocket. There were several comfortable seats inside, sprays of flowers and a uniformed usher to look after the guests. The front shelf had been decorated with fresh flowers and, unlike the other boxes, heavy velvet drapes would frame the occupants. It would become a highly ornate sarcophagus once the killer carried out the attack.

'One minute, Tom, no longer...'

'I'll try to delay them!' Tom passed the phone to Zahir and pulled a police walkie-talkie from an inside pocket. He began to plead with royal protection officers to delay the party's entrance, but the whole theatre was on its feet now, all heads craned towards the royal box.

All but one.

Zahir was too low down to see over the heads of members of the audience, but he strained to see the auras of those who were closest to the box. Immediately he saw that one of the auras was black and throbbing with a chilling mix of fervour, anticipation and deadly determination. *'There Tom! At the end of the row! The one who's still sitting down!'*

The usher in the royal box moved to the door, ready to open it to admit the royal guests. The orchestra began to play the first notes of the introduction to the national anthem. Tom called to his men already in position in the four corners of the theatre: 'We have a bandit. End of row 8, below the royal box. Use maximum force if necessary!'

Immediately two men moved from the end of the front row and started to walk briskly up towards the eighth row, drawing guns from holsters concealed beneath their jackets. Tom used all his strength to push Zahir as rapidly as he could to the exit at the rear of the theatre. He leaned over the boy to use his own body as a shield against the blast of the bomb. Their progress was impeded by more of Tom's officers running down the aisle to provide back up to the other two. Members of the audience nearest to the action were beginning to realise that something was wrong and some of them began to leave their seats and stand in the aisles feeling confused. They were seconds away from a mass panic.

The person they were trying to arrest still had not been identified. No-one had seen the suspect's face, but the movement of armed men had not gone unnoticed by the person they were hunting down. The assailant realised that it was all going wrong and began to make an escape. And, in the growing confusion, no-one noticed the slim girl in the long black skirt who slipped from her seat and slid quietly up the side aisle towards an emergency exit.

The first armed officers arrived at the end of the row and stared at the empty seat.

'There's no-one here, sir!'

'What!'

'It's empty!'

'Hold your position! Don't let anyone move!'

As Tom barked out orders, Zahir had the chance to spin his chair round and look down the auditorium to where the action was. He realised instantly that the person with the aura that had scared him was gone. He let his gaze move down towards the stage and it was then that he noticed the emergency exit. He immediately recognised the person opening the exit door as the one whose aura had so disturbed him. For a lingering second, the girl's dark eyes stared into his and he knew that she had seen him also. In that single second, something had passed between them and she knew that this innocuous looking boy in a wheelchair had played a vital part in her discovery. They would meet again.

But then all hell broke loose. One of Tom's officers made an alarming discovery. 'SIR! A package! There's a package under the seat!'

'Evacuate the theatre! Get everyone out! FAST!'

As a pre-recorded public address announcement asked everyone to leave the building calmly and not to panic, Tom steered Zahir out of the foyer and into the road outside. Within seconds they were back in the car. Quickly, Tom filled Hilary in on what had happened inside and then called in the bomb squad that had been waiting discreetly two streets away. The royal car raced past them with its escorts on its way to the safety of Kensington Palace. The people leaving the theatre were beginning to crowd the road, even though police were urging them to move on. Hilary decided that it was time for them to leave, while it was still possible to drive freely down the road. As they turned the corner and began to speed towards the motorway, the car suddenly juddered and they heard a loud long 'kerrump' noise. The bomb had exploded and blown half the auditorium to smithereens.

16. AFTERMATH

Beth was full of praise for her two friends. 'You were well cool! George – you were great! Zahi – did you see him?' Their eyes were sparkling and they were all elated with their success. The mood darkened slightly as they heard Tom on the phone to his back-up teams.

'Any idea of casualty figures yet?'

They heard the crackling response over the car speakers: 'We're checking now, sir. Most people got out, but the exits were blocked by people trying to leave in a hurry.'

'Roger. Are you inside?'

'Yessir, but it's hard to see. The electrics are out and it's full of dust and rubble.'

Another voice: 'Paramedics are bringing in emergency lights. We'll have a better idea soon...'

'Roger. Listen – if you can find anything that might have been part of that package, bring it to Foxes Hollow. Keep it out of the bomb squad's hands!'

Hilary looked at him approvingly. 'Good work, Tom. There may be something that Beth can use.'

The three children were quieter now. In their elation at having succeeded in such a critical task, they hadn't realised that some might not have been saved. As the news filtered in from the bomb site, it became clear that, though a major tragedy had been avoided, some of Archie's vision had become a reality. Not everyone had had time to escape. It was already clear that there had been loss of limbs and possibly of life. A fleet of ambulances was ferrying away the injured and every large hospital in the central London area was gearing up to receive the casualties.

As they reached the gates to Foxes Hollow, the outriders halted and moved aside to let them pass. The electric gates opened noiselessly. As the car turned onto the long drive to the house, the first news broadcasts came through on the car radio.

This is the BBC. We interrupt this programme to bring you an important news report from the BBC news room in London.

A woman's clipped voice took over. *Reports are coming in of an explosion in the Princess of Wales Theatre in the West End of London. The theatre was hosting the royal premiere of a new production. Initial reports confirm that there have been casualties, but that all members of the royal family are safe. Police sources have told the BBC that without the timely intervention of our intelligence forces, this could have been a far greater tragedy.*

Acting on information received, the theatre was evacuated before the bomb could be exploded and most of those attending the premiere were able to leave the theatre safely. London hospitals have declared an emergency alert and are treating those who remained inside. We'll bring regular reports throughout the night as more information becomes available...

Once back in the house, they gathered in the dining room. A white damask cloth was laid with mugs of hot chocolate and plates of warm muffins and fresh cream cakes. Hilary told the three of them to help themselves while she checked on Archie. As George attempted to stuff a muffin and a chocolate éclair into his mouth, both at the same time, Zahir turned to Beth, who was eating much more gracefully. 'Can I tell you a secret?'

She nodded. Her eyes asked what it was, while her mouth continued to chew the muffin.

'I saw the bomber, I think,' he whispered.

'Have you told Hil and Tom?'

'No.'

'Why not?' she asked as she spluttered a few crumbs in surprise.

'I don't know. I might be wrong.'

'How sure are you?'

'Pretty sure, but she...'

'She!!! It was a woman?'

'No, no ... it was a girl!'

'WHAT!!'

Just then Hilary re-entered, with Archie in tow.

'Here he is, right as rain! Once he heard that there were cakes to eat, it was impossible to keep him in bed!' Hilary laughed and released Archie's hand so that he could get at the food.

'I'm starving,' he declared, taking a muffin in one hand and a cream cake in the other. He sat down next to Zahir, his new best friend, and he began to eat happily, all his traumas of the day forgotten.

'Sleep is a great healer,' said Hilary to herself, quietly.

'Go on – tell her!' Beth hissed to Zahir.

'Tell me what?' asked Hilary. Not having had walkmans or iPads in her teenage years, she had not damaged her hearing by listening to over-loud music and so her ears were as keen as a sixteen year-old's.

Beth took matters into her own hands. 'Zahi thinks he saw the bomber!'

'Really? Hold on, we'll need Tom.'

Tom came in almost immediately. There was a subtle change in him, Zahir thought. Or maybe it was just in the way he viewed him. Up to yesterday he was simply a friendly security guard who was always kind – even to two rather silly boys trying to capture an army of ants. For the first time now Zahir looked at him more closely. He realised that this was a very intelligent man and one whom, away from Foxes Hollow, commanded considerable respect, as well as a considerable paramilitary force. He was still learning to interpret the many different hues of the auras that he saw round people, and Tom's, he recognised, contained a still, green hue that suggested calm authority. Tom was carrying a notepad and asked Zahir to tell them what he had seen.

'It was just before your men found the package. I saw someone at the emergency exit...'

Tom scribbled on his pad. 'This was before the announcement to evacuate the theatre?'

'Yes.'

Tom and Hilary exchanged meaningful glances.

'Then it could well have been the person we are looking for. No-one else would have had a reason to leave early.'

Hilary was excited and wanted to know more. 'What did he look like, Zahi?'

'It wasn't a he!' said George, eager to be part of this and not to allow Zahir and Beth to be the centre of attention.

Tom began to scribble. 'It was a woman? You're sure?' He sounded dubious.

'Not a woman!' exclaimed Beth. 'A girl!' Zahir was glad that he was not the one revealing this information. He had problems with what he had seen, with her reaction to him

'Are you sure, Zahi?' asked Tom, writing rapidly.

Hilary could tell that he was discomforted. 'What's the matter, Zahi? Was there something about her that worries you?'

'She looked straight at me. I think she knew that I had found her out...'

Hilary sounded firm. 'All the more reason that we trace her and find her quickly.'

He told him all he could of the tall slim girl with the dark hair and the piercing black eyes that had looked deep into his soul. Why did he feel so bad at doing it? Strangely, he felt that he was breaking a bond that had formed between them. It was almost as if he was in league with her, as if she had established a sympathetic link with him when they exchanged that brief but meaningful glance. He felt no pleasure at what he had done and was relieved when Tom cast doubt on this new suspect.

'I am sure that you saw something, but this doesn't fit with any of our information from other sources. We have no hint at all that girls are being recruited in the UK. Think, Zahi – could it have been a young man dressed as a girl? You said that she looked very tall.'

Zahir hesitated. 'I suppose it could have been...' But he knew it wasn't.

Tom looked thoughtful. 'It's happened before - instances of gunmen wearing long black dresses and using them to hide AK47s. We'll put out some feelers, but we'll be careful not to give away that we may be on to something. In the meantime we're pulling in all known suspects. It's a huge operation. There is good news – we have a couple of pieces that we think came from the package that contained the bomb. They'll be here by the morning, so maybe Beth can cast some more light on things.'

'I'll try!' Beth was pleased that she might at last be able to take an active part.

Tom glanced at his watch. 'It's time for the ten o'clock news. Turn on the television, George, and let's see how much is being reported!'

The explosion was, of course, the headline item and though the reporters had little in the way of facts to report, they managed to stretch out what little they knew to almost twenty minutes. Almost everyone had escaped – that was the good news. The bomb squad had deployed one of their robotic devices to investigate the suspect package. It had rolled down the side aisle to the seat under which the bomb was hidden and the soldiers were at a safe distance viewing images from the robot on CCTV when the device exploded. It was estimated that eighteen or twenty people had been injured – some seriously – when part of the ceiling collapsed. Several hospitals were treating a range of injuries. These included loss of limbs. Archie chirped, 'Told you so!' and was disappointed when no-one seemed to take any notice. Several possible witnesses were interviewed, at least two of whom were obviously embroidering their account of events to make it sound as if they had seen more than they actually had. Hilary was relieved that no-one mentioned seeing a suspicious car near the theatre, or a boy in a wheelchair acting strangely.

For the moment at least their cover was safe.

Then there was a statement from Downing Street. The Prime Minister was grave.

This evening an attempt was made to assassinate members of our royal family, along with very many of our fellow citizens. These potential victims had done nothing wrong. They were cruelly targeted in a vicious and evil plot. Fortunately our intelligence forces were too good for the terrorists and not only detected the plot, but were able to pinpoint the actual location of the explosive device and arrange for the evacuation of the theatre. It is entirely due to their brilliant insights and to the heroic actions of the police, fire and ambulance crews that a major tragedy has been largely averted.

Our thoughts are with the families of those innocent people who are now suffering in hospital, some with life-threatening injuries. We thank God that there were not more and send our condolences to all who have borne the brunt of this evil and cowardly attack. Let those responsible be sure that we shall leave no stone unturned until they are brought to justice. And anyone who thinks that our wonderful country can be brought to its knees by acts of terrorism – know that we will not be bullied or beaten. The British people will stand firm. We will uphold the values of our great nation and of democracy no matter how hard the enemies of freedom and free speech try to intimidate us. Good night to you all and God be with you.

As his words faded, the occupants of Foxes Hollow sat in silence. In most cases, this was because they were taking in the enormity of what had happened. In Archie's case it was because his mouth was too full for him to speak without losing several grams of cream cake. He was, however, the first to break the silence. 'Wharabout me? I found it! He never even mentioned me!'

Hilary tried to smooth things over. 'You all played a vital part in the operation, Archie. But we can't allow your names, or even your existence to be known by the world. You'd be media celebrities without any doubt, but you'd also be targets for everyone with something to hide. And you'd also be little use to us any more because you'd be recognised everywhere you went! So for the time being at least you have to stay hidden and safe, but one day there'll be books written about the OSIRIS Project and you'll all be famous!' Archie was unconvinced.

'But important people know that the entire nation owes you all a debt of gratitude,' Tom assured them. 'We've already been contacted by Number Ten to ask you to come to Chequers, the Prime Minister's country estate, at the weekend so that the PM can thank you in person. And you are assured of a reception at the palace when we can work out how to keep it out of the media spotlight!'

Hilary smiled. 'So don't worry, your contribution is being fully recognised!'

'Will we get medals?' asked Beth.

'I'm sure,' laughed Tom, 'and a knighthood at least! Arise Sir Beth of OSIRIS! But we have lots to do tonight. We're going to go through hours of surveillance video looking for Zahi's young lady. I won't get much sleep tonight. But there's no reason for you all to stay up any longer. Bed all of you. You've had far too much excitement for one day.'

And secretly they agreed as they made their way upstairs to the comfort and safety of their beds. Or so they thought.

17. A NIGHT OF TERROR

The others were very excited at all that had happened, but Zahir was troubled. Hilary knew at once that he was feeling disturbed and so, after Beth, Archie and George had run upstairs, she stopped Mary beside the rickety lift. Mary pulled the chair back out and looked questioningly at her. She knelt down beside him. 'Is something worrying you, Zahi? You look anxious about something.'

'The girl...' Zahir wasn't sure how to explain.

Hilary tried to reassure him. 'Are you worried because you might have got her into trouble? You've no need to be. If she's innocent, she has nothing to worry about. Tom will just check out the tapes and we'll try to watch what she did tonight. Nothing will happen to her because you pointed her out to us. It will all swing on whether or not she carried that package into the theatre.'

'It's not that.'

'No?'

'No. I'm sure she left the package.'

'So what is it? Share it with me...'

'What they said about it ... on the telly and the radio ... it wasn't really like that...'

'I don't understand. You saw what happened!'

'Yes but they said ... evil ... done by cowards...'

'It is evil, isn't it, to try to kill all those innocent people?'

'I suppose ... but that girl, she was so sure that she was right...'

'Right?'

'That it was the right thing to do ... a good thing...'

'Oh I see. She thought she was on a mission?'

'Sort of. That it was a sort of equalling up. A pay back for what had happened to her family...'

'Zahi, nothing can make it right. Listen. If we find her, she'll be able to tell us what drove her to this. She'll get a fair hearing. Trust me.'

'I do but...'

'Go on. Tell me what's on your mind.' She was gentle and coaxing. She liked Zahir very much and felt guilty in some way that he had become so involved in these terrible events. She wanted him to be happy with his part in it.

Hilary's manner encouraged him and made him confident enough to voice his concerns. 'They said she was a coward. She wasn't a coward, Hilary. You should have seen her. She was so brave!'

'Of course. To agree to take part, to carry that package to the theatre when it could have exploded at any moment...'

'Hilary,' Zahir was determined to make his point. He interrupted her for the first time ever. 'There's more. She was going to stay to make sure it happened as planned. She would have died for what she believed in. How could they call her a coward?'

'Sometimes people have to say things that people want to hear.'

'Even if it's not true?'

Hilary thought hard. It was difficult to explain. 'It would be dangerous to praise those who plan to blow up public places and kill any number of men, women and children. It would send the wrong message, don't you see?'

'I suppose so...'

'Come on, Mary – take him to bed. Maybe by tomorrow Tom will have more to tell us. He's got a dozen officers working on the video tapes and Beth will have some artefacts to examine. Don't let this spoil things for you, Zahi. You've been a hero tonight. After a good night's sleep, you'll feel better.'

And she truly believed this would be true. It only goes to show how wrong even the cleverest of us can be.

Zahir felt confident to use the bathroom on his own now, so Mary put two large cushions in an armchair so that she could stay in the room in case he needed her in the night. When he came back into the room, she helped him into his bed, hugged him and then settled down for the night. It was dark outside and when Zahir leaned across to switch off the bedside lamp the room turned black – darker than he remembered it being the night before. The blackness was so thick he could almost feel it. The room felt very cold. He was very tired and as he pulled the duvet over his face and closed his eyes, he was quickly asleep.

Sometime after midnight he awoke, with a strange feeling of dread. It felt as if icy fingers were brushing across his face. The hair on the back of his head bristled and stood on end. He used his arms to raise himself up and peered into the darkness. There was a grey misty shape at the foot of the bed. Without meaning to, he began to moan quietly with fear. The shape was vague and shifted and shimmered. Eerily it formed itself into a gigantic head and two empty eye sockets stared darkly at him. He tried to raise his hands to protect himself and cover his eyes, but his arms were frozen. The sockets filled and became two eyes staring at him. Dark eyes. Black eyes. With a chill of fear he recognised them – they were the eyes of the girl in the theatre.

The large grey shape began to form into a face. There was her nose. There was a mouth, with dark scarlet lips. Slowly it opened wider and wider until the whole face was distorted by a terrifying scream that at first was soundless and then became louder and louder. Zahir's eyes bulged out in fear and he tried to cover his ears to protect himself from the dreadful cry of a soul in torment. And then objects around the room began to rise into the air as if floating up on an invisible column of air. Things he had loved and treasured – a toy plane, a railway locomotive, a football – hovered in the air and then with a terrible screech were hurled towards him as if by an unseen hand. All the while the eyes glared at him with hatred so strong that Zahir could feel it, chilling him to the very core of his being.

Mary was awoken by his cries and rushed from her chair to the doorway to switch on the light. Zahir heard the piercing screaming and realised that the noise wasn't coming from the ghostly face but from his own mouth. His skin was cold and damp. He looked for his toys – they weren't where they had always been. Mary was holding him. 'It's OK, Zahi. It's okay. It was a nightmare. That's all.'

Zahir clutched her as his eyes darted round the room in fear. 'I saw her, Mary. She was here.'

'Who?'

'The girl in the theatre. The girl with the bomb!'

'There's no-one here but us, dear. It was just a bad dream...'

'She hates me!'

'But Zahi,' she hugged him in delight, 'something wonderful has happened! Your legs moved!'

Under the shock of seeing his nemesis in the room with him, a broken part of Zahir's brain had been triggered into action and his legs had been drawn up, as he curled into a foetal defensive position. Mary straightened them again. 'Try again! Try to move them!'

Zahir grunted as he struggled to do what she asked, but his mind was still very distracted by what he had just been through. The legs remained determinedly motionless. Mary hid her disappointment. 'Don't worry, Zahi. Now we know you can do it, it'll happen again. It's a great breakthrough!' And she gave him a big squeeze. But she was worried by his silence.

She pressed her hand against his forehead to check his temperature and then took his pulse. 'I'll get you something to help you sleep.' She was gone only a moment, but it seemed to him an hour. Even in the glare of the light bulb, the room still seemed to be full of menace. He stared at the floor. The toys were lying on the floor where they had dropped. *If it was a dream,* he wondered, *why aren't the toys still on the shelf?* He said nothing of this to Mary when she returned. She had been so dismissive of what he had seen that he thought that she would take little notice of him now. He took the glass of milk she offered him and the sleeping tablet. His eyes closed again and he fell into a dreamless sleep. Mary, as soon as she was sure that he was settled, left the room and went to wake Hilary. The sleepy woman thanked her for letting her know what had happened and told her that it was only natural that he would be disturbed after what he had been through.

Meanwhile, unknown to everyone, the dead spirits of the house stirred and surrounded the sleeping boy to protect him from a danger they recognised as very real.

18. BETH'S DISCOVERY

When he awoke the next morning, Zahir was still shaken by his strange unsettling dream – if a dream it was. Mary attended to his every need, reassuring him that everything was fine. He joined the others for breakfast and found them much more confident and ready for the meeting with Tom than he was. He tried to put the image of the girl out of his mind, thinking that he was being less brave than his friends. But what Tom was about to show them would bring it flooding back.

They went up to the school room where Fenton had set up a projector linked to a laptop so that Tom could use the computer for his presentation. Zahir was gradually realising the full complexity of the arrangements at Foxes Hollow. Fenton was not an ordinary teacher. He was linked in some way to Tom and the security force that was more and more clearly an offshoot of MI5. They were able to call on police and army resources with ease and, though they seemed ordinary civilians, they were obviously high ranking and trusted at the highest levels.

Once Hilary and the children were settled, Tom switched on the projector. It showed a picture of the inside of the theatre. It was a scene of devastation, with large sections of the ceiling crashed down onto the seats below and the area around the royal box totally wrecked.

'Thanks to your efforts,' Tom began, 'a dreadful loss of life has been avoided. Very few were left in the auditorium when the bomb exploded. You can imagine how different it would have been if this theatre had been packed with men, women and children. Archie – it's thanks to you that we were forewarned about a possible disaster. Hilary, your faith in him and your quick thinking helped us identify the possible target.

Zahi and George, your courage in going into the theatre and your special skills enabled us to find the bomb and evacuate the building. Beth too will play her part when we move on to look at some of the items we've brought here from the scene.'

His expression was firm. 'But there are things that are very worrying about this terrorist attack.' He brought up a new slide. 'One: the person who planted the device escaped and we don't know where the bomber is. Next slide: Two: if it was the girl that Zahi saw, she's not on our radar. This could be a new cell totally unknown to us. Three: the explosive used was particularly effective.'

He brought up a new image, taken from a website. 'This is the kind of chemistry we are accustomed to seeing used. It can be horrendously effective, especially if mixed with nails and bits of metal that tear victims to pieces. But it's very crude and they need large quantities of chemicals to make a decent bang – that's why they go for car bombs. This bomb was small but highly explosive. A package the size of a shoe box tore a huge hole in the theatre and could have killed hundreds. We're still analysing it, but it looks like it was a highly sophisticated liquid explosive. You can imagine why this is very worrying. It means this group has access to cutting edge science. We can make explosive devices as small and powerful as this, but we didn't realise that the technology had been leaked. It makes these groups much more dangerous, because the bombs will be both more powerful than ever before and harder to detect. It also means we have to retrain our sniffer dogs. They aren't currently able to detect this new chemical, which helps to explain how the bomber got past the security in the queue.'

Then his voice went quiet and grave. 'The next picture is one that I'd rather not show you, but we've got a good reason for sharing it with you. This shows what happened to the two in the audience who received life threatening injuries. If we hadn't intervened, this is what would have happened to almost everyone trapped in that building when the bomb went off.' The picture showed part of the seating near the rear exit. The seats had been flattened. Dust and small pieces of rubble were everywhere, but just discernible in the debris were pieces of something that had once been a human body: a hand grey with dust, no longer connected to an arm; a foot and part of a leg, the shoe still in place. Beth gasped, 'Oh my God...'

Archie was excited. 'That's what I saw! I saw that!' He was still too young to associate pictures of death with pain and misery. To him, it was just exciting.

'I think some of you may be wondering whether or not we should hunt down the people who did this.' He exchanged a meaningful glance with Hilary. Zahir knew that this was meant for him and understood for the first time how closely Hilary and Tom worked together. He also noted how Beth stared at Tom and hung on his every word. This was only the beginning of his third day at Foxes Hollow, but already the complexity of the human relationships within it were becoming clear to him.

Tom continued. 'It's vital for the security of our country and the safety of everyone across the world. This act of terrorism was done to gain maximum impact. Even though we managed to minimise the collateral damage, the publicity it has gained across the whole world has been immense. It's been headline news on every television station in every country on Earth. If we don't track down and arrest the perpetrators of this atrocity they will strike again and again. They will want to build on this success – and the horror you see here will be repeated on a bigger and bigger scale.'

Zahir looked across at Hilary. She smiled at him. He tried to smile back, but he felt dismal and sluggish. It could be that the effects of the sleeping pills had not fully worn off yet. Hilary frowned and glanced at Mary.

Tom brought up the next slide in his power point presentation. 'Now let's turn to the possible suspect – the girl that Zahi saw. Well done, by the way, Zahi – this is a great lead.' Zahir tried to smile back at him, but it came out very weakly. 'Unfortunately, the bomb destroyed the CCTV cameras in the theatre and damaged the recorder, but we're working to see if we can rescue anything from the hard disk.

The camera in the street outside was working and we found this – is this the girl?'

Zahir stared at the screen. He saw a blurred picture of part of the queue outside the theatre. The shot had been enlarged and centred on a slim dark figure in a long black dress with a short coat over it. A chill went through his body as he gazed at the top of her head. Tom asked again. 'Is this the girl? We have a few other shots similar to this, but none of her face. She kept her head down to hide her face.'

Zahir took in the long dark hair and nodded. 'That's her.'

'Good. If you look closely, you'll see a bulge at her tummy. If she had been carrying anything, it would have been examined by the security people in the foyer. But she must have strapped the package to her stomach so it looked as if she was pregnant. Clever – no-one's going to suspect an innocuous looking girl who is heavily pregnant. Now that you've identified her, Zahi, we'll track her back using all the street cameras in the area to see where she came from and hopefully get a better view. Once we have a shot of her face we can use our face recognition software to identify her, or at least to help us to spot her next time she ventures out. Now Beth, this is what we've got for you. It's not much, I'm afraid.'

And it wasn't. He opened a small bag and produced a charred length of wire, a scrap of plastic and the deformed remains of a small, cheap, plastic alarm clock. Beth took them from him as if they were treasures and bit her lip in concentration. She was determined to do her best and impress them all. And especially, thought Zahir, she wanted to impress Tom!

She selected the wire first, cradled it in her hands and then began to stroke it as if it were a stick-like baby. She began to rock to and fro gently. They all waited quietly.

'They're just fragments...there's not much coming through,' she began at last and Tom switched on a small recorder the size of a mobile phone to catch her words. 'This wire was cut and wrapped round something. I'm not getting much from this. Wait, I can see someone! It's not a girl. It's a man, a big man, with a dark beard ... not a cut beard ... a rough, untidy one...'

'Can you see where he is?' asked Tom, urgently.

'Inside ... somewhere ... he's by a window ... the glass is dirty ... no ... there's something ... bars ... or a grid ... across the glass. That's all I can get!'

'That's good, Beth! It's more than we hoped!' Beth glowed with pride at this praise from him. 'Now, try the other things!'

She put the melted clock and the scrap of plastic together. Zahir realised that they were probably part of the same thing. Again she cradled them and began to rock. She made no sound. The silence seemed never-ending – especially to Archie. It exceeded his concentration span.

'I'm bored!' he announced. 'I wanna play with Lego!'

'SHUSH!' hissed George, not wanting him to break Beth's concentration. Fenton smiled and passed Archie the Lego box from the activity shelf in the school room and crouched down with him as he began to link the brightly coloured plastic bricks together. He put his finger to his lips to remind Archie that he must be quiet.

Beth spoke at last. 'It's hard 'cos the surface is all burnt. The memories have been wiped out by the blast. I've got to go in deeper...'

'Anything, Beth,' said Tom gently. 'Anything will be useful.'

'It's been handled by three people, their memories are caught up on it. One is the man with the beard. Another is a man in a white coat, like a chemist. And there's another ... with dark eyes, so very dark ... black...'

Zahir shuddered. He knew who the third person was.

Tom moved the miniature recorder closer to Beth. 'That's good, Beth! Anything else? Where are they? Can you tell?'

'Big, big place... Lots of windows...'

'A block of flats?'

'No... I don't think they live there. They go there to make things...'

'Is it an office? A factory?'

'I don't know... It's big, empty ... dim and ... dingy...'

Beth dropped the pieces of the clock and put her head in her hands. The strain had been too much for her. Archie squealed in dismay as the distorted lumps of plastic fell on his half built model. Beth opened her eyes to look at him. 'What's the matter?'

'You bombed my buildin'! You spoilt it!'

Beth dropped to her knees and examined it closely. 'What's that?' she asked, pointing to a pulley.

'It's a crane, stupid!'

Beth looked up at Hilary and Tom. 'There was a thing like that, on the building I saw...'

Tom knew immediately what this meant. '*A warehouse!*' he cried. 'An old warehouse, possibly semi-derelict. They're using it as a bomb factory!'

'But where is it?' asked Hilary. 'It could be anywhere!'

'We'll track the girl using CCTV images!' Tom picked up his phone. He gave the news to his team gathering CCTV footage and told them to try to track the girl back to any tube station that she may have used to get to the theatre. Now there was nothing they could do but wait. Fenton soothed the wailing Archie and helped him to mend his model. Zahir was wheeled away by Mary for more physiotherapy. There was still much work to be done to further strengthen his arm muscles and she wanted to try again to trigger his legs into some kind of response.

George was tempted to join in with the Lego, but felt it may be beneath his dignity. He was glad that Archie had bonded with his new friend, Zahi. George wanted to reposition himself as a mature young man. He secretly envied Beth, who, though slightly younger than George, seemed to him much more grown up. He went over to his work tray and picked up the folder with his topic book. The project he was working on was about famous F1 racing cars and he was currently researching the McLaren team. With Fenton's help he was finding out all he could about the development of their cars, including how they improved the aerodynamics of the body and souped-up the engines. George liked cars – and the faster the better. He hoped Hilary would let him take driving lessons when he was old enough and dreamed of owning a sports car one day. As he switched on the computer to download more information on engine design, he turned the screen away from Archie. He didn't want any more adventures just yet.

Tom winked at Hilary and walked out of the room to go upstairs, where he would get a better signal on his phone. Beth gazed at his back as he walked away. Hilary put an arm around her.

'Nice, isn't he?'

'Yeah ... he's well fit,' breathed Beth, dreamily.

'And well old enough to be your dad!' laughed Hilary. She was secretly pleased at the way that Beth was growing into an attractive, well-balanced teenager under her care, despite her terrible childhood. She was a lemon when Hilary found her, but a lemon, with a little sugar added, can become a wonderful fruit. Hilary confided in Beth, 'I don't blame you for liking him. He's handsome enough! If I were ten years younger, I'd make a play for him myself!' George snorted under his breath. Ten years, he thought, was wishful thinking on a grand scale. Forty years perhaps, he thought wickedly.

George's presence wasn't even registering on Beth, she was in a bit of a dream.

'Was you ever married, Hilary?'

'No. I had offers of course.'

'Why didn't you then?' Getting married to someone like Tom seemed very desirable to her.

'The offers didn't come from the right kind of man. And anyway, I was married to my career. It didn't seem a good deal

– to give up my university career in exchange for dirty nappies and washing and ironing some man's pants!'

Beth laughed. 'I'll make sure I get a man who'll share the housework!'

'Well I hope you do! Mark my words though – they'll promise the Earth to get you, but once they've got you, it'll be all change!'

'Awhh, Hilary!'

'No, don't worry – you're going to be very pretty in a year or two and you'll be able to take your pick. There'll be suitors queuing at the door for you!'

Beth spoke quietly and seriously. 'I'm sorry you didn't find the right one for you.'

'I'll tell you a secret,' she whispered. 'I was too clever for my own good. Lots of men are scared of very intelligent women. They don't want to feel stupid. Alpha males and all that. They want to be top dog. I could have played the dumb blonde and had men by the hundred. But why should I? I'm proud to be me. Take me or leave me. I'm not going to pretend to be someone I'm not, just to please some man!'

'Hilary, you're ... awesome!'

'You're pretty awesome yourself! What you did with those bits of junk was just mindblowing! I know Tom was very impressed!'

'D'you think so?' Beth blushed.

'Absolutely. And speak of the devil...'

Tom came back into the room, looking excited.

'I hope your ears were burning!' Hilary said. 'We've just been having a meeting of your fan club!' She tipped her head towards Beth, who turned an even deeper shade of red.

'I should be so lucky,' Tom joked. 'Fenton, can you get Skype on your laptop? We've got a breakthrough!' Fenton nodded and left Archie, who pouted in pretend annoyance, and got to work on the keyboard.

'Do we need the others?' asked Hilary, suddenly brisk and business-like.

'Yes, we'd better have everyone here.'

Hilary left to fetch Zahir and Mary, while George reluctantly turned away from his data on turbo chargers. While they waited for the others to return, Tom connected the laptop via Skype to a police computer in London. The projector was powered up and a picture of an incident room filled the screen.

Tom leaned towards the laptop's microphone. 'Jack! Can you hear us?'

In the incident room, a man detached himself from his desk and pushed his glasses up onto his forehead. He had designer stubble on his face and his arm muscles, visible under his short sleeve shirt, indicated that he could look after himself. Beth looked at him critically. He looked a bit younger then Tom. She wondered if he was married.

'Yes, Boss, loud and clear!' the man barked, briskly. 'We've got an update ready for you. Just a minute, I'll turn the camera so you can see one of our screens.'

Beth gave a small sigh as she lost sight of Jack. The picture now showed a flat screen television. Hilary, Mary and Zahir entered quietly and settled down to watch with their friends who were already in the schoolroom.

They heard Jack's voice again. 'We found the girl – we've codenamed her Lucretia – on two cameras in Covent Garden, walking towards the theatre district. This is what we got. (The night pictures were dark and fuzzy, but they showed clearly the tall, slim girl walking with her head bowed.) No luck on her face. She kept her head low. She's been well trained, whoever she is. These pictures were taken between 18.15 and 18.20, so we looked at a string of streets around Covent Garden between 18.00 and 18.30. We couldn't find her close to the theatre, but got this picture (a shot came up of the outside of a tube station) of her leaving Tottenham Court Road.'

'Where is she Jack?'

Jack used a ruler as a pointer. 'Not easy to see. Just a dark figure behind this group leaving the station.' Most of those gathered in the room found it impossible to see anything that resembled a girl, but Zahir could spot her easily – a dark menace in the background. 'We knew that the cameras in the station are higher definition. They were upgraded after the tube train bombings. So we looked at the platform cameras and that's when we got a view of her face.'

The picture changed to a close up of a girl's face, side on. 'We put this through our face recognition software, but there wasn't enough of her face on view to get a match. So we're getting an identikit artist to do a full face impression from what we've got here and we'll see if we can get a match from that.'

'Jack – can you track her back from Tottenham Court Road?'

'It's not been easy, Boss. This girl seems to vanish into thin air. She ought to be on the street between this station and Covent Garden, but we've searched every camera image and we just can't find her. It's the same between Covent Garden and the theatre. Our Lucretia had to walk between them, but she's just not there. It's as if she disappears. She's weird.'

Zahir moaned inwardly. He didn't need CCTV cameras. He could have told them already that this girl was weird. She appeared to him in his bedroom in the middle of the night, threw things at him and then vanished. How weird was that?

Jack continued. 'We checked which trains had come into the station just before Lucretia appeared on the screens. There were two; a westbound train on the Central Line and a southbound train on the Northern. We tracked the northern line all the way to the terminus. No sign of her getting on to a train. Mind you, with this girl it doesn't necessarily seem to mean anything! Then we followed the Central Line train back towards Ongar. We found Lucretia again – getting on the train at Bank. You can see her here...'

The picture changed to show the girl, now codenamed Lucretia, stepping onto the Central Line train. Again, though, it wasn't possible to see her face. But that wasn't the only thing that was strange.

Tom asked the question: 'Jack – what's up with the picture? She looks like glass!' And it was true. It was possible to see the slim dark shape of the girl, but the outline of the train carriage could be seen through her.

'You tell me, Boss! Either Lucretia is transparent or she's moving incredibly fast – so fast that the camera is seeing her and the train behind her as she moves past. We brought in our imaging man, Fred.' The view swung round back to showing the room again and a geeky looking man with thick spectacles swung his chair round to face the camera.

'Hi, Boss, y'OK?'

'Yes thanks, Fred – what do you make of it?'

'It's a mystery, Boss! Never seen anything like it. She'd be having to move as fast as a jet plane to make this double image and she'd be blurred – but this shot of her has a sharp outline. It's got me baffled. We're checking the camera for a malfunction.'

'Let me know what you find out. Jack – where did she go from Bank?'

'Nowhere. We couldn't find her anywhere.'

'There must be twenty cameras inside Bank station and in the street outside. One of them must have seen her!'

'I know. We checked every camera, over and over again. Nothing. Then we had an idea. Jill!'

A woman in the room's farthest corner looked up. She was the only one in a police uniform. She looked very tired. 'Hi, Jack! Hello, Boss!'

'What've you been up to, Jill?'

'Well, Boss, when we got no leads on the route in, I thought what about her route back? After the bomb went off she might have retraced her steps. The explosion was timed at 19.50, so I checked every Central Line train stopping at Bank from that time onwards. I've been at it all night. I've been through over twenty hours of video.'

'Sorry about that, Jill – we'll make it up to you.'

'Just find Lucretia, that'll be all the thanks I need!'

'So what have you found?'

'We got a glimpse of her at 20.40 leaving the Central Line platforms at Bank and moving towards the exit for the Docklands Light Railway.'

'Great! Which train?'

'Lucretia did her vanishing act again. No sign of her on any platform. But we struck lucky. We tracked every train leaving Bank from twenty to nine onwards, following them station by station. You've no idea how my eyes ache!'

'But did you find her?'

'In the end we did. We saw her leave a Docklands train at Pontoon Dock.'

'Pontoon Dock? Never heard of it,' protested Hilary.

'Oh it exists all right – but I've never been there.' Tom chewed on his bottom lip as he considered this new information. Then he barked out an order: 'Jack, get the largest scale map of the area round Pontoon Dock that you can find and highlight every building that might be a warehouse.'

'OK, Boss, but that's in the docklands. There could be hundreds of warehouses. It could take weeks to search them all.'

'I'm hoping we won't need to. I've got a few people here who may be able to help us quite a lot! Get the map, pull the team together, and meet us at Pontoon Dock station. We'll need a squad of armed officers.'

'Righto, Boss. We'll let you know when we're ready to move.'

19. BACK TO THE SMOKE

Tom turned to face them all. 'Well, guys. Ready for action again?'

Zahir was. He wanted this girl safely behind bars – if bars would actually hold her. Beth slid off the desk and ran towards her room. A little make-up wouldn't go amiss, especially if she was going to meet Jack. A girl likes to look her best when she goes out! George reluctantly slid his project back into its folder. He was as excited as anyone at the idea of action, but he was playing it very cool. This was an important part of the new mature image he was developing. Archie wasn't cool at all. He threw a Lego brick across the room in a sulk.

Hilary watched him, slightly exasperated. 'We won't really need Archie,' she whispered to Fenton. 'Stay here with him, will you?' Fenton nodded and Archie squealed with glee. 'We'll let him get on with his career as a great architect!' Archie's building, tastefully constructed of bricks of many colours, had already reached forty centimetres in height. It looked perilously top-heavy. Its jagged top was vaguely reminiscent of The Shard. As Zahir was wheeled round by Mary, he was slightly worried for anyone who ended up living in any building designed by Archie. He was glad that Hilary was only joking about his likely career.

Tom drove up to the side door in the 4x4. This was going to be a lower key dash into London than the last. Just one vehicle would be used, leaving four officers at Foxes Hollow to keep an eye on things. Zahir was helped into the back and his wheelchair folded and packed. George stomped towards the car with his iPod, earphones in his ears, thinking he looked cool. Hilary got in the front alongside Tom and they waited for Beth. She finally made an appearance. She had changed –

hipster jeans and a short-sleeved white top with **LOVE** written on it in sequins. 'Very pretty...,' said Hilary, with only the very slightest hint of amused sarcasm. Beth stuck her tongue out at her and slipped into the back of the car, flashing a toothy smile at Tom.

'Right. Let's go!' said Tom, decisively. He was eager to make a start and the time the children had taken to get organised had annoyed him a little.

The car purred across the gravel, along the long winding drive, under trees that were heavy with leaves. The dappled sun shone brightly through the branches and Zahir put his hand up to shelter his eyes from its flashing light. As they left the lovely grounds of Foxes Hollow, two squirrels raced across the lane in front of them and it was hard to believe that, away from this green and calm countryside, danger and death could be stalking the streets of the capital. The electronic gates slid open and Tom accelerated away in the direction of London. He switched on the blue flashing lights as he accelerated to warn other drivers out of his way. His passengers settled back into the soft comfort of their leather seats as the Range Rover whisked them almost silently towards the dual carriageway.

Zahir was snuggled between Beth and George. George was listening to an album Zahir didn't recognise and Beth was checking her Facebook pages on her phone. He knew that everything she wrote was checked by security before it was released to the server. This was to ensure that it did not give away either her location or what was happening at Foxes Hollow. Security need not have worried. It appeared to Zahir, who was not yet old enough to be interested in social websites, that she wrote and received nothing but meaningless drivel. He sighed as the car raced down the slip road onto the major highway and roared directly into the fast lane. Tom put his foot down on the accelerator and the six cylinder engine went into turbo drive. There wasn't much traffic on the arterial road so far from the capital and the slow lorries and family saloons were left standing as he accelerated to well over an hundred miles an hour. George now had his eyes closed and may have been asleep. Beth was busy tapping away at her tiny phone screen.

Zahir gazed glumly out of the window as the miles ticked away to their destination. He was very worried. Everyone else thought they were dealing with a normal terrorist cell and that once they had tracked them down they would be easy to apprehend. Zahir suspected that the truth was very different. This girl, now nicknamed Lucretia in a joking allusion to an infamous criminal who lived five hundred years ago, was not going to be easy to track down. She seemed able to appear and disappear at will and, more worryingly, seemed to have identified him as a target.

The car radio was playing quietly: classical music from Radio Three. This was Hilary's choice and Zahir found it soothing even though much of it went over his head. Hilary had her head back and was humming along to a piece by Tchaikovsky. Suddenly the lyrical music from Swan Lake was interrupted by a call on Tom's phone. It was connected by Bluetooth to the car's audio system. As Jack's urgent voice filled the car, Zahir saw Beth's fingers freeze in mid-texting and her eyes shot up. Zahir smiled to himself. He wondered if a girl would ever pay him this much attention. To his surprise, he found himself hoping that one day one would. He thought that his disability would be a disadvantage to say the least. Next time he had a session with Mary, he would try even harder to get some response from his legs, which hung beneath him like lumps of lead.

'Boss ... can you hear me?'

'Go ahead, Jack.'

'OK. We've set up a satellite incident room in a disused office at Pontoon Dock. We have two minibuses of armed officers from the Met on their way, including a snatch squad. They'll be parked a good distance away waiting for orders from you. We've alerted the bomb squad in case they're needed and they're coming from Sandhurst. We should have everything in place by the time you reach us.'

'Good work, Jack. Mark the concentrations of warehouse type buildings on a map and we'll go to the areas of heaviest concentration first. Hilary?'

'Yes.' Hilary spoke to the microphone concealed by the reverse view mirror. 'Hello, Jack.'

'Hi, Hil.'

'We'll visit the areas you identify in order, the heaviest first. We'll tour in the car so that we can see if Beth can recognise any of them. Zahir may be able to help too if he gets any bad vibes from them. If we have a suspicion about one, we'll try sending George in first to recce it. It's vital we don't cause any suspicion. It seems that Lucretia has seen Tom and Zahir, so they need to keep out of sight. The blackout on the rear windows of the Range Rover should keep Zahir safe...'

Zahir wasn't sure.

It took ages to negotiate their way across London, even with the sirens wailing and the blue lights flashing. Some drivers seemed to be both deaf and blind and it took a lot of effort to persuade them to move out of the way. In places, the traffic was so congested that even when the cars, taxis, lorries and buses tried to move over, there was no space for them. George seemed to be dozing and Zahir eventually nodded off. When he opened his eyes again, they were to the east of the city and heading into Docklands.

He was amazed at the amount of rebuilding that was happening here. Whole blocks of buildings were being torn down and replaced with modern light contemporary housing estates, with green grass and young trees, or with pale coloured commercial buildings with enormous car parks. Lumps of the old docklands still stuck up here and there like bad teeth amongst rows of shiny white ones. These remnants were largely derelict, with jagged broken glass in the windows and boarded up frontages. Some of the domestic buildings were space-age modern. Zahir thought this would be a fine place for him to live when he was older, in a penthouse apartment with a balcony and floor to ceiling windows giving spectacular views of the Thames. If he lived that long, he thought glumly, remembering the evil threat of Lucretia still hanging over him like a menacing black cloud.

'Nearly there!' said Tom at last, and Beth, George and Zahir looked out of the darkened windows at an ultra-modern railway, high in the sky on concrete plinths. To their surprise, when they reached Pontoon Dock, the station itself seemed to be floating in the blue sky, white and clean and quite beautiful. When they had been told they were going to Pontoon Dock they had imagined something Dickensian. They had visions of dark alleyways, crumbling tenements, open sewers and soiled washing hanging on lines stretched across from one window to the next like satanic bunting. The reality was quite a shock. Beth looked round in dismay. Where was the large, old, warehouse-like building that she had seen in her vision? Maybe she had been completely wrong. Or maybe Lucretia had completely outwitted them. Maybe stopping at Pontoon Dock had been a feint, and her real destination had been somewhere much darker. They drove past a slender, tall, blue and white Docklands railway sign like a giant lollipop that gave the name of the station and then the car went under the railway to a modern office building on the other side. Here Tom pulled up and wiped his brow with his sleeve.

'At last! Glad I don't have to do that drive every day! Can't understand why people want to live in big cities ... I feel sorry for them!'

Hilary opened the doors to let the children out and Beth preened herself, glancing at the dark windows of the 4x4 to check her reflection. She was just in time, because the door of the office opened and Jack strode out.

'We're all ready for you! Come in!'

20. DEEP IN DOCKLANDS

Tom opened up the wheelchair, settled Zahir into it and they all walked through the office door. It wasn't really wheelchair width and Tom had a struggle. In the end, he had to lift Zahir out of the chair and through the door while Hilary collapsed it and brought it through empty of its occupant. Zahir thought sadly that this was not the most dignified way to enter a building.

Jill was there and smiled a greeting. 'Kettle's on! Cup of tea?'

Jill was small and rather mouse-like, with bright, piercing eyes that missed nothing. Although her small, rather pointed face made her look like a mouse, she was actually a little dynamo. Full of energy and very bright, she ran the office with great efficiency and the men depended on her more than they ever admitted. As she set out the mugs, she thought wryly to herself that it shouldn't always be automatically the woman who made the tea, but she knew that if she hadn't offered no-one else would have done. Men did not think of ordinary hospitality often enough. Hilary asked for Earl Grey tea, but she was disappointed. Neither was there any lemon, so she had to settle for a steaming mug of strong, milky Yorkshire tea and be grateful for it.

The room was about six metres by four and the far wall had a long bench along it. A row of computers had been set up there and two men that Zahir had not seen before were working at them. Three screens were locked into a range of surveillance cameras in the neighbourhood and the pictures changed every few seconds as the computers switched automatically from camera to camera. Beth watched the screens for a while but none of the buildings she saw looked familiar. One of the screens showed an unchanging view of the station platforms at Pontoon Dock. One of the men was watching this screen constantly, in case Lucretia reappeared. Zahir knew somehow that she wouldn't. He got no sense of her presence round here. He wondered if maybe they were in the wrong part of London altogether.

A large table dominated the centre of the room with a map on it. Uncomfortable plastic chairs were ranged around it and this is where they all sat to drink their tea. Beth asked rather sweetly where the ladies' was, and Jack pointed to a unisex symbol on a door in the corner. 'Sorry, miss, we all have to share!' Beth blushed prettily, a little embarrassed but rather impressed at being called 'miss'. She went away (it had been a long journey) while Jack updated Tom on their progress so far.

'We've got the snatch squad and the armed unit in position. They're both at Camden Town – close enough to get here in a few seconds when we need them, but far enough away to be out of sight. We don't want to make anyone suspicious. The bomb squad isn't here yet. They needed some extra equipment from Aldershot, but they've promised to be in range within the next twenty minutes.'

'What's the bomb squad for?' asked George, rather nervously. He had had enough of bombs and didn't like the sound of this.

'If what Beth saw is right, explained Tom, it could be that the base we're looking for is a factory making IEDs. If it is...'

'What's an IED?' George was still confused.

'IED stands for Improvised Explosive Device,' said Tom patiently. 'It's the technical term for a bomb made by terrorists, rather than an official one made for the military in a proper armament factory.'

'Oh,' said George, looking less confused but more nervous.

Beth emerged from the rear, having made herself more comfortable and run a comb through her hair. She entered rather grandly and then sat down, feeling very disappointed that no-one had even looked at her.

'If it turns out that bombs are being made here, we'll need to send the bomb squad in first to make sure everything's safe before we can do a proper search. There may even be booby traps.'

Now Beth was confused. She had missed most of this conversation and had no idea what they were talking about. She knew boobies was another word for breasts, but didn't think they could be trapped. She decided not to ask. She set her face into a picture of intelligent interest, as if she was perfectly on board with all this.

Tom turned to Jack. 'What've we found out about the local area?'

Jack smoothed his hands over the large scale map they had found of the area. It covered the entire table and went over the edges on every side. There were brown circles on it where tea and coffee cups had rested. 'Most of the area has been redeveloped over the last ten years. It's a mix of new housing developments and industrial areas. Any one of these could be being used by the gang we're looking for. The largest industrial zone seems to be off the North Woolwich Road and Dock Road. There must be thousands of warehouses, factories or distribution depots. It could be any of them. And this map isn't even up to date – more have been built since.'

'We don't think it's a new building, so we don't need to worry about very recent buildings,' Tom reassured him

'No,' offered Beth, seeing a chance to make an impression on Jack. 'It looked well old!'

Jack made no comment to this. 'Well let's make a start to the east of the station. If they are here, they've picked a key area to set up shop in. It's chock full of possible important targets.' He gesticulated off the map. 'There's the Thames Barrier this side – if that were breached most of central London could go under water when there's a specially high tide. The City Airport is just over this side. We have main stations and major traffic routes everywhere – and even the new city park – a prestige project.'

'Where do you think we should begin?'

'Let's drive to Bell Lane and zigzag through the industrial areas from there. We'll be reasonably close to all major buildings. Close enough to give your wonderkids a fighting chance.'

Zahir detected a sharp intake of breath from Beth. She didn't appreciate being described as a kid, wonder or not!

'The sooner we start the better,' urged Tom. 'We'll only have one chance. We can't cruise past these buildings over and over again without giving the game away.'

'We've got a bulletproof car ready for you with a video camera mounted on the dash so that we can follow your progress from here,' reported Jack.

'Bulletproof!' exclaimed George. This sounded scary.

'Just a sensible precaution,' Jack assured him. 'We can't afford to take any chances with you!'

Tom, Hilary and the three children got into the new car while Jack contacted the support groups, telling them to ready themselves for action because Operation Lucretia was ready to begin. The heavy doors with their thick dark glass swung soundlessly shut. The powerful engine purred into life. George was impressed with the keyless ignition and the array of dials and switches on the dashboard. 'Dual zone air-conditioning and cruise control!' he whispered to Zahir, who tried hard to look impressed without actually knowing what he was talking about.

Tom heard him and turned. 'Three point eight litre in-line turbo-charged diesel as well! And we'll need that power to shift this, with all its armour plating!'

'OK, boys, let's concentrate on the job in hand!' Hilary was no more interested than Beth in the inner workings of cars. 'Beth, tell us straight away if you recognise anything. Zahi, you too – if you see or sense anything strange or suspicious, speak out straight away!'

They drove back under the high arches of the station and then turned left towards large complexes of industrial buildings. Another left turn took them into Bell Lane. Beth was nonplussed. None of this looked anything like the glimpses she had of the room with the two men. These were modern concrete blocks, or large rusting containers being used for storage, or modern low-built office buildings. George took in all the cars in the many car parks they cruised past. He was unimpressed. There was the usual mix of Ford Fiestas and Vauxhalls along with the cheaper models from Honda and Toyota. Zahir took his role seriously. He scanned the buildings carefully, although this was not his strength. Occasionally he could pick up a glimpse of someone's aura through an open window, but the people, he sensed, were just ordinary folk, bored with their work, waiting for home time.

The car took another turn and, still keeping to a steady ten miles an hour, skirted a large vacant lot. The open fence allowed them to view a field of ground-up rubble and a couple of abandoned supermarket trolleys. Once past this wasteland, they were into an area where new buildings were being constructed. A crane swung slowly round swinging large sewage pipes across the sky whilst two workmen sunbathed and dragged on cigarettes. Beth shuddered. The men were bare-chested and had large hairy stomachs that hung out over their belts. She wondered what it would be like to be kissed by a man who smoked? Stained teeth and breath that would smell of tobacco ash ... gross!

Beyond this, as they continued their zigzag route through the industrial estates, was another road that was almost a carbon copy of the first. Pre-cast concrete buildings in monotonous rows. The windows were all closed and had security grids in front of them that cut out half the daylight. An assortment of signs identified them to visitors and they had a range of meaningless names – Amoto Ltd, Conco PLC, Wongat Inc. – that gave no clue what went on inside. They passed a car rental outlet with a row of uniform white, freshly washed cars for hire.

They cruised towards a faceless two storey building, again built of precast concrete sections but with its windows covered with thin metal sheeting. George almost jumped out of his seat. 'LOOK AT THAT!!' he squawked, considerably excited. The car thudded to a halt as Tom slammed on the brakes. Beth examined the building curiously and Zahir searched in vain for any sign of an aura.

'What is it? What have you seen?' asked Tom, already reaching for his phone to call in back-up.

'Look, look!' exclaimed George, suddenly realising that he had given them the wrong impression of what he had seen and so trying to justify his excitement. 'A Ferrari and - and a Lotus!' And it was true. Unlike the nondescript cars that had graced every other car lot, here were two very new, very shiny, VERY expensive motors that had George on the edge of his seat with excitement.

'George!' said Beth in disgust. 'You are so pathetic!'

'Girls...' muttered George to Zahir, as if this was all that needed to be said.

'Is that all, George?' asked Hilary, to be sure that nothing suspicious had been detected.

Tom spoke quietly. 'I don't think George intended this to be anything to do with what we're looking for, but we should check anything that's unusual. We need all the leads we can get. It is odd to see such high value cars in an area like this. It doesn't look like the sort of building that would be generating enough income to allow the owners to drive cars like that. And have you noticed,' he asked Hilary, 'it has no name board, no signage at all? If it's a respectable business, they'd be getting deliveries and mail – how could they do that without any signs to say who they are?'

'Well, George,' responded Hilary, 'your obsession with cars might prove useful after all! You can be even more use now! Tom, get as close as you can without giving us away and George, try to go in and tell us what you can see.'

Tom used his phone after all, calling in the snatch squad and the armed police as well as updating Jack and his team in the incident room. Jack said he would run a computer check on the building to see if it was registered as a business address and if so, what the business was. Tom radioed the snatch squads to position themselves just out of sight round the corner and then moved the car quietly and slowly alongside the building, on a blind side where there were only two small blocked up windows.

'Are you ready, George?'

'Yeh...' replied George, looking rather pale and drawn now. Intuitively, Beth understood some of the strain that he was now under and began to care for him as she had done outside the theatre. She massaged his shoulder and spoke soothingly to him as his eyes gradually went blank. Minutes past, but they seemed like hours to the occupants of the car. Hilary watched Beth approvingly. She was pleased with the way that her charges were measuring up. Eventually, George's eyes flickered back into life – he was back with them again.

'Did you see anything?' Tom asked, his hands on the phone, ready to call in the snatch squads.

George blinked his eyes and looked confused. Hilary was worried. 'Are you OK, George?'

'Yeah ... think so...'

'Tell us, George. What was inside?' Tom was eager for information. It was more important than he was telling the children that they found the terrorist cell. Military intelligence services and the police anti-terrorism units were under enormous pressure from politicians to produce results. Whilst the bombers remained at large, the security of the country was in danger and the population as a whole was, understandably, extremely nervous. The government felt under pressure to show that it was dealing competently with the threat. They reacted to this by turning the pressure on the police.

But before George could say anything, Jack's voice came over the car radio.

'Boss?'

'Yes, Jack?'

'We've got something on the building. It's leased to a firm that calls itself Johalko. They claim to be import and exporters. We checked with company records at Companies' House and there's no such firm.'

'It doesn't exist?'

Jack sounded excited. 'If it does, it's not filing any records. It isn't registered. And Customs and Excise have no record of it either. It's not paying any taxes and if it's importing anything, it isn't doing it legally. This looks like a goer, Boss!'

'OK, Jack. I'm calling in the snatch squad with armed backing. Just wait till I see what info we have on the inside.' He turned to George. 'What's it like inside, George? We need all the help from you we can get. The more we can tell the officers who'll be forcing an entry, the safer they'll be!'

George looked as if he was going to cry. Beth put her arm around him.

'Upstairs ... I couldn't ... it was just ... black...'

'You mean blacked out?' Hilary tried to help him. 'Black because the windows were covered over?'

'I suppose... There was nothing. Just blackness... and something thick and soft on the floor...'

'Carpet?'

'No... Much thicker than carpet. Deep, well deep...'

Hilary looked puzzled. Tom tried to probe further. 'Downstairs ... did you see into the ground floor rooms?'

George looked desperate now. 'It was ... so different ... white...'

'White?'

'Like a blinding light...'

'Could you make anything out? See anything?'

'No ... nothing ... but light...'

'Weird!' exclaimed Beth.

'There's something very odd about this.' Tom, too, was confused. It didn't sound like a bomb factory, but, if George was correct, it was something highly suspicious. 'I think we've found out enough. Let's take them out. Jack – we're going in!'

'Right, Boss. We'll monitor you from here!'

Tom left the car and walked towards the door, all the time barking instructions into the phone. The occupants of the car watched with bated breath as he was joined by six policemen wearing flak jackets and helmets, one of whom was carrying a metal battering ram. From the other side, a group of heavily armed officers burst into view. The whole operation was soundless. These were professional, highly trained men who understood their roles thoroughly. The men lined up each side of the doorway, pressed against the wall so that they were invisible to anyone on the inside.

One was holding a megaphone. On a sign from Tom he raised it and pointed it at the door. The man with the battering ram had it poised to strike just above the door handle. The megaphone screeched into life. *'ARMED POLICE! We're coming in!'*

What happened next was dramatic and very fast. The occupants of the building, whoever they were, were given no time to react to the police warning. If they had been given more time, they could have done a runner, hidden the evidence or exploded a bomb. Two thuds with the battering ram were enough to cause the metal door to burst open and two of the armed police were running in, wearing full body armour. The megaphone blared out, *'STAND STILL! Keep your hands in the air!'*

Even many metres away from the open door, the blast of heat could be felt like a furnace opening. The snatch squad stepped back in confusion. Although it was bright and sunny outside, the light from inside was blinding. The second pair of armed police officers went in after the first two and were met by an amazing sight. Through the mist that was forming on their visors they saw batteries of intensely bright lamps packing every metre of the ceiling. There was steam everywhere and, as it swirled away from the fresh air coming in through the open door, they made out tens of thousands of broad leafed plants in large pots standing in shallow troughs of water. It was like a jungle, except that the lush plants were in ordered rows, each one reaching almost to the ceiling. Three individuals, two women and a man, thin, almost naked and streaming with perspiration, were standing shivering with fear. Their hands were straining upwards in surrender.

Outside, they heard one of the officers yelling. 'POLICE! YOU'RE UNDER ARREST! LIE ON THE FLOOR WITH YOUR ARMS SPREAD!'

Seconds later one of the officers came out and gestured for the snatch squad officers to enter the building. He turned to Tom. 'Situation under control, sir. Three arrests. But it's not the bomb factory we hoped for. It's a weed mill!'

Tom returned to the car. 'Well done, guys! I think we'll have to drive you lot round London every day if this is anything to go by.' But his face displayed disappointment.

'It's not what we wanted, is it?'

'No, Hilary. Under normal circumstances, this would be a major crime scene and we'd expect promotion and a mention in dispatches.' He shook his head sadly. 'But these aren't normal days and we're after much bigger fish.'

'What is it?' Beth spoke for all of them. They didn't understand what they had found.

'They're growing weed,' Tom explained. 'Tons of it. It's a drugs factory, supplying cannabis to most of London by the looks of it. It's an important find. We'll pass this over to the Met. There'll be enough information here to put dozens of traffickers behind bars.'

'Those bright lights?'

'Arc lamps to simulate the heat and bright sunlight the plants need to grow quickly. The soft material in the upper floor that George saw will be wadding to insulate the lower floor and stop heat escaping.'

'To keep the plants hot?'

'Partly, but mainly to make sure that helicopters with heat sensors don't spot the factory. It would glow in the dark like a beacon otherwise and give them away. They probably tap electricity from the mains, bypassing the meter, so as not to alert suspicion by having sky-high power bills.'

Hilary wondered about the occupants. 'You've made arrests?'

'Three so far, poor kids. They're probably illegal immigrants being used as slave labour. They're so scared they'll squeal all they know. But let's leave this to the Met now. We need to move away. There's been so much noise we have no chance of continuing any sort of covert operation. But well done, kids. This is quite a coup for you!' With that he swung into the driving seat and turned the car away from the building and back towards Pontoon Dock, just as a dozen police cars, sirens wailing, raced up to the crime scene to continue the investigations.

It was a subdued quartet that drew up at the incident room. To their surprise, Jack came out to greet them, smiling and excited. 'Good job, Boss! The Met's been looking for them for the last two years! They've been trafficking drugs to most of the East End! The commissioner's over the moon!'

'But the bombers are still at large, Jack. And they're what we came for.'

'We've got good news for you there as well, Boss!'

'You found them – they were hiding in the cannabis plants?' Tom joked wryly.

Jack laughed. 'Not quite! But we've got a trace on Lucretia! Come on in and we'll fill you in!'

21. LUCRETIA

Excited, they rushed into the incident room, Hilary quickly erecting Zahir's wheelchair and pushing him in after the others by skilfully wriggling it through the narrow door. Jill was busy organising some refreshments for them – it had been a long day and they had had nothing to eat. She made some tea, opened a packet of biscuits and then left to buy burgers for the children and a salad for Hilary. Meanwhile Jack swung a computer screen round for them to see.

'Remember that the CCTV images weren't good enough to get a match for the face recognition software? We decided to let an identikit artist have a go at Lucretia. Not much work for them nowadays so she was able to get a quick likeness to us. She had to use the image we had of part of Lucretia's face to work out what the rest might look like, and then do a full face picture we could put in the computer.'

'And it worked?' Tom asked, impatiently.

'Sure did! This is the picture she came up with!'

They all gazed at the face that stared at them from the screen. It was a thin, sallow face with a dark complexion, long, straight black hair and dark black eyes that sent shivers running up and down Zahir's spine.

'Is that the girl, Zahi?' Hilary asked.

'Yeah ... except her hair is pulled back from her ears and her ears are a bit pointed at the top.'

'We'll get that changed straight away!' promised Tom. 'It'll be put right before we release this to the force.'

'Great!' enthused Tom. 'At last we have a good likeness. This will make finding her much easier!'

'It gets better! Face recognition has given us two matches!'

'Two different girls?'

'No, better – the same one in both cases! We got a match from the passport database and another from the DVLA.'

'DVLA?' asked Hilary.

'Yes, driving licences. Now we have pictures on the card part of the licence it gives us a huge database to work from.'

'Has she any form?'

'No, she's clean. Nothing on record at all.'

At this moment Jill returned from the burger bar and there was a pause while snacks were distributed. Tom managed two bites of his cheeseburger before curiosity got the better of him and he had to ask. 'A name? You've got a name?'

'Yes, Boss, and a bit more! We're building up quite a file on her!'

'Name, Jack – give us a name!'

'Lucretia's real name is Irna Khan. She's 28 years old, but looks a lot younger. She was born in Britain, the birth was registered in Leicester and she was born in hospital there.'

'Family?'

'Ah, that's the crunch, Boss. We checked her parents' names from the birth certificate and tried to track them down. They left the UK for an extended holiday in Pakistan last year.'

'Still there?'

'Not exactly. Well, yes I suppose they are. But they're not living there if you see what I mean.'

'What happened?'

Jack looked grave. 'They were visiting their family home close to the Afghan border. A big family gathering was organised and relatives came from miles around for a three day celebration to welcome them.'

'And?'

'Unfortunately all this traffic was picked up by American spy satellites. A quick decision had to be made about how suspicious it was, and the decision was wrong. The Americans assumed that militants were gathering on the border to organise a strike into Afghanistan. They ordered a drone attack. The house was hit by two Hellfire missiles and thirty members of the extended family were killed, including twelve children and Lucretia's parents.'

Zahir felt numb. He had already sensed some of this, but the full extent of what had happened to Irna's family still came as a shock to him. No wonder she was set on revenge.

Jack continued. 'We've got a picture here of the outcome. It was covered by Al Jazeera.'

Hilary gasped as she took in the outcome of the drone attack. Hardly a single brick of the large house was left standing, and long rows of bodies wrapped in white sheets lay in the foreground, the sad victims of a tactical error. 'So American intelligence thought it was a gathering of insurgents?'

'I guess so. Some trigger happy general and a location too close to a sensitive border. That turned out to be a tragic combination.'

'What about Lucretia ... err Irna?' Tom asked. 'Has she been to a terrorist training camp?'

'Not sure, but she applied for and was given a British passport so that she could travel to Pakistan for the funerals. The application was fast tracked for humanitarian reasons. Funerals happen quickly in Muslim countries, so there was no time to waste. She was there for all thirty funerals and saw the devastation of the family home.'

'It's not surprising she was radicalised,' Hilary mused, 'but that's no excuse for what she tried to do...'

'She stayed in Pakistan for eight months, according to immigration. We've no idea where she spent her time, but we're contacting our agents there to try and track her movements.'

'If we have her driving details, we'll have her address.'

'Yes, Boss – a flat in Newham. We sent a there an hour ago, but they say the flat seems to be empty. A forensic team's on its way so we'll see what they can pick up. We're also checking mobile phone records for that address – we should have something to go on by tonight.'

Tom sighed. 'We should have known it wouldn't be straightforward.' He turned to Beth, George and Zahi. 'But if we can get a further lead we may well have to use your skills again, kids.'

'They can't do much more this evening.'

'No, Hil, but I don't want to drive you all the way back to Foxes Hollow tonight and then back here tomorrow. Jill, can you get us somewhere to stay?'

'I've been looking at possibilities, Boss. I thought you might ask. The Ecohotel in Canning Town has four rooms free tonight. I'm holding them for you.'

'Great work guys! We're making progress! Let's check out the hotel and find somewhere to eat tonight.'

'I'll let Fenton and Mary know what's happening.' Hilary rang them and explained why they would be staying the night in London. Fenton asked whether or not they should join them, but Hilary told them to stay at Foxes Hollow and be safe. Beth whispered to Hilary that they may need some fresh clothes and it was decided that they would, to her delight, do a little gentle shopping in the mall across the river after checking in to the hotel.

This was a plan that was doomed never to be put into practice.

22. MILLENIUM MILLS

As the five of them left the incident room, Hilary suggested to Zahir that, as there were only four rooms, they would take a room with two single beds and she would stay with him in case he had any more bad dreams. Zahir was as pleased as the other two were. It meant that George and Beth would have rooms to themselves. They thought this very grown up and would perhaps allow them to watch television as late as they liked! Neither Beth nor George had ever stayed in a hotel before. And to be able to shop for clothes first – this was very heaven!

Hilary manoeuvred Zahir into the back of the car, with a little help from Tom, and then settled back into the comfort of their 4x4. The hunt for the bomb factory temporarily on hold, they no longer needed the bullet-proofed car. All four of them felt relaxed and hopeful for tomorrow as they drove once again beneath the tall columns that held Pontoon Dock station high in the sky and headed north towards a road that would take them to their hotel. As they turned towards the bridge across the massive dock, Beth let out a scream...

'STOP!! THAT'S IT! THAT'S IT!'

Tom slowed the car and pulled to the side of the road. 'What? What is it?'

'That's the building I saw! I'm sure it is!'

'Jack!' Tom barked urgently into his phone. 'There's a large old building here almost on the waterfront. What do you know about it?'

'That'll be Millennium Mills, Boss.'

'Why wasn't it on our search list?'

'It's derelict, Boss. It's not safe to go in. It's full of asbestos, decaying beams and rusting girders. It's not even fit to use as a doss house any more. All the windows are smashed and rain leaks in everywhere. Even the squatters moved out years ago. The rats left shortly after.'

'Is any of it habitable?'

'Don't think so. It was going to be redeveloped as luxury apartments but the plan fell through after years of wrangling. It was just not worth saving, but Newham Council put a listing order on part of it. It's not just one building: it's a complex. It's been used as a setting for pop videos, films and TV, but you can't live in it.'

'There's a chance our bombers are based there!'

'It's a huge site, Boss. We'll need back-up.'

'I'll take the kids in as close as I can and we'll see if we can narrow things down a bit!'

'OK, Boss, good luck! The snatch squads have gone off duty now, but I'll get all the back-up I can for you!'

'Thanks, Jack. I'll keep you in touch!'

The occupants of the car looked up in amazement as the car pulled up alongside the old flour mill, well over a hundred years old and described, in its heyday, as a palace of industry. It towered over them in all directions, ten storeys high. The grey concrete was stained and crumbling. The windows gazed out sightlessly, many of them smashed and gaping open. This had once been a bustling workplace where thousands had spent their working lives. Now it was eerily silent and empty. In the darkest corners, bats had made their homes and hung from twisted metal struts waiting for darkness to fall. Birds roosted in broken cable ducts. Now and again they would emerge and fly down the long empty corridors squawking angrily. Only when they got as close as this could Hilary and the children fully understand why Jack had dismissed this as a target for their search. No part of it looked habitable. And it was so enormous that it would take days to work through all of its floors.

Tom looked grim. 'This looks bad, guys. Beth, how sure are you that this is the place?'

'I don't know. I can't be completely sure. I only saw bits of it. But this is the sort of place I saw.'

'I reckon it'll take at least an hour – maybe two – before we can get armed back-up. And we'll need to isolate the most likely places to search. If we go in indiscriminately we'll warn the bombers. They're sure to notice squads of armed police crawling all over the building. Then they'll either make a getaway or blow the place sky high!'

Hilary was worried too. 'If it doesn't blow up, this place could fall down on top of us anyway.'

'We need some sort of clue on where to look,' mused Tom.

Beth was keen to help Tom all she could. 'Should we just glance inside?'

'Would that help?'

'I might recognise something...'

Hilary took her 'in loco parentis' role seriously, even though technically Beth had no parents. She objected. 'You can't take her in, Tom! It can't be safe!'

'I think it's the only way. We could just stay on the main staircase. If we keep out of the main structure we'll be safe. Armed support will be here soon. The first hint of trouble and I'll bring her out.'

'I don't like it.'

'I don't think we've any choice. We need something to go on. And we need to get in before it gets dark. How do you feel, Beth?'

'Yeh, let's do it!' Beth felt safe with Tom looking after her.

They opened the doors and stepped out of the car. Beth suddenly felt the enormity of what they were doing. In the vast open space of broken tarmac, untidy shrubs and weeds, she felt very small and insignificant. The huge, broken building towered over them and she heard a spooky wail as a gust of wind blew through the empty rooms. Hilary, George and Zahir watched anxiously as the two of them walked almost on tiptoe to a gaping entrance.

Tom motioned to Beth to stay back as he entered and peered into the darkness. As his eyes adjusted to the contrast between the bright sunlight outside and the dim interior, he looked at a picture of devastation. Beth joined him and she too stared at the first floor of the old mill building. A long room stretched hundreds of feet away from them. The floor was covered in dust and small bits of debris. Long lengths of thick rubber wire wound along the floor like snakes. The walls were painted up to waist height in peeling dark green paint. The air smelt damp and foul. Along the ceiling, metal struts, rusting and stained, supported long metal shafts that carried rusty pulleys at regular intervals. Beth pointed at them excitedly. 'That's what I saw!'

Tom looked doubtful. 'You could find them in many old buildings. They would have had belts round them and they drove machines of some kind.'

'It looks right, Tom.'

'But there's no sign of anyone having been here. Look at the floor. If men had been walking here they would have left marks.' And he was right. Looking at the mess on the floor, only rats and mice could have walked over it without disturbing the layers of filth. Despite the danger, Beth rather liked being on her own with Tom.

'Let's try the next floor!'

'OK. Be as quiet as you can!'

They tiptoed slowly up the wide concrete steps and peered into the next long corridor-like room. This was as derelict and abandoned as the one below. Huge metal spirals, like helter-skelters, stretched from floor to ceiling. Thin metal pipes were partly attached to the ceiling, but lengths of them had come away and were hanging drunkenly down, like long thin arms. The floor was covered in dust. Even Beth could tell that no-one had walked across it for months. Tom took his phone out of his pocket as Beth began to climb up to the next floor. He was putting a call through to Hilary when suddenly he heard a piercing scream from above him and Beth came stumbling down the stairs. Instantly Tom caught her with one hand and, dropping his phone, drew a gun from under his jacket with the other.

'What was it?'

'A bat!' cried Beth. 'It flew straight at my face!'

Tom gave a sigh of relief and, putting away his gun, picked up his phone. He replaced the battery which had fallen out when it clattered to the floor. 'Shush ... listen!'

'What for?'

'If there's anyone here, that scream will have stirred them up! Can you hear anyone moving?'

'No...'

They listened for perhaps two minutes with bated breath. An acrid smell drifted into their nostrils – an unpleasant mixture of damp and rat urine. Above them somewhere, a broken blind was creaking scarily in the breeze. Beyond the staircase they could hear a slow steady drip of water falling down through the building from the roof. There was no sound that could possibly be human. Tom checked his phone. To his relief it still worked.

'Hilary?'

'What's happened, Tom? We heard a scream!'

'Beth had an argument with a bat!'

'Who won?'

'I don't think that bat will go near a teenage girl again!'

'What have you found?'

'There's no sign of anyone being here for some time. It's safe. Bring the others in if you like.'

Hilary turned to George and Zahir. 'Do you want to look inside?'

'Yeah!' George was up for it. Zahir wasn't so sure but he went along. Hilary, with George's help, opened up the chair and they both helped Zahir out of the car. George, rather gallantly, offered to push Zahi. As they neared the entrance, Tom and Beth came out to greet them.

'Looks like we've drawn a blank. I'll let the armed police do a quick search when they arrive to be sure, but there's no sign of anyone here.'

'I was so sure,' said Beth, apologetically. 'But I suppose it must have been another warehouse after all.'

'Don't worry, Beth. No harm done.'

George was already through the doorway exploring the inside. 'Crrreeepppeee!' He called back through the doorway to them. He pushed Zahir towards the stairs, and then left him by the side because it was going to be impossible to take him up with him. Seven steps up, he heard Zahir hissing to him.

'George! George!'

He stopped and looked down at him.

'Wot'sup?'

'There's something down here...'

'Where?'

George stepped down to Zahi and looked around. 'I can't see nothin'.'

'There!'

Zahir was pointing to the side of the steps. There was a narrow gap between the stairs and the wall which no-one else had noticed. It was a dark passage, but to Zahir it looked very dark indeed. 'There's someone there, George....'

George looked doubtfully into the darkness. 'Where?'

'I dunno. Move me round a bit...'

There was just enough room to squeeze the wheelchair between the wall and the staircase. George guided his friend into the tight space and they peered into the darkness. At the end of a short passage was a metal door. The floor in front of it was clear. It had been used recently and they saw multiple footprints in the dust.

'Someone's in there,' Zahir whispered.

'Are you sure?'

'Yeah. Put your ear to the door and listen!'

Feeling very nervous, George went up to the door and pressed his ear against the cold metal.

'Can you hear ought?'

'There's summat...' George whispered. Then, 'They're cummin!'

In a panic, George tried to push Zahir back along the passage. His wheelchair banged and scraped against the wall as they tried to make their escape. When they emerged into the entrance hall, he swung the chair round and raced into daylight where Tom and Hilary looked at them in surprise.

'They're in there!'

'I think they heard us!'

'Who? Where?' Tom tried to make sense of what they were saying.

'There's a door behind the staircase!' Zahir tried to explain, but the words were tumbling out. 'We heard someone!'

'Footsteps!' George added, almost talking over his friend. 'They were cummin' for us!'

Tom lifted his hand to silence them. He put his hand in his jacket to grip his gun as they waited in silence. 'I can't hear anything. You're sure someone's in there?'

'We saw footprints going to the door. Lots of them.' Zahir was sure this was the place Beth had seen. 'And ... darkness...'

'Not just ordinary darkness?' Hilary prompted him.

'No, Hil ... something bad...'

She turned to Tom. 'Sounds as if we ought to investigate it. Have we got back-up yet?'

Tom assessed the situation quickly and professionally. 'There must be another set of stairs going down! There's a basement! A perfect cover for them!' He used his phone. 'Jack, have we got back-up yet? We may have something here!'

'Yes, Boss. I've got teams in place. How much do you need?'

'We've got to force an entry. We'll need an armed squad and road blocks to make sure they can't get away. We don't know how many there are or if they're armed, but we have to assume they are.'

'We've got all the Met on standby! The hunt for the bombers has top priority. We'll have the road blocks in place in five minutes. Armed squad with you in two!'

'Thanks, Jack. Call me when we're ready to go.' He turned to Hilary. 'While we're waiting, can we get some idea of what's inside?'

'You need George?'

'Yes. What do you think, George? Can you do your trick and have a look inside?'

'I'll try,' said George doubtfully. He had never gone underground before. He wasn't sure about this. And he felt anxious because while he was travelling he was helpless. If the men came out and attacked them he wouldn't be able to move or defend himself until he had rejoined his mind to his physical self.

Zahir was worried too and confused. 'I'm sure they heard us...' he said. 'Why haven't they come out?'

'They'll have thought it was just kids playing about,' Tom reassured him. He was keen to get on, now that he felt they may be close to a successful outcome.

George sat in the back of the car, with Beth behind him. She massaged his shoulders to relax him. His eyes closed.

Two police minibuses came to a halt beside the car. They had bars on the front and grills over the windows. An officer came out of each and one walked up to Tom.

'Where do you want us, sir?'

'Through here...' Tom indicated the entrance to the mill, 'there's a stairway. Down the side of it is a passage. There's a door down there – what's it like, Zahi?'

'It's got a sort of metal plate over it. It looks strong.'

'So are we, son!' smiled the officer. He called into one of the buses. 'We'll need the ram, Bill – and bring an explosive charge just in case!' He turned back to Zahir. 'There's no door anywhere that we can't get through.'

'Get your men ready. Go in as soon as I give you the word. We're trying to get some idea of the layout.' Tom wanted him away from the car. He didn't want anyone to know about the special skills these children possessed. He trusted these men, but the fewer who knew, the safer the children would be.

'Yes, sir!'

'Position a group of men by the door ready and keep the others in reserve.'

The officer went back to the two minibuses and spoke urgently to the men inside. Five men went into the entrance with a ram. They were heavily armoured and carried automatic weapons. The other occupants of the two vehicles spread out around the area ready for action.

Back in the car, George's eyelids began to flicker. He was coming back. Suddenly his eyes opened wide. He tried hard to convey the urgency of what he had seen, but he was confused and it took a few seconds for him to fully regain consciousness.

'The back! The back!'

'What is it, George? What did you see?'

'A door! There's a door at the back!'

'Facing the river?'

'Yeh! They're getting away!'

The two men had heard the noise made by George and Zahir. Suspecting trouble, they had set the room where they worked to destruct and were putting in place their escape plan, using a door at low level and hard to spot that led directly to the dockside. Tom began to run round the massive mill building to the waterside, calling other men to follow him. As they turned the corner to the dock frontage, they were in time to see one of the fugitives disappearing down a distant steep slipway to the water's edge. They called out to them to stop and warned them that they were armed. But the sound they feared disturbed the early evening calm of the still, black water in the dock. An outboard motor kicked into life. A small power boat that the men used to travel back and forth to their bomb factory began to nose off the tiny disused jetty and edged out into the immense dock alongside the City Airport runway.

Within seconds the boat was at the entrance to the Royal Albert Dock. It raced through the water at the side of the runway as a small passenger jet roared along beside them before its wheels lifted off the tarmac and it soared into the sky. The tide was in and the dock gates to the marina and docks were open to let small boats enter and leave. The powerboat zoomed through the massive gates and into the swirling waters of the Thames, forcing a small pleasure boat to crash into the dock wall. Tom cursed. He should have done a full survey of the area, but in fairness they had had little time. Luckily, main roads run along both banks of the river for miles in both directions. It took only seconds to inform the traffic police, who were operating the road blocks, of the new situation. Almost immediately their cars were on the road, keeping the boat in sight and monitoring its progress as it turned and swung upstream towards the heart of London.

In the incident room, Tom's team swung into action. A police helicopter was waiting in reserve at the nearby City Airport. It was airborne in minutes and sweeping the river to keep the boat under surveillance. The first bridge over the river was at The Tower. They dispatched an armed squad there in case it was decided to fire at the boat if it reached that far. Meanwhile, to Hilary's alarm, the events were beginning to attract a lot of public attention. Passers-by on the river banks were excited by the sudden rush of police activity. They couldn't help but notice the helicopter buzzing the small boat, the two men crouching down to avoid being recognised, the police convoys, sirens wailing, chasing the boat up the river. She was worried that the children might get caught on one of the many videos that were being shot on mobile phones, but within a minute the action had moved round a bend in the river. She sighed with relief. The children had not yet reached the river bank on the far side of the building and their identity would remain a closely guarded secret.

Tom was in a quandary. The nearest police launches were at Tower Bridge and Greenwich. Neither could get into action quickly. While the two men remained on the river they were frustratingly safe. The police marksmen could hit them from the river banks, but police in the UK are under strict orders not to shoot at unarmed civilians. These men may have guns, but they didn't know. Without evidence of weapons, the police were powerless. All they could do was to follow the boat and wait for them to come ashore. Attention swung to the basement rooms of Millennium Mills. He ordered the squad with the battering ram to break down the door. While they were waiting for the bombers to land or run out of fuel for their boat, at least they could explore the bomb factory. It could give them valuable clues. There was still the mystery of the elusive Lucretia. As he turned to walk back to the building's main entrance, he met George, looking anxious.

'Tom! Those men! Before they ran away they were...'

That's as far as he got. He was interrupted by a deafening explosion. In the stairway, the two men breaking down the door to the basement were blown off their feet by a powerful blast that scorched their clothing and melted part of the plastic on their visors. All hell broke loose. Their companions shouted, 'Officers down! Get the medics!' Ambulances were called. Men fought their way through the dust, trying to reach their companions. The injured men were coughing and choking in the dust, but were still alive.

George looked crestfallen. 'They were ... I think ... rigging it to explode...'

With a wail of sirens the first ambulance pulled up and two medics ran out. As they burst into the hallway, the building shuddered. Beneath their feet, age old timbers began to groan and crumble. There was a long low screech as metal girders began to move against each other and give way. A long crack opened up on the floor beneath their feet. The explosion had compromised the stability of the old mill and years of decay had at last come to a head. After attempt after attempt by developers to get permission to demolish the old structure had been refused, the old mill had decided to take matters into its own hands. It was demolishing itself.

The paramedics were close to panic. They didn't know what injuries the two officers had and so their training told them that they couldn't be moved until a full assessment had been carried out. Pulling, twisting, turning in the wrong places could lead to more serious injuries or even death. But if they delayed moving them, they could all be crushed to death under the collapsing building.

Out on the river, the desperate race was still being run. The boat was small but very fast and the police cars were having trouble following it as they approached the city and heavy traffic. The helicopter was still flying low, buzzing the fleeing men and trying to spot any weapons they may be carrying. The men were running scared, zig-zagging their boat wildly across the broad river in a vain effort to throw off their pursuers. They were close to Tower Bridge now, and the police marksmen, shielded by the bridge's metal girders, had their guns trained on the tiny, weaving target.

The officer in charge was on his phone, waiting for permission to fire, when the Upper Thames police launch roared under the bridge, spray shooting from its sides, blue lights flashing from its superstructure. Armed police wearing flak jackets were gripping the sides ready to board the power boat when they got alongside. The men they were trying to arrest saw the danger and swung the boat around. They began to flee downstream, helped by the receding tide, leaving the men on Tower Bridge powerless to stop them.

Beth was crying as the children were moved away from the old mill. She knew that the men inside were in mortal danger and she was desperate for them. Hilary was comforting George, who was heartbroken that he hadn't managed to warn everyone in time. Zahir watched in horror as dust began to swirl from the gaping, glassless windows of the crumbling building. Deep underground, old concrete pillars that had been supporting the ground floor had been blasted apart and the reinforced cast beams that had stretched between them were groaning as they gave up the ghost and dissolved into dust. The brave paramedics with their injured charges were relatively safe in the tall stairwell. Nevertheless the situation was becoming critical and visibility by now was almost zero. They made a decision to evacuate and move the injured to safety. The two officers were rolled onto stretchers and then half carried, half dragged through the clouds of dust into the fresh air outside. The sun dipped down behind the blocks of flats on the horizon.

There were now two helicopters over the Thames tracking the fleeing power boat. Their floodlights were switched on, spotlighting it as it weaved to the right and then the left in a vain effort to escape. The race was now down river and, unknown to the occupants of the boat, a trap was being prepared for them. The Greenwich police launch was ready in the centre of the river, with chains attached to buoys connected to the river banks. If the power boat refused to stop it would hit the chains and be upturned. Police marksmen lined the banks. The Upper Thames launch, still in hot pursuit, was also part of the trap. It was preparing to swing across the river when Greenwich was reached to block any escape back upstream towards the Tower.

The police operation was intended to give the bombers every chance to surrender and remain alive. But if it was necessary to take severe action to protect the public, all had been made ready for that contingency. As the tiny powerboat, bouncing across the water, came into view of the Greenwich police launch, loudspeaker warnings blared out across the Thames. *'ARMED POLICE! BERTH YOUR BOAT NOW AND COME ASHORE! YOU ARE IN DANGER OF DEATH IF YOU CONTINUE!'*

The fugitives spun the boat around again. They appeared to be assessing their chances. The boat went into a tight spin and then they seemed to decide that their best chance was to tackle the upstream launch head on. In the incident room, Jack finally got permission to use armed force to stop the pursuit. As more and more bystanders turned their phone cameras on the drama unfolding around them, Tom called the chief of the team of marksmen.

'Neil, we've got permission to use all necessary force!'

'Roger! We're ready, sir!'

'Tell your men to aim at the outboard motor. If we can cripple the boat we can go alongside and get them out!'

'Sir!'

Three of the Metropolitan Police's best marksmen were given the order to fire. They strained to keep the small craft in their sights as it bucked and swayed in the water. After several seconds of agonised waiting, they had the boat's engine in the cross hairs of their sights.

Back at Millennium Mills, the two injured officers were out of the damaged building. The ambulances were still parked where they had slid to a halt, while the paramedics worked on their patients. Only when they were sure that it was safe to move them would they be taken to Accident and Emergency. One of the paramedics nodded to Hilary to assure that the men would survive. She turned to Tom.

'The children have been through enough for one day.'

'You're right.' Tom's mind was on the news coming in from the river. 'I'll drive you to the hotel and then go on to Greenwich.'

A third long, low rumble emanated from the innards of the old mill as it suffered another death pang. The car purred away from this desolate part of London's docklands and crossed the bridge over the dock as it took its passengers to the comfort and safety of their hotel. The sky flamed red as the sun sank into the west.

Back at the river, things were not going well. The first marksman's shell hit the drive mechanism of the outboard motor and it jerked into the air, slowing the boat's progress though the water. This meant that the other two shots, which would normally have blown the motor to splinters, missed their targets by a tiny, but deadly, margin. The bearded man was using the handle from the motor to steer the boat. As the motor stalled, he was thrown back and the second bullet went straight through his arm, shattering the bone. The third bullet too went astray. It went directly through the small fuel tank that was attached to the motor. The engine exploded in a flash of flame. The two men were blown out of the boat into the water. Both were unconscious. By the time one of the police launches reached them, the bearded man had died of his injuries. The launch raced them to the riverbank where paramedics were waiting. There was a slim chance that the smaller man might have survived.

23. WHERE IS SHE?

An hour later the four were huddled in Zahir and Hilary's room, welcoming the warmth and light of the hotel room after the chill wind of the darkness outside. Even Beth had to agree that it was too late for shopping and in truth had little appetite for it after the catastrophic events of the day. Jill had called in to ensure they were settled comfortably. It was agreed that they were too tired to go out for a restaurant meal so it was another snack before bedtime. They sat on the two single beds eating Subways and drinking diet coke. George still thought he should have done more to warn the men of the danger of entering the basement, but Hilary told him he wasn't to blame. He'd done all he could. Beth kept wiping her eyes and was worried that they would be red and sore in the morning.

Tom arrived, looking worn and tired. He brought good news of the two police officers hurt in the blast. They were both concussed, but their protective clothing had saved their lives. They had suffered some minor fractures and had lost a lot of blood, but they were out of intensive care and should be out of hospital within the week. He broke the news to them of the bombers. Hilary and the children knew nothing of the excitement on the river and the dramatic end to the chase. He gave them a quick outline of what had happened and told them that one of the men had failed to make it. His life had been taken by the river before he could be picked up. The other man was now in hospital under police guard. He was critical and in a coma. He was getting the best possible care, but only time would tell whether or not he would survive.

It was time for the evening news. They switched on the large flat screen television. Both Hilary and Tom knew that a mass of amateur video would be available to the news organisations and they were nervous in case any of it showed Hilary and the children. They need not have worried. They had been sheltered behind the huge mass of the mill building and anyway most of the footage was of such low quality that it was impossible to make out distant faces. The chase up and down the Thames dominated the news, of course. It was hailed as a triumphant success for the police and intelligence services. Two of the bombers had now been found and accounted for. The people of Britain could now sleep safely in their beds. The London theatres that had been closed since the bombing would open again next week.

Television reporters and experts were confident that the terrorist cell would be wound up quickly now. Nobody mentioned Lucretia, Zahi noticed, and he worried about that. Many eyewitnesses were interviewed and the chase became more dramatic and wilder with every account. It was amazing what people could imagine they saw when they had the chance to appear on national television. They took full advantage of their few seconds of fame. No mention was made, of course, of the part played by OSIRIS. Hilary chuckled. She wondered what the great British public would make of the Occult Surveillance and Intelligence Recording and Investigation Service if they had known of its existence and its role in this success. Even more – what would they think if they had known that OSIRIS gained most of its information from the psychic skills of four children! Archie would be watching this with Fenton and would, no doubt, be sulking again because his part in the capture had not been recognised. Would the part played by his Lego tower, she wondered, ever be known?

Tom told them that Jack and the rest of the team were going to work through the night to gather clues as to Lucretia's whereabouts. They'd all meet up again over breakfast to agree on tomorrow's priorities. In the meantime, he suggested that these young people should be in bed. No-one objected. He guided Beth and George to their rooms before retiring to his nearby. He had several conference calls to make before settling down for a few hours sleep. It seemed astonishing that only twelve hours ago they were sitting in the schoolroom at Foxes Hollow watching Archie build his stunted Shard.

George was not going to let this chance go by to watch some unsupervised, grown up television. He flicked through the channels looking for something interesting and finally settled for a repeat of a Top Gear programme he had watched last year. Beth lay down on her bed, switched on her television and was asleep before the first commercial break was over.

Hilary tucked Zahi into bed and then went into the bathroom to freshen herself up. She wished she'd brought a toothbrush. Then she settled down under her duvet and hoped that he slept well. She didn't want visions of the dark girl to disturb his rest. She need not have worried. He fell into such a deep sleep that the devil and all his demons would not have woken him. She wondered about this strange girl. How did she make herself so difficult to spot? How did she manage to torment Zahi as she did? Under different circumstances, Hilary might have welcomed her into their little family. She might have skills that would be fascinating to study. But most of all she wondered, 'Where is she?'

24. STRANGER AND STRANGER...

2 am. Both Hilary and Zahi were fast asleep. Slowly and sinisterly the darkness around them seemed to thicken. The light by Zahi's bed had been left on, in case he woke in the night. The blackness in the room appeared to thicken and wrap itself around it. Mysteriously, the light from the bulb seemed to dim, gradually fading away until all that was left was the faint glow of the element. The steady breathing of the two sleepers was the only sound that could be heard. Then the temperature in the room began to drop as if someone, or something, was drawing energy from the air around the two sleeping bodies. The heating in the hotel bedroom came on and tried to compensate for the sudden unexpected chill. A steady whine could be heard now as the room heaters fought to respond. When, after a few minutes, the thermostat readjusted and the whine ceased, a listener would have heard a new sound. There was no longer the sound of two people's breath. There was a third. It did not come from any specific place, but seemed to permeate the entire room. It was a deep, rasping sound. It was the sound of someone breathing heavily as he – or she – struggled to use all their strength to perform an action that meant a great deal: an action that was cold and calculating and evil.

Along one wall of the room was a wide shelf at waist height. The ice cold presence in the room moved towards this and seemed to be searching for something. The shelf held the flat screen television and its remote control. It also included a large, moulded plastic tray with all that was needed for making hot drinks. The dark presence seemed to pause by this a moment and then one of the cups rose a millimetre into the air, rattled gently and then sank back again. As if satisfied by this test of strength, the spectre moved on. At the end of the shelf was a folder covered in dark, imitation leather that contained advice and instructions for hotel guests, along with a few sheets of monogrammed writing paper. The cover of the folder rose almost imperceptibly. Within the fold was a cheap plastic ballpoint pen with the hotel's logo on its side. Slowly the pen slid out of the folder and hovered above it for a moment before – menacingly – floating across the room towards Zahir's bed. It appeared to stand on its end, 40 centimetres above one of Zahir's eyes, the point threatening to plunge down and bury itself in the boy's eyeball.

It stayed there for a few seconds and then rose another thirty centimetres into the air. The two beds were side by side and just over a metre apart. Behind them the wall was painted a smooth dove grey. The pen turned through ninety degrees and then lunged at the wall above Zahir's head. It began to write in large letters, up to half a metre high. When it had written seven letters, it floated back to the start and began again, going over and over the letters so that they were strongly marked and gouged into the hard wall plaster.

The wraith had done her work and sighed with satisfaction as she returned to her physical body. She had said what she had to say. It was impossible for her to understand how this boy could have allowed himself to be led so far astray. She remembered how she had been smuggled from Pakistan into Syria to become part of the ISIS training camp. There she had learned the truth about the West. Her masters had taught her of the battle that raged across the world – something that previously she had barely understood. Islam was threatened everywhere by pernicious forces: by evil men driven by greed. These servants of Satan used the liberality that Christianity gave them to corrupt the world, spreading pornography and capitalist materialism. Only Islamic law could bring about the ideal state, in which good would triumph over evil. This boy had become an unwitting agent of the forces of the devil. Perhaps the message she had left would bring him to his senses!

Hilary woke early and went to use the bathroom, tiptoeing so as not to wake Zahi. She washed her face and looked critically at herself in the mirror. She had not set off from Foxes Hollow with any intention of spending the night away. She had not brought any make-up, not even a hairbrush. She was going to feel very self conscious today, not like herself at all. The sooner she could get back home the better! Very carefully and quietly, she opened the bathroom door – and then stopped in horror as she stared at what had been written over Zahi's head!

How could it have happened? Who could have done it? She swung round to check the bedroom door. Tom had insisted, to Hilary, Beth and George, that, for the sake of security, each of them close the safety catch on the inside of their door so that no-one could possibly enter their room during the night. She had done so, and the catch was still closed. An icy hand gripped her heart as she slipped back into the bathroom and drew her phone from her bag.

'Tom...'

Two doors away, Tom had risen early and was writing notes on what had happened yesterday before filing a report. He too had not come prepared for a long stay and had not brought a razor. He ran his hand across the stubble that was forming on his chin. He was just about to call Jack for an update when Hilary rang.

'Yes, Hilary, what is it?'

'Tom ... can you come round? I don't want to wake Zahi, but something very worrying has happened here...'

'On my way!'

Hilary made a quick decision. She couldn't chance Zahir being awoken by Tom's arrival and seeing what had happened. She went over to him and shook him gently. 'Zahi! Time to get up! Let's get you to the bathroom first!'

He grunted sleepily and was too tired to take much notice as she carefully moved him into his chair and pushed him into the bathroom, always ensuring that she was between him and the wall. Once in the bathroom he could manage for himself. She pushed him in.

'Run some water in the bath. Can you lift yourself in? I'll come in for you in a few minutes!' Then she exited the room, closed the door and breathed a sigh of relief. Tom tapped quietly and she let him in.

'What's happened?'

'That has!'

Tom's jaw dropped and his mouth gaped open in shock and horror. Scored in to the wall above Zahir's bed were seven large letters. They spelt the word, 'TRAITOR!'

Hilary was desperately worried. 'If Lucretia has done this, how? And why? No-one could have got into the room.'

Tom agreed. 'Not by any normal means!'

'This means Zahir is in danger. For some reason, this girl wants to destroy him. If she could do that to the wall – what could she do to him?'

Tom took charge, calmly, but inside he was more mystified and alarmed than he wanted to reveal. 'He mustn't see it. Bring him backwards out of the bathroom and we'll tell him we need to go to the incident room quickly. That'll give you an excuse to wheel him straight out to the lift.'

Hilary did as he suggested, while Tom fetched the other two to the car. Beth was not pleased. She had fallen asleep fully dressed. Waking, she felt grubby and, worse, her *LOVE* top was crumpled and creased. Tom would not give her time to get changed. Grumpy, she squeezed into the car alongside George. He was plugged into his music again and much less concerned than Beth about not being able to change his clothes or clean his teeth. With Zahir safely seated at the other side, the car drew away from the hotel back towards Pontoon Dock. Tom had cleared the damage with the hotel and was eager to get to the incident room to see what the team had discovered during the night. As they approached Millennium Mills, they saw the police tape screening off the area. Emergency vehicles were still present as the area was thoroughly searched and made safe. It brought back to all of them the horror of the day before.

It was a subdued quintet that drew up outside the incident room. Jack came out to greet them looking tired and drawn. He helped to get Zahir into his chair and told them that they had some breakfast ready for them inside. Tom took him to one side and brought him up to speed with what had happened to Zahir at the hotel. Jack, a very practical man, couldn't believe that there was a supernatural explanation for this. He agreed with Tom that he would send a forensic team to Zahir's room to carry out a full investigation. Hopefully, they would uncover who had carried out the atrocity and how they had entered the locked room. His Sherlock Holmes-like rational approach pleased Tom, who wondered whether he himself was falling too much under Hilary's spell and beginning to believe in spooks.

When they joined the others the mood had lightened. The drinks machine was working overtime, pouring out cups of coffee and hot chocolate. The weary incident team was joining Hilary and the children in consuming piles of croissants and bacon sandwiches. They were all beginning to relax and chat and joke with each other. Beth was pleased to see Jack join them and did a Princess Di pose, head slightly down and to one side, smiling as she looked up at him, giving him the full benefit of her large blue eyes. Hilary noticed it and smiled. As long as it went no further, fourteen was not too young to begin to practise flirting skills. Jack was too tired to even notice.

Tom gave them all fifteen minutes to enjoy this time free from pressure before calling them to order. 'Right, Jack – I know you're all shattered. I want you out of here in an hour and home getting some well earned rest. But first – let's have an update on progress since last night.'

Jack looked glum. 'We haven't got as much as we'd hoped, Boss. Forensics are raking through the basement of the mill, wherever it's safe enough to tread. The damage is pretty extensive. You were right about the explosive they're using. It's a lot more advanced than we've seen before: some kind of super-refined nitro-glycerine. It's made a right mess of the old mill. We're afraid any evidence they left down there may have been completely wiped out by the blast.'

'What about the two bombers?'

'Nothing on them to identify them by. We've taken photographs and we're trying face recognition again. Once we've got names, we should be able to get an address.'

'And the one in hospital?'

'Still unconscious. The doctors don't hold out much hope, but if he does come round, we'll be on to him straight away.'

'This has top priority, Jack. If the doctors tell you he's too sick to talk, get him to a prison hospital so we can work on him without interference.'

Hilary drew in a breath but made no comment. She knew that the man would not be tortured and understood how urgent it was that any information he had was made known to MI5.

'Will do, Boss.'

'Now, what about Lucretia's flat?'

'Well, Boss – I think we've had this all the wrong way round. From the start we assumed that Lucretia, because she was a girl, was a mule.'

'I beg your pardon!' This sounded rather offensive to Hilary!

'Sorry, Hil – a mule is our slang for someone who is forced to do something bad – like carrying drugs or a bomb – against their will or having been talked into it, perhaps by a boyfriend. But it seems now that this girl is very bright indeed. It looks to me as if she could even have been the mastermind behind it all. Her flat was so clean that a professional hitman couldn't have done a better job of hiding himself away.'

'There was nothing?'

'No clues at all as to where she may be now. No phone records, no letters, no diaries, the place was clean. But there were fingerprints, plenty of those.'

'Any match?'

'No. She's got no record at all.'

Tom was thoughtful. 'Still, the prints will be useful. They'll help us to track where she goes from now on.'

'We've got good pictures now from DVLA and immigration records. They've been sent to every police force and there's a nationwide hunt going on now.'

'If we don't find her by tomorrow, we'll go for national TV coverage,' Tom asserted.

'Right, boss. The commissioner's giving a news conference this morning to talk through yesterday's business. He'll reassure the public that we have two bombers captured and good leads on the third.'

Tom grimaced, wrily. 'That should reassure the media. I wish it reassured me! Close this room down and go and get some rest. Take a few hours off.'

'Thanks, Boss.'

Tom dragged a weary hand across his eyes. He had not had much sleep. 'We'll visit Lucretia's flat before we go back to Foxes. We'll let the kids see what they can pick up.'

Hilary crouched down in front of Zahir and put her hands on his shoulders. She was grateful that Zahir had not seen what had been written on the hotel wall, but she felt guilty that she was exposing him to more danger than, perhaps, he realised. 'Are you OK with that, Zahi?'

'Think so...'

'If when we get there, you're worried – just say. I'll stay with you in the car.'

'Thanks, Hil!'

The incident team was packing everything into two cars as the Range Rover drove away from Pontoon Dock for the final time. They drove along Prince Regent Lane, over the busy dual carriageways of the A13, and parked in the grounds of Newham Hospital. From there, it was an easy walk to the large house, divided into multi-occupancy living spaces, where Lucretia had lived.

It was a large Victorian villa divided into flats and bedsits. Two police cars were parked outside and a very determined female police officer was standing at the gate to prevent anyone entering. Tom showed her his card and they were admitted. The garden was overgrown. The lawn was patchy and full of weeds. It had not been cut all summer. The grass was knee high and beginning to look like a hay meadow as the flower heads turned gold. A mint plant, put there at some time to provide a herb for the kitchen, had run everywhere and so there was a pleasant minty smell as they walked up the overgrown path. Two enormous sycamore trees cast deep shade down the side of the house. The front door was formidable-looking, with dark green paint beginning to peel and stained glass panels in the small windows. There was a heavy, black metal door knocker in the shape of a lion's head. A panel at the side contained a row of push buttons and small pieces of paper with the residents' names written on them. One announced tersely, 'I Khan'. Tom did not bother to ring the bell of course, but gestured to his small team to walk right in.

The hallway was dark and forbidding. The walls were panelled in dark brown wood that had not been changed since the Edwardian era. A single light bulb dangled where once a gas lamp had provided a welcoming glow. The light bulb was of the economy variety and gave only a little cold light. Faintly, on a dark, ochre-coloured door at the end of the passage way, could be discerned the word 'kitchen'. The other three rooms off the entrance hall were each individual bedsits. The house smelt damp with a faint aroma of excrement, partly explained by a small pile of dog dirt on the checker board floor tiles. The overwhelming impression was one of despair. Only in London, where accommodation was so difficult to find, would people pay to live in conditions such as these.

The stairs were carpeted in a patterned, rust coloured covering that showed evidence of a number of greasy, black stains. Carefully, to avoid any further dog mess, the OSIRIS team mounted the steps to the first landing. The lighting, such as it was, was on a timer so that it didn't stay on too long, in order to avoid large power bills for the owner. As Tom stepped off the top stair, the lights clicked off and he was plunged into darkness. He told the others to wait on the steps and ran his hand over the walls searching for a switch. Before he could locate it, a light came on at the top of the next flight and a voice asked, 'Is that you, sir?'

'Neil?'

'He's inside, sir. It's Colin.'

'For God's sake keep the light on while we get up there!'

'Yessir!'

He had known it would be difficult to get Zahir up all the stairs and so he had been left with George in the car, watched over by the woman constable. Hilary, Tom and Beth walked past the door marked 'Bathroom' and the three rooms on the first floor and climbed the final set of steps up to the attic bedrooms. Nine rooms all sharing one bathroom – it didn't bear thinking about. Tom had a low opinion of greedy landlords who exploited desperate people like this. Was there a fire escape from the top floor? Would everyone have to use the one internal staircase in case of fire? If so, this was a criminal fire hazard. He would get this landlord somehow, he vowed to himself. At the top of the final staircase was another single bulb, hanging from old twisted wire. The door to Lucretia's room was open. Inside the two forensic officers were taking the final digital images before wrapping up.

'Hi, Neil – how's it going?'

'Nearly done, sir. We've got plenty of clear prints. Not much else though. Sorry.'

'It's OK – not your fault. Go out and get some fresh air. Take half an hour off.'

'Thanks, boss, I'm parched!'

'You too, Colin. There's a coffee bar at the corner.'

Colin and Neil were comically different. Neil was rather petite without his white lab coat and was impeccably dressed. He had a liking for designer clothes and highly polished, pointed shoes. His hair and nails were immaculate and he was full of energy and almost pubescent humour. Colin was tall with feet that seemed too large for his body. They came before him as he lumbered along, as if they didn't quite belong to the rest of him. He was dour, with a lined face that made him look older than his 48 years. Most of the team called him gramps, at least behind his back, if not to his face. He knew his job, though. If there was evidence to be found, he would find it. The two men took off their white coats, glanced curiously at Hilary and Beth, and descended the stairs for a well-earned break.

As the two men left, the OSIRIS team peered into Lucretia's room. It was set in the roof, so the walls sloped steeply, almost from the floor at the edges, up to a high point along the inner internal wall. A skylight let in some light, but it had not been cleaned for years and was covered on the outside in oily dirt and bird droppings. The far wall was entirely taken up by a single bed, covered with a cheap duvet and a mismatched pillow. Both looked clean. The flooring was bare boards and a small grey rug that might have been another colour once. There was a small 'flatpack' wardrobe on the tallest wall. The door was hanging off because one of the hinges had given way. Next to it was a tiny, cracked basin that served both as kitchen sink and for personal hygiene. A small cupboard and a single chair completed the room's furnishings.

Tom sighed. He looked for something personal to Lucretia that might provide Beth with something to work on. He opened the wardrobe door fully and the small cupboard. There was little there. Their girl lived very frugally if this was her only home, but she was clean. Every surface had been dusted, the pots and pans were scrubbed and the sheets on the bed were clean. He asked Hilary and Beth to make themselves comfortable and they sat next to each other on the bed. Did Lucretia spend much time here? Did she have another home where there would be more to search? He called Neil.

'A quick word, Neil.'

'Yes, Boss?'

'There's not much here, mate. How sure are we this is her home?'

'We interviewed the other people who live there, first thing, before they went to work. They said she's here most days, although they don't often see her come and go. She has the radio on a lot – stuff in a funny language they said.'

'No car?' asked Tom. It seemed impossible that she could live with so little.

'No, they see her walk to the station or down towards the river. No visitors that they've seen.'

'So it seems that this is it?'

'Yeah, Boss.' He could no more understand it than Tom did. It was very difficult for these men who had lived all their lives in a consumer society, where people were judged not by their worth as people, but by how much they owned, to accept that there are societies where one can be content with so little.

'OK. Thanks, Neil.'

He looked round at the sparse room, thoughtfully. He saw one or two objects that maybe Beth could use to give them more information about this elusive woman. He selected a spray deodorant and a hairbrush from the small cupboard and a plain black shoe from the wardrobe. These would do for a start.

Beth was still on the bed, gazing at the room in bewilderment. She could not believe that a young woman could live in such a place and make no more mark on it than this. There was nothing to give a clue of Lucretia's interests or character. The grey walls had once been off-white. There were pale rectangles where a previous occupant had pinned up pictures. There was no colour, no warmth here. It was the spartan room of a woman focused on something other than comfort.

Tom offered the objects to Hilary and she selected the deodorant spray to pass to Beth.

'This is the least likely because it's something she hasn't had long enough to make much impression. Let's get rid of this one first. Ready, Beth?'

Beth nodded. Here was another chance to make a good impression on Tom. She smiled at him and took the can, cradled it in her hands like a precious doll. Hilary sighed. She would have to nurse Beth through this period of making eyes at men. She knew that children who have been deprived of affection when they are young are likely to seek attention when they grow up. Beth could be vulnerable to any man who showed an interest in her. She was very safe with Tom and Jack, but Hilary would need to advise and protect her as she met more boys and men.

Beth closed her eyes and relaxed. She murmured to herself as she stroked the can gently. Gradually she seemed to connect with some memory that the object held. Tom and Hilary moved closer to her, struggling to catch her words. *'Hate ... hate them ... kill...'*

'Are you OK, Beth?' Hilary was worried that Beth was dealing with emotions that could deeply upset her. But Beth did not seem to hear her.

'They tried to stop me ... let them try ... I am the avenging angel ... an eye for an eye...'

Tom was worried now. The spirit of Lucretia seemed to be taking over Beth and her eyes were narrowing, her face twisting into an evil grimace.

'Let them try ... nothing will stop me ... I will revenge all those who have been taken...'

'Beth, can you hear me? BETH! Where is Lucretia? Can you tell us?' Suddenly Hilary was very, very worried. Beth had never reacted like this before. It was not her voice that they were hearing. Hilary realised that she had no experience of dealing with anything like this and she just might be out of her depth. And she was right.

Everything was about to go terribly wrong.

A cold wind rushed through the room and wailed as it swirled past the back of the wardrobe and under the bed. Beth's eyes were fixed on the door and she started to get to her feet. Tom grabbed her and held her down. Beth turned to look at him and moved her head towards him as if she was going to kiss him on the lips. With her face only centimetres away from his, she suddenly let out a loud scream and spat at him, full in the face. Hilary tried to pull them apart. Beth held out her arms, one hand still holding the deodorant can. It began to vibrate – gently at first and then violently. She parted her fingers and the can, instead of falling, hovered in the air. Beth was still screaming – a low, hoarse scream that curdled Hilary's blood. Tom reached out to grasp the can, but it floated out of reach of him. Then, with a speed that took him completely by surprise, it flew at him with incredible force! It struck him on the face and he let go of Beth and clutched at his cheek, where blood was beginning to run down his jaw. Alone, Hilary was finding it difficult to hold Beth and was being swung round as the demented girl twisted to free herself from her grip. Her strength was unnatural – the strength of ten.

The brush rose up from the bed and began to spin in the air. The shoe shot into the air, bounced off the walls and struck Hilary on the back of the head. The wardrobe tottered and the loose door swung crazily on its remaining hinge, then the whole wardrobe crashed down onto Tom's back, knocking him over. The small cupboard began a crazy dance and the taps on the sink turned on by themselves. Hilary was terrified, grappling with Beth, striving to keep her still and pull her down onto the bed.

Then the ice cold wind picked up again and stirred the small items of clothing that had fallen out of the wardrobe onto the floor. Tom was trying to get back to his feet but he was dazed by the knock he had just taken. A sound came from deep in Beth's throat and then left her, to whirl around the room, deep and throaty. *'Ahhhh ... the boyyy...'*

The wind gathered force and as Beth finally fell back onto the bed, limp and exhausted, the eerily moving air exited the room, roaring through the open door, blowing papers, clothes and a white ghostly bedsheet out of the room, through the door and down the first flight of stairs.

'My God...' said Tom, still holding his head and trying to stop the blood. He collapsed onto the bed beside Hilary and Beth. They looked at each other, bewildered and not a little scared. Hilary put her hand gently on Beth's arm.

'We're so sorry,' Tom whispered to her. 'If we'd known, we'd never have put you through that... Are you all right?'

Before Beth could reply, Hilary leapt to her feet, her face as white as a sheet, so that her make-up shone brightly making her look like a demented clown. '*Zahi!*' She screamed, '*She's after Zahi!!*'

'I'll go!' cried Tom and he ran to the doorway, closely followed by Hilary and then by Beth – she was not going to stay up there alone, even though she felt totally shattered. They stumbled down the stairs, Beth slipping down the last few, only to be caught by Tom before she injured herself on the hard tiled floor. When they reached the front door, they saw the 4x4 surrounded by whirling dust and litter. The woman constable was looking scared and confused. She was holding on to one of the door handles as the car rocked wildly from side to side.

Hilary screamed, 'NO!!'

The WPC turned round. 'I'm trying to open the door ... to let them out!'

'No! Leave them!'

The woman let go of the door and the car almost leapt away from her. The wind wound up to a frenzy and seemed to howl in frustration. They could see Zahir's and George's faces at the rear windows, pale and frightened, calling out to them for help. Tom ran up to the car and called out to them. 'You'll be all right! Stay where you are! You're safer there!'

'Keep the windows and doors closed!' cried Hilary.

But Lucretia was not going to be defeated so easily. The whirling wind moved to the front of the car and seemed to be looking for a way in. At the top of the bonnet it found the ventilation grills that led to the car's air conditioning ducts. The disturbed air calmed around the car and the litter that was flying everywhere began to fall and settle. The car stopped rocking about and for a moment they thought that Lucretia had given up. Two bystanders who had stopped to watch the action shrugged and began to walk away.

Beth had left her bag on the back seat of the car. As she walked towards it, she saw the bag begin to rise into the air. It turned on end and the objects inside fell a few centimetres and then hovered in thin air in front of Zahir's face. Beth turned in panic. 'Tom! She's in there!'

Tom ran to the car, pressing the key fob to unlock the doors. As he did, Beth's mobile phone moved a metre through the air towards the dashboard, and then was flung by an invisible force straight at Zahir's head. He threw his hands up to defend himself, but he was too late and the phone caught him a glancing blow on the side of his head. Tom reached his door and pulled it open. He yanked Zahir out of the car as Beth stood by screaming. George stumbled out after him. Tom pulled Zahir to him to protect him and for a while the wind tore at their faces and clothing. Hilary held on to George and Beth and tried to calm the hysterical girl. Then, as suddenly and mysteriously as it had arrived, the evil force was gone, with another frustrated howl.

They hurried into the car. Tom accelerated away, onto the A13 and out of London towards the Dartford crossing. He was determined to put distance between them and whatever had attacked them, and regain the relative safety of Foxes Hollow as soon as he could. Surely Lucretia couldn't find them there? He glanced at the clock – 14.30. That meant at least a three hour journey ahead of them. He put his foot down. By his side, Hilary was desperately worried. The care of these children was in her hands. It seemed that Lucretia could strike at will. How was she doing it? How could she defend them against attack?

25. TOGETHER AGAIN

Foxes Hollow, Southwest England.

Archie was thrilled to see them. He'd been at the window for an hour, hoping to catch a glimpse of his friends' car returning. When it turned round the bend in the drive, away from the tall chestnut trees that had been shielding it, he shouted out in delight. He ran to the front door and threw it open so that he could greet them on the front steps. When the car finally glided to a halt, five very tired faces broke into smiles to see Archie's obvious pleasure at their return. Hilary got out and gave him a hug. Then they opened the rear doors so that George and Beth could greet him. But Archie did not follow them into the house. He climbed into the car to sit next to his new friend Zahir, as Tom drove round to the side door. He half helped, half hindered Tom as he retrieved Zahir's chair from the back of the car and then helped him into it. Oblivious to the danger and excitement that his friends had been through, he chattered away. Zahir listened with genuine interest to Archie's tales of how high his tower had become before he ran out of bricks and the games of Junior Scrabble he had played with Fenton, with great success. Zahir laughed. He was glad that Archie had become so fond of him so quickly and was far too kind to tell Archie that Fenton must have been losing the games on purpose! For a while he could relax and enjoy being back at a place he was happy to think of as home and put behind him the horrors of the last two days.

Hilary was waiting indoors by the rickety lift. She told them that they all had a chance to change and freshen up before supper. After they'd eaten, she would call them together for a council of war. They were all happy with this. It sounded as though they would soon have a plan of how to move forward and they felt reassured. Tom could tell that this was largely a bluff on Hilary's part. He touched her arm. She put a finger to her lips and whispered, 'I need time to do some research before supper!'

Back in her room she showered and then restored her make-up. Several items of gold jewellery and a skirt slightly too short and much too tight later, she felt human again. She sat at her computer desk and began to search through research papers from across the world.

She was late down to supper. The others had finished their first course before she appeared. 'Sorry...,' she explained, half truthfully. 'I must have fallen asleep!'

They forgave her. They were giving Archie a blow by blow account of the way they had been attacked by a violent wind that made phones and cans and shoes fly at them. Now they were back at Foxes Hollow they were much more relaxed and the fears of the day seemed far away. They enjoyed their first decent meal for what seemed like ages, but was actually less than two days. The lasagne was delicious. Even Archie pronounced it tasty and made a decent attempt at the green salad that accompanied it. Hilary and Mary finished with yoghurt, whilst the others revelled in sticky toffee pudding. It was a very contented group that met in the drawing room for coffee and soft drinks at 8.30 that evening.

Once they were all comfortably seated, Hilary began to discuss with them the threat they were facing. She kept it low key, but wanted to be sure that they understood the care they had to take until the threat could be allayed. Tom stood by the computer to bring up images and text when they were needed. A cosy fire was burning in the grate, even though it was a warm summer evening. Hilary was keen to make them feel safe and warm before she began her account. When she was sure of their rapt attention, she began.

'All of us, except Archie, experienced some strange and quite frightening things today. Beth was the first to suffer...'

'Yeah, it was well bad... Things were flying at me...' Now that she felt out of danger, Beth was rather pleased to be the centre of attention.

'And there was a screaming wind,' added George, not to be outdone.

Hilary shushed them. 'That's right. Now first, let's understand that this is not the first time there have been events like this. They've happened all over the world, with the earliest accounts dating back to the beginning of recorded time. There is even a name for them. Students of the paranormal describe the things we experienced as poltergeist activity. It's a German word. It means a noisy spirit.'

She paused for breath. 'We recognise a poltergeist by loud noises, objects levitating, rising off the ground, flying through the air for no apparent reason. Sometimes, a poltergeist will write on walls. Now, I'm sure that you'll recognise some or all of these as things we saw or heard today. There are many, many accounts of poltergeists, in Britain, Germany, the United States, Borneo, even Japan. It happens everywhere, so we mustn't think that this is something highly unusual. Many have been thoroughly investigated.'

Even Archie was listening carefully now. 'Some scientists dismiss them as fake, but they'd be determined not to believe, no matter how convincing the evidence was. I've met scientists who wouldn't believe in a poltergeist if one hit them in the face!'

'Do they kill people?' asked Beth, rather more concerned now.

'Ah Beth – a good question! The answer is no. They seem to want to frighten people. And it's people they pick on. They don't belong to a particular place. They seem to attach themselves to a person or family and attack them in some way. Most who've studied them assume that the poltergeist is the evil spirit of someone long dead. But I suspect that where there is activity that we designate as a poltergeist, it is most likely to be psychokinesis.'

'Psychowhat?' George liked long impressive sounding words.

Hilary laughed. 'Psychokinesis! It's a Greek term that means the ability to move objects with the mind. It was used by American parapsychologists over a hundred years ago, when they were investigating the claims of people who said they could make objects move just by staring at them and willing them to move. This led other investigators to suppose that their previous ideas were wrong. What they had once thought was the work of ghosts could actually be being done by living people. And maybe they didn't even know they were doing it.'

'And so,' suggested Zahir, 'sometimes it could be people sort of haunting themselves?'

'My, Zahi, you are quick today! Yes, it could be that psychokinesis is actually a talent that some people have – just like each of you has a talent that would seem to many people to be supernatural. What I think is that our Lucretia can use her mind to make objects move and draw air into currents of wind and make strange sounds...'

Tom had a distant look in his eyes. 'Wasn't there a similar case about 40 years ago in London?'

'Yes, Tom. I won't tell you I was part of the team that investigated it – it would give my age away!' Hilary laughed. George snorted. Hilary ignored him. She didn't really care who knew her age.

'It was called The Enfield Poltergeist! It's a strange and spooky tale,' Hilary whispered. 'Ideal for a dark night like this! Would you like to hear it?'

Zahir and Archie were sitting each side of Mary. They snuggled up against her. All of them were hanging on to Hilary's words, totally absorbed.

'The lady called us in when the strange things that were happening to her family became absolutely impossible to bear any longer. Peggy she was called. Peggy Hodgson. She had two girls, called Janet and Meg. The first time she saw something strange was when she heard shouting in the girls' bedroom. She ran in to find a large, heavy cupboard had been moved across the wall and was partly blocking the door. She pushed it back to where it should be, thinking the girls had somehow done it. And then she stood frozen to the spot as she saw the large wooden cupboard move back across the wall all by itself - without anyone touching it. That night things got scarier still. Heavy objects rose into the air all on their own and then they were thrown with great force across the kitchen, narrowly missing the children. There were strange frightening noises in the house.'

Hilary felt Beth shiver as she continued. 'They were so frightened they called the police. Two officers arrived and took notes, but they thought the children were making it up – until, as they turned to leave, a chair in front of them rose up and hovered a few inches above the ground. That convinced them that something weird was happening, but they had to leave. This was nothing to do with them and there was nothing they could do. As far as they could tell, no crime was being committed.'

Zahir stirred, 'So they couldn't do anything to help?'

'No. But experts came and went. Many of them were convinced that a poltergeist was at work in this small Enfield house. They saw objects appear and disappear. They heard strange groaning noises that were frightening and no-one could explain. Some thought the two young girls were to blame, but no-one could explain how they could move heavy objects without even touching them. And then two passers-by saw something truly inexplicable...'

Hilary looked round at her audience. She didn't want to frighten them too much before bedtime, but all this was true and she wanted them to know what they were up against. Everyone was listening, their eyes fixed on her, their mouths open in astonishment.

'A passing baker and a crossing patrol lady were walking past the house one evening when they saw a strange light coming from the girls' bedroom window, accompanied by what they described as an 'unearthly noise'. To their astonishment, they saw Janet through the window floating above her bed. She spun round in the air and screamed as her head crashed over and over again against the window. They rushed into the house and ran upstairs with the girls' mother. There they saw Janet, alone in her bedroom, lying unconscious on the floor. As they tried to wake her, she began to speak in a man's voice, shouting and swearing at them. Only when the family were moved out of the house by the local authority did the poltergeist activity end.'

Beth was on the edge of her seat. 'A man's voice? Why a man's voice?'

Hilary paused a moment. She seemed to consider something and finally decided to tell them about the man.

'It seemed to be a man's voice and not a very nice one. He was swearing and telling them his name. It was Bill.'

'Bill?'

'Yes. And the records showed that a man with that name had lived in the house thirty years before. And he'd died there. He'd taken his own life.'

There was silence in the room for a long time as they all digested this extraordinary story. The only sound was a gentle crackle from the logs burning in the fireplace. Zahir shivered. He knew how persistent Lucretia was, and how clever at seeking them out. How were they going to protect themselves from her?

Hilary tried to reassure them. 'To start with, we'll make sure that everyone has someone with them at night to cover their backs. For some reason, Zahi seems to be the one she's going for the most. Tom, can you stay in his room with him tonight?' Tom nodded. 'Beth had a bad time with her as well, so I'll stay in your room, Beth. I'll call Fenton and I'm sure he'll drive over and stay with you, George. Mary – can you look after Archie?'

'Of course!' said Mary. Archie looked delighted.

'In the longer term, we need to see if we can grow the skills we need to defend ourselves. Beth – you have an extraordinary affinity with objects of all kinds. It's not impossible that you could move them with your mind. Have you ever tried?'

She shook her head.

'Well, let's start tomorrow. If some of us can do it, we could try to counter Lucretia if she tries it again. As she lifts things, we could use our minds to push them down again. I don't know if it will work, but it's worth a try. When you think of the amazing things you four can achieve, this is fairly minor!'

'She's very strong, Hil,' said Beth, doubtfully.

'I know. It's not going to be easy. But remember – poltergeists are scary, but they have never done anyone any real harm.'

'Yet...,' thought Zahir, but he kept it to himself.

Temporary beds were set up in all the rooms and Foxes Hollow prepared itself for a night of siege. Outside in the cool, dark night, the spirits of the house left the family graveyard. They drifted through the moonlight to the cold stone walls of the ancient building to form a last line of defence. They would protect their home and its occupants in every way they could. As the living drifted into a troubled sleep, believing that their weak plan may help them, the long dead took their places at every door and window, prepared to battle to protect their own.

26. A DIVERSION

Did Irna, known to them as Lucretia, come in the night and attempt again to take revenge on Zahir? Was she determined to destroy him because in her mind he had turned on his own kind? Did she circle the house in the dead of night and sense the ghostly guardians were ready to defend it against her? Did she decide to fight another day when the OSIRIS team would be away from Foxes Hollow and be easier targets? We'll never know, but there was no attack on the house that night. However, Zahir did not sleep well. As he tossed and turned in his bed, he saw a flash of flame; a home destroyed by a rocket attack; mothers crying for the souls of their dead children; uncles and aunts in hospital beds in terrible agony from burn wounds and torn limbs. Voices were crying to him: '*These are your own kind! These are your kindred! Why have you forsaken us?*'

He woke feeling exhausted, damp with cold sweat all over his body. Tom was worried and called Mary. She took his pulse and temperature but could find nothing physically wrong with him. She promised to check him regularly through the day.

His friends were much better today, relieved that the night had passed quietly and that they had slept well, despite their fears. And Hilary had good news for them all. Tomorrow was their visit to Chequers to be thanked by the Prime Minister for their part in saving so many lives. They had forgotten all about it and the news excited all of them. None of them had any interest in politics – they were too young. However, it was a day out – without, they hoped, any more explosions to dodge. More important, Hilary announced that for such an important visit they would need smart, new clothes. Today – shopping!

Tom was fully occupied that morning. The pictures of Lucretia were going global today. They had been with the police for twenty four hours without any reported sighting. She had apparently disappeared off the face of the Earth. The hope now was that with her face on every television station, MI5 could rely on the 60 million people of the United Kingdom to spot her somewhere. There was a news conference this morning and Tom would feature in it. He would emphasise how dangerous this young woman was, using her real name of Irna Khan, and appeal for help from the public to track her down.

So it would be after lunch before he'd return and they could hit the shops. In the meantime, Friday morning was a school day. An hour of maths was highly eventful. Fenton had Beth, George and Archie measuring the height of everything in the schoolroom and then working out the mean. Lots of tape measures and recording and calculating later, Archie decided that his friends were also objects and insisted that he must measure Beth and George. He stood on a chair to measure Beth, the chair tipped and he fell to the floor. Fenton examined the chair and declared that luckily no damage had been done! Archie squealed, 'What about me!!' Fenton was not interested, declaring that little boys bounce, chairs break. He was only joking and eventually the teacher put a sticking plaster on the part of Archie that the boy claimed was broken. Then, to Archie's delight, Fenton blamed the chair for the accident and relegated it to the naughty corner. It was the first time anything but Archie had been in the naughty corner.

Maths was followed by English and Beth, helped by Archie, had to imagine that she was a reporter for the Enfield Herald and she wrote a news item on the Enfield poltergeist, researching facts from the internet. George continued with his racing car project. Poltergeists are interesting enough, but you can't drive one. Zahir had been excused lessons today. He spent the first hour with Mary and to their mutual delight made some progress. He was able, by the end of the session, to move his legs very slightly. She said that from now on they would use a walking frame every day to get movement and strength back into his legs. It was with the aid of a walking frame that he half staggered, half stumbled up to Hilary's door, with Mary keeping him steady. She knocked and Hilary beamed with pleasure when she opened the door and saw Zahir standing there. 'It's just a little movement and the control isn't there yet,' explained Mary.

'But it's a wonderful start!' exclaimed Hilary and gave him a big hug that made him feel wonderful. 'I was just about to have coffee – come in and join me!'

Zahi had never been in Hilary's room before. He liked the curtains with pretty flowers on them and the matching duvet cover. The room was full of colour and light and smelt of Hilary's heavy perfume. There were books everywhere – Zahi had never seen so many. Two sets of bookshelves each side of the fireplace were packed with volumes, most of them learned works on the paranormal. The fireplace was filled with a vase of roses. A large stereo unit from the 80s with speakers on small stands was playing pretty piano music – Chopin, though Zahi did not recognise it. Every table was heavy with more books and papers. Hilary swept a dozen books off the small chintz sofa to make space for them to sit. A lady – Zahi had not been at the house long enough yet to learn the names of all who worked there – brought up a tray of coffee and a can of cola for him. Chocolate biscuits too. For the first time for two days he thought of his mother and realised he was missing her. He wished that she were here to see this.

'Have you read all these books?' he asked, wide eyed.

'Almost!' laughed Hilary. 'In fact I'll tell you a secret ... I wrote some of them!'

'Really?!!' exclaimed Zahi. It had never occurred to him that books were written by real people that you could meet. 'Which ones?'

'Here's one,' she told him, picking up a book with a picture of a ghost on the cover, holding a piece of scientific equipment. The book was called 'Science versus the Supernatural – an ongoing feud' by Dr Hilary Fleischmann. 'Would you like it?'

'For me? Really?'

'Of course,' she smiled. Picking up a beautiful fountain pen with a gold plated nib, she opened the book to the title page and wrote on it: 'To Zahi, a super – natural boy, from his friend Hilary.' He clutched it to his chest, overcome with gratitude. Mary was touched by his obvious pleasure. It was the first real book he had ever owned. 'It has been a good day! Mary smiled. You've made your first steps and been given a first edition, signed by the author!' Zahi smiled back.

'At last!' beamed Hilary. 'That's the first time you've smiled for two days! I've been worried about you. Are you unhappy here, Zahi?'

He shook his head. She looked him straight in the eyes. 'Are you feeling lonely?'

'No.'

'Missing your mum? Or is it Lucretia?' The look in his eyes told her that she had hit the mark. 'You're worried about her, aren't you? She seems to have it in for you...'

'Yes ... she's so angry with me...'

'Don't worry, Zahi. She won't harm you. You're going to live a long and happy life. Trust me. I know about long life. My grandfather lived until he was 92. When people asked him the secret of his long life, he ascribed it to a weak bladder. He said that running to the lav had kept him fit and healthy.'

Mary laughed and Zahi smiled. He wasn't sure what was funny about a weak bladder, but it sounded slightly silly.

'Another smile! It's getting better! But come on, tell me about Lucretia.'

'What happened to her and her family ... was awful...'

'Yes it was. They were unlucky. They lived near the mountains between Pakistan and Afghanistan. No fault of theirs, but this region's a key target for NATO air strikes, because the mountain passes are used by terrorists and they have bases there. When the satellites showed people gathering near the family home the US forces just assumed that it was terrorists gathering ready to strike at allied forces. So they sanctioned a rocket attack. They shouldn't have done it.'

'But why did Lucretia try to bomb the British royal family?'

'Because we're allies. Although only American forces were involved, in her mind we're just as much at fault.'

'So Lucretia is right to take revenge... Innocent people were killed and so innocent people should suffer...'

'If you believe that Zahi, I'm sorry. There were other things she could have done. She could have gone to the press with her story. We are shocked by what happened, so would millions of others have been. She could have sought justice through a war crimes court. There are international laws, and these laws are there to protect people and punish those who break them. She could have used the democratic process to bring pressure to bear on those who regard some people's lives as cheaper and more expendable than others. In our country we have freedom of speech and freedom of the press. These are the ways to change things for the better. No good ever came from bombs and killing.'

'She thinks I betrayed my religion and my culture.'

'Do you think that's what you've done?'

'I dunno...'

'In the end, only you can decide, Zahi. I've told you what I think. The western democracies have lots of faults, but we, the people, have the power to change things for the better. I think that's better than a dictatorship or a government so driven by religious extremism that no-one dare say what they think or protest against injustice.'

'I wouldn't want that. But Lucretia ... Irna ... hates me so much.'

'I'm afraid she does. We're going to protect you all we can, Zahi. You mean a lot to us. Oh, Zahi, don't cry...'

But this was too much for Zahir. He was torn between loyalty to his friends and the country in which he'd been born

– and over a thousand years of tradition, religion and culture. After all that had happened to him, this was too much, too soon. Mary put her arms around him.

Hilary held his hand and spoke softly, 'Oh Zahi, if it helps, think of this. Every Muslim religious leader and teacher in the country is going to appeal for calm this weekend. They all condemn violence.'

'Really?'

'You saved lives, Zahi, rather than took them. I think that's the right thing to do. It's what Islam teaches. And if it comes to a choice between you and Lucretia, I'd have you every time.'

'And now,' Mary offered, 'it's lunch and then our shopping trip!'

Zahir forced a small smile for her sake, although he had no appetite for food or retail therapy. Soon they were downstairs in the dining room and it was difficult to feel depressed when Beth, George and Archie were so full of excitement at the thought of the coming trip. Their enthusiasm was infectious. And Beth was full of information about poltergeists that she was eager to share.

'It was well strong, Hil! Did you know it tore a cast iron fireplace off the wall and threw it across the room?'

'The Enfield one?'

'Yeah! I looked it up – there's loads on the internet about it!'

'It's one of the best recorded sightings. Many experts were called in and lots of reporters got involved. It was a major story for weeks.'

'Some people said the girls were doing it all themselves!'

'Yes – much later, when they grew up, they admitted that they had done some of it – moved things or hidden things and pretended that the poltergeist had done it. They said the pressure put on them by the media to prove the haunting was so great they felt they had to make things happen just to please the reporters.'

'But they couldn't make themselves just float in the air!'

'No. Or send a very heavy fireplace flying across the room. They were only little girls.'

'I found an article in the Daily Mail that says that most of the things that happened can't be explained except by the supernatural!'

Hilary suppressed her doubts about this particular source of evidence. 'Remember,' she said, 'we've had very recent experience of what a poltergeist can do. Most people are in one of two camps: those that want to believe in ghosts and extraterrestrials and those who think it's nonsense. Most scientists are in the latter group. It goes against everything they've been taught. But if you want to learn more, there was a documentary on the Enfield Poltergeist a couple of years ago on Channel Four. I'll try and get a copy for you.'

'Thanks, Hil!'

Lunch over, Tom brought the car round to a side door and the team piled in. Spirits were high and this was a much livelier journey than the last one. Once at the shopping centre, Beth was in seventh heaven. She dragged Hilary into River Island and gazed in wonder at the racks of clothes under the bright white lights. Pop music played quietly in the background as Hilary fought to stop Beth buying half the store and sending Hilary's credit card into overdrive. She was sympathetic, however. After all Beth, for the first twelve years of her life, had not had any clothes that she could call her own.

Nevertheless, she had to be restrained, not only in the numbers of garments she bought, but in the style. Sequins were definitely not appropriate for the next day's meeting with the Prime Minister. Beth's concept of formal attire and Hilary's were almost as far apart as the current political parties. In the end a compromise was reached, whereby Beth agreed to settle for a becoming knee length dress for the meeting, provided she could have three trendy tops and two pairs of jeans, one with a sequined belt, for 'everyday' wear.

This Pyrrhic victory won, Hilary moved on to George. He was in Top Shop, absolutely refusing to accept Tom's advice that a suit or smart jacket and trousers would be the best outfit to wear. Beth offered her suggestions and George, wanting to look cool now that he was aiming to achieve a more mature image, was keener to follow her advice. Luckily, boys' clothes tend to be less outrageous than girls', so George was eventually kitted out in a smart shirt and a pair of chinos. Archie and Zahir had little interest in clothes and so were happy to accept Tom's suggestions, especially as Archie was allowed to move on to a toy shop and purchase a Lego Star Wars set.

The drive home was uneventful. The team spent another night watching and waiting, but there was no sign of anything out of the ordinary. The next morning they dressed in their smart new gear for the Big Day.

Far, far away their nemesis, Lucretia, was making plans of her own. She had reached out to Foxes Hollow and proved that even over vast distances she could move objects with the power of her mind. A detailed reconnaissance had enabled her to assess the most effective ways to destroy her enemies and ensure that her future plans could proceed without their hateful interference. She could not allow herself to feel any pity for these children. Cold and calculating, she must think only of her mission to avenge the destruction of her family. It would not be long before the OSIRIS team would feel the terror her parents must have suffered.

27. THE CALM BEFORE

The road to Chequers, Buckinghamshire, England.

The exit from Foxes Hollow was a quiet one. It had been decided that the convoy of police riders that had been accompanying some of their trips could possibly attract too much attention to the house. So they left quietly and were joined after a few miles by the motorcycle outriders and a plain car. This was the convoy that arrived at the gates to the grounds of Chequers, country home to British Prime Ministers for almost a century. The house is very old, more than a thousand years in parts. It had been granted to the country by its last occupants as a thank you for British success in the First World War. The benevolent owners had realised that the Prime Ministers of the twentieth century were not wealthy, like the royal family. They did not own country houses where they could entertain foreign dignitaries. Chequers was gifted to fill this gap: providing a country retreat for the leader of the government away from the pressures of London. It was also to be a suitably impressive and commodious home for entertaining on a grand scale.

At the gates, Tom showed his pass and the car was allowed through. The rest of the convoy drew aside and waited. Security within the grounds was so tight that no other protection was needed. As they drove through almost a mile of the pastures and lawns that surrounded the grand building, they caught glimpses of magnificent brick gables and enormous windows. A huge conservatory took up enough space for several normal-sized houses. Multiple chimneys towered up into the sky – Beth thought there must be hundreds of fireplaces inside that enormous house. George peered at the garage blocks and wondered what magnificent cars they might contain. They drew up at the grand entrance door, where Churchill had met Roosevelt and Stalin; where Thatcher had greeted Reagan and Tony Blair had entertained Putin.

News of their arrival had been sent ahead and the Prime Minister and his wife were waiting on the steps to greet them. Tom opened the door for Hilary whilst a butler trotted up to let the children out. Archie was sitting at the back with Mary, where two extra seats had been installed to make it a seven seater. Mary helped Zahir to walk up to the steps. It had been decided that he should try to enter using his frame, although Tom brought the chair along behind, because he may need it later. The effort of walking was sure to take its toll.

Hilary was watching Zahir closely. This was partly because she was worried about his strength, but not entirely. She was very aware of his divided loyalties, his confusion over Lucretia's motives and the rights and wrongs of Britain's involvement in the Arab conflicts. She wasn't sure that close contact with the leader of the government was going to help Britain's cause in the youngster's eyes. Zahir was gazing up at the PM with interest. The Prime Minister was no doubt flattered that this young person of another race was looking at him with what appeared to be veneration. Actually, Zahir was staring at his aura and he was mystified by it. It seemed to be doubled up, as if this was someone with two very distinct sides to his personality. The front aura was pleasing and willing to agree with anyone's point of view. The second, deeper aura was focused on self-interest and cunning. Hilary could read Zahir very well. She sensed that this could be very difficult.

It was the Prime Minister himself who took them on a short tour of the house. He thought this was a great honour for them – and of course it was – but the children had to try hard to seem interested. Hilary was impressed by their good manners. They learned more than they really wanted to know. The original 12th century house had been enlarged by William Hawtrey in the16th century and they were shown the room that is named after him. More interestingly, they were shown the room where Lady Mary Grey was kept prisoner in the 1560s after being banished from court by Queen Elizabeth the First. Her crime was to marry without the consent of her family. This caught Beth's attention, especially when she was told that the room is still just as it was when Lady Mary was imprisoned in it.

Less interesting was the collection of objects and pictures that related to Oliver Cromwell. There seemed to be no end to them and it was just lucky that the PM did not notice Archie's suppressed yawns. Then they were paraded down the Long Gallery to admire the stained glass window with the inscription: *This house of peace and ancient memories was given to England as a thank-offering for her deliverance in the Great War of 1914-1918.* Finally the OSIRIS team was ushered into the dark panelled room where Tony Blair had met with Vladimir Putin. The enormous oval table was heavy with finger food of all kinds, from tiny pastries to delicate patisseries that looked far too beautiful to eat. Down the centre of the table were lovely flower arrangements. George was impressed. Minding his manners, he told the Prime Minister's wife that she shouldn't have gone to so much trouble. It must have taken her days to cook all this. She seemed to find this very amusing, which rather confused him.

Two waiters were standing in a corner. They looked very smart, in black tail coats with white shirts and black ties. At a nod from the PM they came forward and offered drinks to the guests and provided them with white china plates with gold edging. The atmosphere improved considerably as the children sampled the fare, squealing with delight at the wonderful tastes they were enjoying. Their obvious pleasure thrilled his wife, who warmed to them as the buffet went on. Twenty minutes and several dozen canapés later, they were invited to sit down so that they could be formally thanked for all they had done.

The PM made a moving speech, recognising the debt that Britain owed to the OSIRIS team for their courage and extraordinary skill in identifying and tracking down the bombers. He marvelled at their skills and promised that the budget for OSIRIS was guaranteed under his administration and would be increased if more were ever needed. He ended by reading out a message from the royal family, personally thanking them for saving so many lives and sincerely hoping that one day they would be able to meet them personally to express their gratitude. George and Zahir felt a little embarrassed by so much effusiveness. Archie was having trouble understanding all this rather formal language, but felt that he was at last getting some credit. Beth had shot a smile at the best looking of the waiters and was feeling delighted – he had winked at her in return.

The PM showed great interest in Lucretia. He asked Zahir what he knew of her and said he was shocked by the terrible tragedy that had befallen her family. He promised to raise this with the US president the next time they talked – which he assured Zahir was frequently. Zahir stared at him doubtfully. His aura and his words were at odds. He suspected that the Prime Minister had known of the rocket attack for many weeks and had dismissed it as an accident of war. His sympathy with Irna increased as they talked, even though she seemed intent on destroying him. The PM asked Tom what had come of the public appeal for information. Tom brought him up to date. There had many calls to the incident room. She had been sighted everywhere. It would take days to filter the information and sort out the most positive leads. In the meantime, CCTV cameras across the country were being monitored for matching images and GCHQ was tracking millions of phone messages to hunt for clues. Everything possible was being done, but so far Lucretia was still eluding them.

The PM shook hands with all of them. It was a contented septet that drove back to Foxes Hollow. Praise is always welcome, even if one has doubts about the person giving it. And after all, this praise came from high places and with the promise of a certain future for the OSIRIS project. OSIRIS was not just an acronym. The team was named after the god Osiris from Ancient Egypt – a deity with supernatural powers. They passed a quiet night. They began to relax a little. Maybe Lucretia had abandoned her efforts to destroy them. A quiet and peaceful Sunday was promised, the hunt for Lucretia was well under way and the team members were beginning to relax.

28. THE STORM

There was one rather special, rather secret room at Foxes Hollow that was always closed and locked. It had been part of the agreement with the family when the house had been leased to the government to house the OSIRIS team. The family had not used the building as a home for many years. Poor health had caused them to move to the south of France. There they had a holiday villa near Nice. For most of the year it was hot and sunny. In winter, when the weather was too chilly for them, they would pack a few trunks and fly to Madeira or the Canaries. The income from their family seat in England helped to allay their expenses. But one room was sacrosanct and so was always out of bounds to tenants.

The room had belonged to a young man admired by all who knew him. He was tall and athletic. His shock of fair hair fell over a handsome young face full of hope and promise. His parents had spared nothing in ensuring that he had every advantage. He had been sent to the same boarding school that his father had attended, one that regularly sent its students on to Oxbridge colleges. He had become captain of the first eleven in his first year in the sixth form and had risen inevitably to head boy the next year. He was intellectually able. He won not just a place, but a scholarship to Cambridge. He was in his final year when war broke out.

The Great War of 1914 – 1918 was like no other. The young men of that golden generation had no fear. They had grown up with tales of bravery and daring. Their heroes were the valiant men who had defended Rorkes Drift and Mafeking. The war stories they read were of a thin red line, of British soldiers in bright red uniforms, of cavalrymen charging into battle with lances, a mighty horse thundering beneath them. Later generations would associate war with the mud and carnage of the Somme, with hails of machine gun bullets and death that came unseen from the *crrrump* of an artillery shell. But not they. All that was still to come.

In the first years of the First World War, Britain was unique in Europe in that there was no compulsory call up of men. There was no need. The best of Britain's youth were more than ready to volunteer. They were eager to fight for their country: *For God, England and Saint George!* From the mills, from the farms, from the factories, shops and warehouses, working men marched to the recruiting stations to sign up for the army or the navy. Towns and cities had their own battalions of friends. Men who had lived in neighbouring streets went to war together and died in neighbouring trenches.

This young man, with a golden future in front of him, signed up with the rest of his year at university in the opening days of the war. Only those not fit for active service were refused. University men were automatically chosen for officer training. This locked room is as he left it. On the wall are team photographs. In his cricket whites he smiles at the camera, gazing out at a world that lies at his feet. There are year photographs from his prep school – in the final one he sits next to the headmaster: head boy of the school, hero worshipped by the younger boys. There are photographs too from Sandhurst, where he did his – too brief – officer training. A large photograph of him in uniform, smiling confidently just before sailing to France, is draped with a black silk.

In one corner you can still see his cricket kit – his whites, his pads and his trusty bats. The score sheets are there for the games in which he scored a hundred for his school or his college. His university cap is there, along with his rugby shirts and boots. Over the fireplace are his guns. He was an excellent shot, but more pheasants suffered from his deadly aim than Germans. There are many learned books in a pile by the bedside, for he was expected to become a great historian. His bed is made, with a quilt that his adoring mother stitched, ready for a return that never came. The room still smells of him, for the window is shut and the air is still: the leather of his boots, the grease on the guns. And, at the foot of the bed, his threadbare teddy bear still clutches a toy locomotive, with the large key still fixed in its clockwork mechanism.

His medals are on display, the telegram from the war office with black edging and a letter from the King. A cutting from the *Times* records the end – his climb from the trench to rescue one of his men stranded in no man's land and the burst of machine gun fire that cut him down.

If you could see this room – and very few ever have – it would be hard to believe that this shrine to a lost son could harbour nothing but memories. It seems too personal, still filled with the presence of the young man who had once filled it with life and laughter.

And maybe you would be right.

For though his body lies on some foreign field, the spirit of Captain Johns still clings to the house and room he loves. And when that house is under threat he is ready to marshal all the forces at his command to defend it. And those forces may be a match even for Lucretia.

Lucretia also had been gathering her strength for a final attempt to destroy the OSIRIS team – and especially Zahir, who seemed to her both a personal threat and a traitor to his race.

But as Sunday evening approached, the occupants of Foxes Hollow were happily ignorant of the forces massing around them. Two nights had passed without disturbance and they were beginning to think that their fears had been unfounded. Fenton was no longer needed, and so he was spending the night at home. Tom was staying in Zahir's room as an extra precaution, but everyone else had gone back to the comfort of their own beds. The house was still, with only the gentle sounds of murmuring slumber to disturb the house cat, Polly. And she too was napping, with just one eye half open in case any tiny rodent scurried past.

The weather was calm and still. The moon shone brightly, giving good light for the surveillance cameras. The one guard on duty was only half awake in the safe room, keeping a sleepy eye on the screens. Outside one of the old barns, a white owl hooted gently. Then he swooped down and a tiny mouse, scurrying back across the cobbled yard to his hiding place, met a swift and painless death.

But the long dead spirits that dwelt around the family graveyard were stirring. They were sensing that all was not well. Captain Johns began to marshal them around doors and windows to form a defensive cordon around the house they loved. He knew the strengths and weaknesses of his troops. Some, like his father who had fought in the South African campaigns, would be resolute, he knew, and had psychic strength. Others, who had lain long rotting in the peaty ground, would need all the help he could give them.

The weather forecast was for a calm and quiet night. And yet, strangely, there was the sound of air being disturbed. Worryingly, this disturbance was not troubling distant neighbours or farmers settling their cattle for the night. The coming storm was centred on Foxes Hollow alone.

29. THE FINAL ASSAULT

If the sole security guard had been more alert, he might have noticed the leaves suddenly stirring in the trees. His eye might have been caught by a garden gate that suddenly swung violently on its hinges. In a corner of a viewing screen, he might have seen invisible feet disturbing the long grass behind the garage block of the ancient house. But he failed even to notice the slim dark figure that seemed to pass through the solid old stones of the barn wall. Too ephemeral to trigger the infrared alarms, Lucretia's spectral spirit slipped undetected into the outbuildings of Foxes Hollow.

Only Captain Johns sensed the intruder. Only he slid silently into the dark lofty space where once his Bugatti had been stored, its dark shiny paintwork set off by chrome fittings and soft leather seats. He remembered the smells of high octane fuel and gleaming cans of oil. He recalled the tools that the chauffeur kept polished and tidy in racks fastened to the thick walls. These same walls once sheltered the fine horses that pulled the estate's carriages and carts. His training in surveillance and reconnoitre stood him in good stead as he hovered, as silent as the two MPVs that occupied the space now. He watched as the dark shape moved stealthily towards the fuel cans, long abandoned in a corner of the garage block that was thick with cobwebs and dust. He narrowed his eyes as one of the lids, on a red can marked 'SHELL', began to turn very slowly, without being touched by any physical hand. Round and round it went, gradually rising until it was free of the can and fell with a clatter to the floor.

An arm, dark and vague, almost too faint to see, reached out towards the can of deadly fuel. It began to sway, slowly, slowly, back and forth, back and forth. Each sway took it closer to the point where it would topple and spill its contents across the floor. The Captain realised with a thud what the dark spectre intended.

In Flanders, in the silence of a military cemetery in the still hours before the dawn, a noise could be heard deep underground. If anyone had been passing in the dead of night, they would have paused in disbelief. Below a white slab of stone, marking the last resting place of Capt. W E Johns, of the Yorkshire Light Infantry, something was stirring in that hallowed ground. The earth seemed to heave as if a gigantic mole was working beneath the soil. The immaculate headstone suddenly cracked from top to bottom and fell to one side. No living soul was there to hear as the air moved strangely. A ghostly, ghastly sound rose as the earth broke apart – to reveal a deep, black chasm that led down to a coffin, with the lid gaping open. No living soul heard the rallying call. No mortal ears thrilled to the sound of the bugle. But in ten, twenty, thirty plots in that cemetery, that had been silent and at rest for a hundred years, the earth above the graves of the Captain's men also began to tremble.

He had been popular with his brigade. They loved him for his courage and for the way he was prepared to die to save a dying comrade. Now he needed them again and the fallen of the Yorkshire Infantry answered his call. Slowly and remorselessly the gravestones toppled like teeth falling from rotting gums. The earth parted and, for a moment, a squad of men with eyeless faces and twisted limbs stood in parade ground order, ready for battle. A ghastly army of zombie warriors, ready to go to war for the final time. Then the blackness swallowed them up and they were gone.

At Foxes Hollow, the sleepy security guard finally gave up the struggle and allowed his eyes to close. As he snored gently, the screen that showed the picture from the garage flickered into life. Motion sensors had been activated and the camera did its job, picking up the image of the falling can and transmitting it to the safe room for assessment. But no one was awake to see and so the camera followed in vain the rivulet of high octane fuel as it trickled across the garage floor and pooled around the wheels of one of the cars.

Another movement triggered the camera's reflexes and it swung round to record it. Dutifully it transmitted the images to the safe room, where no-one was awake to see. A piece of metal, a heavy spanner, was being smashed onto the stone floor. Regular as clockwork it went – crash, crash, crash. No hand could be seen. No arm was lifting or levering the rusty metal. But every now and again the collision would cause a spark to fly across the floor towards the pool of dark, volatile liquid.

Captain Johns drifted back into the garage just as the first spark hit the fuel. It fizzled out. The second spark was enough. There was a flash as fumes from the liquid exploded and then flames shot up towards the roof. A whirlwind within this building, that had once been a stable block, began to fan the flames towards the first of the 4x4s. He moved outside to where his men were lining up in the narrow gap between the garage building and the main house. And in that house the humans slept on, unaware of the silent, deadly flames which, if unchecked, would destroy them all.

Archie had been watching a cartoon channel on the television in his bedroom when he fell asleep. At midnight the channel had stopped broadcasting, but the equipment had remained switched on. The screen was blank, but it was speckled with small white dashes of static. Archie stirred. Something was disturbing his sleep. His eyes flickered open. Anyone else looking at that television would have seen nothing at all. But Archie was drawn towards a picture only he could see – not of random specks but of a darkness that was like swirling smoke. He watched fascinated as the first flickers of flame appeared on the screen and gradually built into a raging inferno. Figures seemed to run into the fire and explode in a flash of flame and smoke. He clapped to see it and laughed as the flames leapt higher – it was like plot night to him as he waited to see fireworks burst into the sky. But then his attention switched to his window. His room was directly opposite the large garage block. Archie was sleepy and confused. The flickering light seemed also to be coming from behind his curtains. The picture on the screen had vanished and been replaced by reflections from his window, where flame-like lights were dancing across the window.

Archie slid out of bed and, rubbing his eyes, he pulled aside the curtains. At first he thought he was dreaming. Flames were coming through the roof of the garage block. Bright orange flames were lighting the windows and throwing flickering shadows across the cobbled yard. He knew something was dreadfully wrong. Archie stumbled to his door and pushed it open. Next to him was Zahir's room. He tried the handle and the door swung open. Tom was asleep, but his eyes opened immediately when Archie called to him.

'What's the matter?'

'I saw a fire, Tom!'

'Where? On television?'

'Yes...'

'Oh Archie! It will just be a programme – like Fireman Sam. Did you leave it on when you fell asleep?'

'Yes, but...'

'It's nothing to worry about. In future we'll have to make sure the TV goes off when you do!'

'Big fire...'

'Exciting, eh? Fire engines and fire fighters? Lots of flashing lights?'

'No ... it's...'

'Come on.' He let one leg slip out of bed and then the other. He sat up and ran his fingers through his hair. He checked that Zahir was all right, still sleeping peacefully. 'Come on ... let's get you back into bed! And this time, stay asleep! I need my rest too, you know!'

He took Archie's hand and led him back to his room. He pushed open the door and then...

'My God!'

He ran to the window. Archie complained. 'I told you...'

Tom picked up the internal phone and called the safe room. 'Tony! TONY!'

When there was no answer, he ran back to his own room and grabbed his mobile phone. The emergency services answered immediately and he asked for the fire brigade, stressing the urgency. Then he ran out into the corridor and broke the nearest fire alarm, before going to Zahir's room to help him and Archie to safety. The alarm woke Tony in the safe room, who stared at the screens in front of him in disbelief.

30. INFERNO

The flames reached the second 4x4. They licked around the petrol tank until the temperature reached a critical point and the tank exploded, sending parts of the car blasting into the garage doors and bursting them open. Fresh air came in from the night and fanned the flames. The dark spirit that was Lucretia stood behind the burning wrecks, calling up a violent wind that blew the fire across the short gap between the garage and the house.

The captain watched, grim faced. He knew that the house had stood for hundreds of years. In all that time, the timbers and plaster had dried out. The wood of the floors had in places been attacked by woodworm and, though it looked solid enough on the surface, beneath it was a pile of dry dust that would burn uncontrollably. The old house was a tinder box. He had lined up his men. They would do everything they could to thwart Lucretia and save his family home. But that dark spirit herself ... they were not strong enough. He would have to tackle her alone.

The dark wraith, the ectoplasm that had emanated from Lucretia wherever she was hiding, had not yet seen the Captain. He was behind her and she was focused on the destruction she was wreaking in front. But as the tongues of flame fanned out towards the ancient building she saw his ghastly squad of corpses, lined up between her and the house. She let out a terrifying scream that sent sparks and fire high into the air.

Tony, embarrassed by his negligence, was collecting fire extinguishers from the equipment room as the rest of the house's occupants stumbled out of the front door, Zahir supported by Tom. In the far distance, on the main road, they could see blue flashing lights and hear the sirens of the fire engines racing towards Foxes Hollow. Archie ran down the central path to where he could see round the west wing of the house to the fire. Excited, he turned back to where the others were walking more slowly towards him. His eyes sparkled, reflecting the flames. 'Tom! Where are the fire engines?'

But the fire engines that could have saved the house had shuddered to a halt, more than a mile away. Normally, high winds happen in winter when trees are devoid of leaves so that the air can whistle through them. Lucretia had brought up winds of great ferocity, when the ancient trees around Foxes Hollow were heavy with late summer foliage. Half way down the drive to the ancient house, two giant oaks had crashed over, their roots ripped from the earth. The emergency vehicles had found their way completely blocked by fallen trunks and branches. The men were scurrying to clear their way, pulling chainsaws from the equipment lockers on the vehicles, so that they could cut the trees into small, manageable pieces. But it would take many minutes to complete this task – time they could not spare. One vehicle left the lane and tried to drive round the obstructions. In the distance they could see the glow of the fire and they were working desperately to reach it.

Meanwhile, the first line of the Captain's infantry marched in disciplined order towards the flames. They were in full battle dress, just as they had fallen in the horror of the carnage in no-man's land. One had only half of his head, the rest had been blown off by a shell fragment. Another was dragging the remnants of his right leg behind him. None had all their limbs intact. Mustard gas had eaten away their lungs. Termites had eaten the eyes out of their sockets. When they had reached a point two metres from the inferno, shielding the house from the flames with their ghostly bodies, The Captain screamed out an order: '*FIX BAYONETS!*'

The line halted. The men slammed the butts of rifles that no longer seemed to have any substance into the earth and fixed long knives onto the barrels. Lucretia swung around and saw Captain Johns for the first time. *'NO!!!'* she screamed, torn between the danger to her plans from him and the infantry waiting to advance on her.

'RIGHT MEN – CHARGE!!!' The Captain looked straight into the dark wraith's eyes as the two faced up to each other, one set upon defending his family home, the other intent on destroying it and everyone in it. Lucretia had to break away to deal with the threat from the men who were stumbling towards her. She drove the flames towards them. Dried mummified flesh ignited as the flames licked over them. Bones seemed to melt in the heat. The first line of men perished and their souls floated free towards eternal rest, their debt to their Captain paid. But valuable seconds had been saved. The second line stepped forward.

The fire engine that had tried to skirt the fallen trees by leaving the lane and driving across the field had come to a halt. A wide ditch blocked its way. It had come across the haha. It tried to reverse and turn back, but its wheels were slipping on the wet grass. A dew was forming. The other engine was still at a standstill. The men tied a tow rope to the front of the vehicle and to a fallen tree. Most of its branches had been removed with the chainsaws. The engine was slammed into reverse. The wheels slipped and screamed on the tarmac. Then it gripped, and slowly the first tree giant tree was swung off the lane.

Tom and Tony ensured that the others were at a safe distance and then approached the fire with extinguishers. They each carried two, but the hopelessness of the task was all too apparent. The garage was burning fiercely. They could not, of course, see the lines of defenders, or the wraith that was intent on destroying them and everything that OSIRIS stood for. Taking one extinguisher each, they squeezed the triggers and aimed them at the conflagration. When they tried to get close enough to douse the flames, the heat burnt their faces and drove them back.

'FIX BAYONETS!! Charge!!' Captain Johns ordered his next line of troops into battle. Some had no flesh on their

faces. Under their helmets, eyeless skulls glared out into the blaze. One arm that held a rifle was nothing but bone. As they began to stagger forward in a ghastly attempt at a charge, shreds of rotting flesh fell from their bodies. Lucretia was furious as this force of zombie infantry threatened to thwart her deadly revenge. She raised her arms to throw fire at the advancing troops. But as she did so, Captain Johns drew his pistol and fired. The bullets went straight through her and her face was contorted with rage. She seemed to grow taller as she swung away from him to hurl flame at the advancing soldiers. But they had made enough ground. As they were sent to their rest in a surge of funeral fire, the blaze was moving back from the house, back towards the garage entrance. Tom and Tony saw the flames retreat, but the ghostly battle that was raging back and forth was invisible to mortal eyes. They tried again to make use of the foam from the extinguishers and made a small advance. Again, the heat drove them back. Tom signalled Tony away – another explosion could cause serious injury. Surely the professionals would be there at any moment? The next line of infantry formed up, invisible to Tom and the rest of the OSIRIS team.

The fire engine that had attempted the cross country route at last made it back to the lane, just as the fire crew completed the roping of the second fallen oak tree to its sister engine. Its motor screamed and its wheels skidded on the road surface as it tried desperately to pull the trunk from the lane.

Zahir turned to Hilary, Beth and George. Mary was holding Archie to prevent him moving any closer to the burning garage block. The cook and the two other live-in staff were still on the steps leading up to the main door of the house. Within, through the rooms and empty corridors, the fire alarms rang and rang, echoing their warning into the darkest corners of the ancient house and sending the bats flying from the rafters. Zahir was looking intense and afraid. He whispered, 'She's there, Hilary ... I can sense her!'

'Me too,' echoed Beth. She remembered the traces of Lucretia she had felt on the objects in her flat and the same feelings were with her now.

'She's in there...,' pronounced Zahir, pointing to the burning building.

'Well, she won't trouble us much longer!' said Mary, wryly.

'No...,' Beth corrected her. 'Her body isn't there ... just her ... sort of ... mind...'

Zahir supported her. 'That's right! We've got to send her away!'

'How?'

He did not know. But with Beth he walked forward until they stood side by side with Tom and Tony. Without realising they were doing it, he and Beth held hands and they both stared into the heart of the inferno. 'There she is!' whispered Beth. She could make out a dark outline in the hottest part of the fire.

'There's someone else as well!' Zahir breathed. He could make out two figures. They seemed to be struggling. As he spoke, the third line of long dead infantry reached the first of the flames and for a moment the fire died back, until Lucretia regained her control and the line perished in a surge of flame. But Irna Khan, the real Lucretia, was beginning to feel the strain. This had not gone as she had planned and her strength was waning. Keeping up this onslaught through her disembodied spirit, at a distance far greater than the OSIRIS team could guess, was taking its toll.

The main trunk of the tree was now off the road. The firemen were clearing the last of the branches and the emergency vehicles began to ease forward. Their way was still strewn with small branches and leaves that made the wheels slip and slide. They turned a bend in the lane and could see the outlines of Foxes Hollow against the starlit sky. The roof struts and rafters of the garage block were burning away. As they inched the fire engines forward, the roof finally caved in and flames shot into the sky.

Beth and Zahir gasped as they saw the fire shoot skyward and they were hit by a blast of heat. Beth turned to her friend. 'Do you think, if we worked together, we could drive Lucretia away?'

'Dunno. But I'll try if you will!'

Beth's left hand clutched Zahir's right tightly. The two turned to face the gaping hole where the large garage doors once stood. They stared into the heart of the blaze and willed the unseen Lucretia away.

The object of their attention was locked in a deadly embrace with Captain Johns. He was trying to pull her away from the building and into the open fields. Her wraith was stronger than his, but she was tiring and her powers were divided as she battled against him and the dead infantry that were advancing again against her wall of flame. It was then that she detected that new adversaries had joined the fight. She hissed with hate and frustration as she recognised Zahir's presence and felt his pull on her, joined to that of the detestable girl who had handled her possessions at her flat. Demented in her rage she threw her last grams of psychic strength into one final strike that sent the Captain howling into the centre of the blaze and made Beth and Zahir stagger back.

'Try again!' shouted Beth. They stood their ground. Zahir's eyes were closed in concentration as he stood, still holding her hand, and facing up again to the woman who hated him so much. They stood firm, using all their combined will to force Lucretia back. Spitting venom, Lucretia's wraith gathered pieces of burning metal and wood and threw them at the two youngsters. A red hot metal splinter was shooting straight at Zahir's head as he stood bravely facing the building with his eyes shut tight. Tom saw it and swung his fire extinguisher into its path so that it was deflected away from him. Lucretia gathered more burning missiles and began to catch them in a whirlwind. They spun faster and faster. They had reached the speed of bullets and she was ready to use them to destroy Zahir and Beth once and for all. But just as she was going to release them, the captain fought his way back to her, used all his remaining strength to push her to one side and the stream of burning missiles flew into the dark sky like an unholy display of fireworks. Archie saw them and cheered with excitement!

Tony was running to meet the fire engines and directing them to where the two youngsters were standing, silhouetted against the bright orange flames. Tom stayed with them for protection in case any more objects were hurled their way. The captain was gone. His spirit had fled to eternal rest. The last stragglers of his troops were still ready to continue the battle and began to move forward. Tom was about to order the youngsters back. He was afraid that he might not be able to fend off the next missile attack on Zahir and Beth. But he need not have worried. Lucretia was near the end of her strength. The psychic power of the two youngsters combined was beginning to tell on her as she weakened. What energy she had left, she turned on the new arrivals as they unrolled the hoses that threatened to defeat her attempt to destroy Foxes Hollow.

31. A VISION OF HELL

The first of the emergency vehicles squealed to a halt just behind Zahir and Beth. One of the firemen tried to shoo them away from the danger, but they wouldn't move and Tom told him to leave them be. Mystified, he went to help his colleagues uncoil the hoses. There was not time to search for a fire hydrant. They would do that once the hoses were operating. For the time being, they would make use of the water stored in the tanks of the engine. As the pumps whirred into life, the second engine raised its hydraulic ladder so that water could be directed down through the gaping roof into the heart of the fire.

As the first jets of water slammed into the burning building, Lucretia was consumed with fury. She turned her energy onto the hoses. The fireman close to Beth suddenly found that the nozzle he was holding began to buck and writhe in his hands. He couldn't hold it onto the flames. Instead, the water began to squirt in all directions, drenching the occupants of the house and spraying across the garden. He cursed and fought to control it so that the precious water would not be wasted. He couldn't understand what was causing his equipment to malfunction so dramatically. Beth closed up on him and reached out to put her hand on the nozzle that was leaping around like a crazy horse.

'Get away, love! You'll get hurt!' the fireman shouted.

'Let me touch it...' pleaded Beth, calmly.

'No, get back!'

Tom intervened. He told the man that, though it sounded stupid, he should let Beth help him. Reluctantly, he allowed Beth to put her hand on the thick brass tube. As soon as she did so, the bucking calmed and the bewildered fireman found that he had control of the hose again. Beth stood next to him, still holding the nozzle, her eyes closed in concentration.

But this meant that she had left Zahir, who was now standing alone, facing the fire. His arms were spread out like wings at his sides, his eyes closed, the front of his body lit orange by the flickering flames. Lucretia saw her chance. The whole of her plan may have failed, but there was still the chance to destroy the traitor that she hated more than anyone on Earth.

George was in Hilary's arms. It was a desperate gamble, but could he leave his body and help in the fight against Lucretia? George was ready to go into battle. She held him while his body went limp and he began to release his spirit from its physical home. He floated free and moved towards the chaos raging in front of him. The fires were just beginning to damp down as the water jets did their work, but now he alone could see Lucretia as she drifted like an avenging devil from the inferno. Her arms were raised high above her, her nails stretched out to rip and tear. George realised immediately that Zahir was her intended prey. He slipped round behind her.

Far away, Irna Khan – the woman they knew as Lucretia, was exhausted. She was using the very last gasps of her energy to complete her task. She had Zahir in her sights. She stretched out her arms and reached for his eyes. Her nails hooked downwards. Like deadly scythes, she swung her arms down towards his face. His eyes were closed. She was going to tear them from their sockets.

Although his eyes were closed, Zahir could sense her presence. He was using all the psychic force he could muster to push her back into the fire. As he did so, George pulled from behind. The nails flashed down, missing Zahir's eyes by less than a millimetre. It was her last act.

Many, many miles away, Irna Khan, from whom the wraith that was Lucretia emanated, collapsed. She had given everything she had in the attempt and finally had failed. As consciousness slipped from her, George, Beth and Zahir saw the black wraith vanish, screaming, into the blackness of the night.

'She's gone, hasn't she?' asked Hilary. The three exhausted youngsters nodded dumbly. She led them back into the house, where Tony was turning off the alarms. He told them that the emergency services would stay on site for the rest of the night, damping down the fire and then investigating how it had started. Zahir laughed hollowly. Tom agreed that they were unlikely to find the true cause, but they had to do their job. In the meantime, the house was safe. They all needed rest. He suggested that they could all go their rooms and sleep. He would stay awake, with the very embarrassed Tony, and keep an eye on things. They were all glad to agree and the now quiet house accepted their tired bodies and lulled them to sleep.

The fire crews completed their work. They found an upturned fuel can, which had obviously been the cause of the fire, but how it had been emptied or what caused it to ignite, they never discovered. The men had strange tales to tell for years after about the fire at Foxes Hollow. They would entertain anyone who would listen with tales of trees that crashed down across a road when no wind blew; of hosepipes that writhed and bucked like crazed horses and were tamed by a girl's delicate touch. One fireman, ashen-faced, would tell of what he had seen in the height of the blaze. *'There were figures in the flames,'* he swore. *'Spectres I tell thee! They were marching right into the fire, with rifles pointed into the inferno! They had 'elmets on their heads like in 'First World War ... and under the 'elmets there was no faces – just grinning skulls...'*

Of course, no-one believed a word.

32. CALM AFTER THE STORM

It was after ten before they met for breakfast the next morning. Still tired and spent, they were quiet but were feeling safe at last. Hilary agreed with Beth that the threat from Lucretia seemed to be over. There was no sense that she was still watching over them. The battle the night before seemed to have resulted in an unconditional victory. If she was still alive, and she may well not be after what she had gone through, she was totally defeated. The OSIRIS team had won the final battle and in so doing had won the war.

It was agreed that there would be no school this Monday morning. The young people would be allowed to relax until lunchtime and then Tom and Hilary would organise an excursion for them – a surprise. They discussed excitedly what it may be. Archie hoped it would be a trip to Legoland. Beth would be happy with another shopping trip, whilst Zahir suddenly realised that he had not seen his mum for over a week and his heart ached for her.

They were about to disperse to play or rest before lunch when Tom got a call on the intercom from the guards at the gate. After a brief exchange, he turned to Hilary. 'There's a car at the gate – two Americans. It's got diplomatic plates. I'd better see what they want!'

Hilary nodded, but this news disturbed her. MI5 worked closely with American intelligence agencies, of course, but she had not realised that the OSIRIS project was known to them. More worryingly, they seemed to know of the existence of Foxes Hollow – a place she had tried to keep totally secret. She had no choice but to leave this to Tom. She picked up a couple of morning newspapers and sat down in the drawing room with a pot of coffee.

Half an hour later, a very worried Tom entered the drawing room leading two well-fed and burly men in sharp suits. 'Hilary – I've two colleagues to introduce to you. This is Harry Ipson, lead agent for the CIA in Britain.'

Harry Ipson had a ready smile and twinkling eyes. His broad shoulders led to a very short neck and a large well-tanned face. His suit was well tailored and of a slightly shiny material. Italian, Hilary decided.

'Howdy! Great to meet you, Doctor Fleischman!'

She accepted his outstretched hand and he shook it warmly.

'How do you do…,' she responded guardedly.

'And this,' continued Tom, 'is Craig Dean, personal aide to the American Ambassador in London.'

'It's an honour to meet you, ma'am. I've heard so much about you.'

'None of it true I hope!' Hilary looked him over. He was black, tall and less well built than the CIA man. If anything he was smarter, in more ways than one. His shirt was dazzling white. He had black and gold cufflinks and a diamond tie pin. His suit was made from the most expensive cloth – probably from one of the mills left in Bradford still weaving cloth for the most exclusive tailors. His shoes were so shiny they dazzled the eye. She had noticed before that successful black African men seemed to take amazing pride in their appearance, as if to put the days of poverty and slavery firmly behind them. This man, Craig, was also, she could tell, very clever. This was a well-educated man with a formidable intellect. She admired him, but was concerned as to why he was here.

She invited them to be seated and they settled into the comfortable arm chairs. Hilary got up and glanced out of the window. Zahir and Archie were on the grass outside, Zahir attempting to throw a ball to his younger friend so that he could bat it. She smiled. They were beginning to relax. A great weight had been lifted off them all.

'We saw the fire damage as we drove up to the house. No-one hurt, I hope?' asked Craig.

'None of us!' Hilary smiled back.

Tom walked across to her. 'The CIA have some rather surprising news for us. It's about Lucretia.'

'Cute name you've given her!' joked Harry.

'There was nothing cute about the real Lucretia,' responded Hilary drily.

'Well, we've got a real embarrassing confession to make!'

'You'd better sit down,' said Tom.

She did. 'Well this is a first. It's usually the CIA who extract confessions from other people!'

'Now don't you go believing all that bullshit about us nice guys at the CIA using torture and stuff – that's just bad spin!' retorted Harry, with a twinkle.

'Well, let's agree to differ,' responded Hilary, icily. She was comfortable running this man down. She felt no threat from him. Craig was watching her, appreciatively. He recognised that her rather bizarre appearance hid a formidable intellect. And a strong maternal need to protect her charges.

'Now – what have you come to apologise about?' Hilary continued.

'Not us!' Harry protested. 'It was Homeland Security who ballsed it up!'

'How exactly?' A very worrying possibility was forming in Hilary's mind. She hoped she was wrong.

Craig took over. 'Five days ago there was a bomb attack on one of your London theatres. It was carried out by a new group that neither MI5 nor the CIA was aware of. Two members of the cell were apprehended – we understand that your group takes much of the credit for this.'

'Who told you that?' Hilary asked, furious that someone had revealed their existence to the Americans. She turned to Tom. If Zahir had been in the room, he would have seen her aura turn a steely grey. 'I was promised that the existence of

OSIRIS was to be a closely kept secret. The more people who know of us, the more danger for these youngsters!'

'You know, Hilary, that we've always worked closely with our American allies.' Tom was trying to ease the atmosphere. He was not responsible for this security breach but suspected that it happened at a very high level. 'We both have full use of GCHQ. We can't have secrets from each other for long.'

'I see,' said Hilary, coldly.

'The point is,' continued Craig, eager to move the discussion onto safer ground, 'we discovered yesterday that Irna Khan, the woman you call Lucretia, applied for an ESTA the day after the bombing.'

'An ESTA?'

'British citizens don't need a visa to visit America. They can apply for visa exemption, known as an ESTA. Provided that there is no reason to refuse it, the ESTA is granted automatically,' Craig explained. He had taken charge of the dialogue, overruling the CIA man with an ease that suggested significant authority.

'But we had identified Irna by then!'

'Yes, Ma'am. Unhappily, the database at Homeland Security let us down. The ESTA was granted. Later that day she boarded a plane and then landed at JFK.'

'Where she was arrested?'

'If only.' Craig looked grave. 'We spend billions of dollars on immigration controls. All it seems to do is make entry to the USA a miserable experience for tens of thousands of innocent tourists. Irna Khan was waived through.'

'You're joking!'

'I wish I was.'

'So where is she now?' Hilary asked, astonished at this incompetence on the part of their allies.

'We don't know, ma'am. She had to give an accommodation address when she entered. We sent agents round to pick her up as soon as we realised what had happened. It turned out that the address was a fiction. It doesn't exist. This isn't our finest hour.'

'So she's somewhere in the United States of America, but no-one knows where?'

'That's about the size of it.'

'Well, there's one good thing about this. At least she's your problem now. We're free of her!'

Tom spoke quietly. 'Not entirely, I'm afraid.'

'What do you mean?'

Craig coughed and looked apologetic. 'We've come here because we want your help. We believe that this woman is planning to continue her campaign of violence in our country. Your team, the OSIRIS team, is the only one with experience of dealing with her. We want you to come to the States and join up with us to catch her and stop her.'

'Absolutely not!'

Tom tried to intercede. 'Hilary, these are our allies. MI5 and the CIA work together to combat international crime and terror. This request for help has come from the President himself...'

'I don't care if it's come from the Virgin Mary. These children stay here!'

Harry stepped forward, looking oddly smug. Hilary decided that he was wearing a toupee. There was a flash of gold tooth as he smiled a false smile at her. She didn't like him.

'Well ma'am, I'm giving you heads-up on this. It's out of your hands. Your PM has given the go ahead. You're booked on a flight tomorrow morning.'

Tom was writhing with embarrassment. 'I'm afraid he's right, Hilary. I knew you wouldn't like it. I've got a call booked to Downing Street if you want to explain your reasons why this should be stopped to the...'

'You bet I do!' Hilary was seething. 'Have it put through to my room!'

She spent twenty minutes on the phone. She began arguing rationally, explaining the reasons for her refusal to co-operate. She pointed out what these young people had been through over the last few days. She was sure he would understand that they were exhausted and stressed. She reminded him that all four of them had suffered terrible trauma in their lives that had left them vulnerable and extremely sensitive. Foxes Hollow had become their home and provided them with security and love.

When the Prime Minister made noises that sounded sympathetic, she went on to express her distrust of the American military. She outlined to him the dismal failure of their previous attempts at psychic warfare, the ill-fated 'Men Who Stare at Goats' project. Too much funding and too little command oversight had resulted in experiments with LSD that almost wiped out an entire regiment. The men, high on drugs, had gone crazy with guns and driven armoured vehicles wildly all over the camp, demolishing anything in their way.

The PM sounded so concerned that she genuinely thought she was winning the argument. Then, when she had finished, he told her he fully understood her point of view. They had anticipated that she may not feel able to take the OSIRIS team to America. She breathed a sigh of relief. And so, he told her, another expert on the paranormal was standing by to take her place. She could submit her resignation that afternoon.

It would be hard for most people to imagine that a lady like Hilary could use such language. As she slammed down the phone, the air turned blue as she gave her considered opinion on the PM, his mother, his sexual tendencies and his intellectual ability. What she intended to do with his balls would require at the very least a mincing machine and a Bunsen burner. However, when Tom finally calmed her down she agreed that she would not resign. She could not allow the leadership of the project and the guardianship of the OSIRIS team pass to anyone else. For the young people's sake, she would have to agree to the move – very temporary – to

America. She would call them together after lunch. They'd pack that evening.

Harlem, New York, the United States of America.

In a small, squalid room in a Harlem tenement, a faint morning light filtered through the dirty net curtains. Irna Khan was regaining consciousness. She was drained. Yesterday's battle had used up all her strength. She opened her eyes and her hands moved slowly towards her phone. It was a cheap, second-hand pay as you go that would be impossible to trace. Before her breakfast of coffee and a stale bagel, she had to call her contacts in Manhattan. They would gather that evening at a cheap diner behind the small hotel where she had found a poorly paid, no questions asked, job. Yesterday had not gone as well she had hoped. OSIRIS had not been destroyed – yet. But there were bigger tasks ahead. The United States of America lay before her, at her mercy. These corrupt capitalists had no idea what terrors she had planned. And with that nasty boy and his meddling friends safely in England, there was nothing to stop her...

To be continued...

FIND OUT MORE!

If you have been interested in any of the topics in this book and would like to find out more, here are some articles that will help you to do your own research!

Poltergeists

Lucretia appears to be able to act as a poltergeist.

A poltergeist is a type of ghost supposedly responsible for physical disturbances such as loud noises and objects moved around or destroyed. Most accounts of poltergeists describe movement or the lifting of objects, such as furniture and cutlery, or noises such as knocking on doors. Poltergeists have also been claimed to be capable of striking and tripping people.

Poltergeists have traditionally been described as troublesome spirits who haunt a particular person instead of a specific location. Poltergeists have been reported in many countries including the United States, Japan, Brazil, Australia, and most European nations, with early accounts dating back to the 1st century.

Find out more from *Ask.com* and *Wikipedia*.

There is a long and fascinating article about the *The Enfield Poltergeist* on the Daily Mail (UK) website.

Astral travel

George is an 'astral traveller'. This is the name often given to Out-of-Body experiences or Out-of-Body travel. It is believed by those who claim to practise it that we have an astral body (like a soul), within our physical body, capable of leaving the physical body and travelling outside it. The idea of astral travel is rooted in worldwide religious accounts of dying and travelling to the afterlife – the belief that the soul leaves the body when a person dies and continues to live on as a separate entity.

Many hospital patients – including some famous people – have reported that when they had died (and then were brought back to life) or were near death in hospital they experienced this sensation of leaving their bodies. Sometimes patients who have been brought back to life by doctors insist that while they were 'dead' they floated above their bodies and could see all that was happening around them.

Although many people believe in Out-of-Body travel, there is no scientific proof of it. Most evidence is anecdotal.

Find out more from *Ask.com* encyclopaedia

Telepathy

Hilary claims to have been telepathic when she was a child.

Telepathy is the direct transference of thought and/or feelings from one person to another person without using the normal five physical senses of sight, hearing, touch, taste and smell. Some people believe that it is possible to communicate using only the power of the mind. The evidence, however, is largely anecdotal. Like Astral Travel, there is not yet any certain scientific evidence that telepathy is possible. Believers maintain that humans originally had the natural ability to communicate using only their thoughts, but that this has been lost over time.

This is, however, a fascinating study and you can find out more from *Wikipedia* and *Heroes Wiki.*

Magicians and conjurors often claim to be able to read thoughts and telepathy features in many stories and films, such as *Star Wars.*

Millennium Mills

The building really does exist, just as it is described in the story. But don't ever go there! It isn't safe. You can see pictures of it on line.

The Haunted House

The story that Hilary tells to Zahir, of an old house in which a little girl sees ghosts that hover above her bedroom floor, is based on a recorded sighting. However, I have not been able to find the source for this report.

International Terrorism

Terrorists are groups of people who try to overthrow existing governments by acts of terror in order to impose their own system of government. They are often doing this because they have extreme religious views. This is not a new thing – there have been many terrorist attacks in the past. In Northern Ireland, for example, both Catholics and Protestants committed acts of terrorism (look up IRA on Wikipedia)

More recently, Islamic extremists have been accused of acts of terrorism across the globe. It is important to understand that the vast majority of followers of Islam are peaceful and do not condone acts of violence. Small numbers are involved and chief among them are the Taliban and members of ISIS (Islamic State).

The Taliban are the *mujahedeen* (holy warriors) and they formed to fight against Russian troops in Afghanistan during the Soviet occupation of their country between 1979 and 1989. At that time they received some support from Western countries, who saw them as a thorn in the side of the Soviets.

When the Soviet troops gave up the fight and withdrew, there was a long civil war in Afghanistan. At the end of it, the Taliban took control of the country. They ruled from 1996 to 2001. They imposed strict laws, based on their interpretation of Islamic teaching. Music, television and the internet were banned. Their treatment of women was considered brutal by

Western standards. Girls were refused the right to go to school, for example.

They were removed from power in 2001 by an Allied invasion of Afghanistan led by American forces. They are fighting to regain control of their country. There are strong links with Pakistan and many Taliban hide out in the mountains that separate the two countries.

Find out more from *Wikipedia. Infoplease.com* and *Ask.com.*

Islamic fundamentalists are also involved in action against Israel. Look up Hamas in *Ask.com.*

Al Qaeda

Al Qaeda was formed by Osama Bin Laden around 1989. It is probably the most notorious terrorist organisation in history, responsible for the horrendous airliner attack on the twin towers in New York, now known as '9/11' because it happened on the 11th of September 2001. It changed history. It was the first major assault by terrorists or by any enemy in recent times on American soil. It had a huge impact on air travel for all of us. It was after these attacks that the intensive security that now surrounds international travel began.

Find out more from *Wikipedia; Al Qaeda.*

Jihad

The greatest Jihad for Muslims is the struggle to be close to Allah and to follow Islamic teachings in all you do. Some extremist Muslims see Jihad also as a struggle against other religions and all those who do not live their lives according to Islamic law. They have a very strict interpretation of Islamic teachings. These militant Muslims see themselves as mujahedeen's (see Taliban).

There are many websites that will tell you more about Jihad. There is considerable factual information in *Wikipedia.*

Drone Attacks

Unmanned planes, or drones, are aircraft with no-one on board. They are controlled from the ground and guided to their targets by military personnel, often hundreds of miles away from the target. American Predator or Reaper drones were initially designed for reconnaissance missions but have been fitted with Hellfire missiles. They are a 'safe' way of attacking enemy targets, because if they are shot down, there are no casualties. Pilots will not be killed or taken captive. They are, however, very expensive and very sophisticated aircraft. They have become accurate and effective weapons.

They are also controversial. There have been many claims of civilian casualties. This is usually the result of human error or incorrect intelligence information, causing the wrong target to be hit.

Go to: Ask Encyclopaedia · Images · Videos

Thank you for reading 'OSIRIS'. We hope that this information about the political and religious tensions that are causing so many problems will help you to a better understanding of the world we all share.

Live in peace.